GRAVE STONES

ANDREA FRAZER

Grave Stones

ISBN 9781783759910

Other Novels by Andrea Frazer

<u>The Falconer Files</u>

Death of an Old Git
Choked Off
Inkier than the Sword
Pascal Passion
Murder at the Manse
Music to Die For
Strict and Peculiar
Christmas Mourning
Grave Stones
Death in High Circles
Glass House
Bells and Smells

<u>Belchester Chronicles</u>

Strangeways to Oldham
White Christmas with a Wobbly Knee
Snowballs and Scotch Mist
Old Moorhen's Shredded Sporran
Caribbean Sunset with a Yellow Parrot

<u>Holmes and Garden</u>

The Curious Case of the Black Swan Song

MAP OF SHEPFORD ST BERNARD

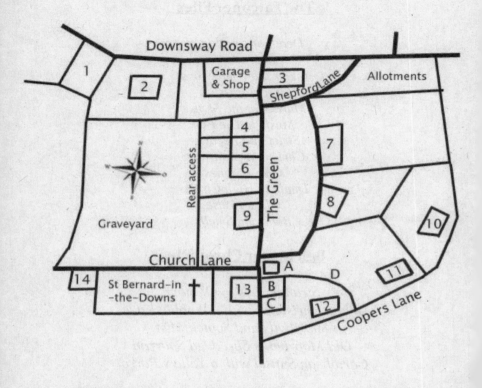

1. Hall 2. The Rectory 3. Three-Ways House 4. Tootelon Down
5. Ace of Cups 6. Carters Cottage 7. The Druid's Head
8. Sweet Dreams 9. Bijou 10. Tresore 11. Khartoum
12. Carpe Diem 13. Robin's Perch 14. Manor Gate

A. Red phone box B. Shop C. Hairdresser's D. Footpath

DRAMATIS PERSONAE

Residents of Shepford St Bernard

Asquith, Maude – an elderly spinster of faded gentility

Bingham, Violet – a widow and best friend of Lettice Keighley-Armstrong

Feldman, Rev. Florence – incumbent of St Bernard-in-the-Downs parish

Fletcher, Bonnie – a commuter and recently arrived resident

Galton, Gwendolyn – an antiques and bibelots dealer

Haygarth – Jasper and Belinda – owners of a failing textiles business

Keighley-Armstrong, Lettice – an elderly virtual recluse

Latimer, Toby – a retired gentleman who collects bibelots and antiques

Twelvetrees, Julius – a retired jeweller

Twentymen, Colin – a newcomer about whom little is known by his fellow villagers

Warwick, Wanda – a white witch

Yaxley, Krystal – wife of Kenneth who left his family on New Year's Day

Yaxley, Kevin and Keith – fraternal twin sons of Krystal and Kenneth Yaxley

Officials

Detective Inspector Harry Falconer – Market Darley CID

Detective Sergeant Davey Carmichael – Market Darley CID

Detective Constable Chris Roberts – Market Darley CID

Detective Superintendent Derek 'Jelly' Chivers – Market Darley CID

Sergeant Bob Bryant – uniformed division, Market Darley

PC Merv Green – uniformed division, Market Darley

PC 'Twinkle' Starr – uniformed division, Market Darley

Dr Philip Christmas – Forensic Medical Examiner

Dr Hortense (Honey) Dubois – psychiatrist, police consultant

PROLOGUE

Shepford St Bernard was another of the area's postcard-pretty villages, but with nothing to really attract tourists. It was a passing-through place, with very few houses, and could only be called a village rather than a hamlet because it had its own church.

As a passing-through place, however, it was ideal, and any trade it did pick up was probably due to the very few facilities that it boasted. It had a very picturesque pub, a garage with a mini-mart attached, a small independent shop, both ladies' and gentlemen's public conveniences, and a truly old-fashioned red phone box.

Thus, it was ideal for the motorists driving through, for they could fill up with petrol or diesel, stop into the pub for lunch or an evening meal or, if they had little time, grab a pasty or a sandwich from the general store, use the conveniences and, as there was a very erratic mobile phone signal in the village's environs, make any urgent phone calls that could not wait until they reached an area with better reception. There were even benches on the Green on which one could sit and eat a picnic lunch, if the weather was sufficiently clement.

The church, which was ancient, might have attracted some interest, had it not been located down a small lane, rendering it invisible from the main road, which was a pity, not just because it was a very pretty old church and eminently photogenic, but because it had probably the most esoteric name of any church in the area: St Bernard-in-the-Downs.

Shepford St Bernard was a quiet village with very few commuters rushing to and fro to Market Darley every weekday. Only one of its houses had been a weekend bolt-hole, and even that now had a more or less permanent resident.

For the ladies of this tiny watering hole there was even a minute hairdressing salon that catered for the shampoo-and-set and blue-rinse brigades. All in all, it served admirably for both those who lived there, and those who only made its acquaintance on four wheels, and life ticked over there sleepily and peacefully.

Chapter One

Friday morning – Shepford St Bernard

Rev. Florence Feldman (Florrie to her friends) sang loudly and tunelessly as she prepared for the next day's Special Occasion, which definitely had initial capitals whenever she thought about it. 'All Things Bright and Beautiful' echoed tunelessly in her flat but surprisingly strong alto voice, as she beat the cake mixture for some of her offerings for the next day. The sound echoed mercilessly round the vast, high-ceilinged kitchen of The Rectory, but of this she was totally unaware as she worked. This was her first parish and, even a couple of months after her Induction she was engulfed in enthusiasm and joy for her new position.

Her appointment at St Bernard-in-the-Downs in Shepford St Bernard had been a shock for the parishioners, even those who did not attend services, and a few of the old guard had even had the brass neck to walk out of her Induction service, once they realised that the replacement for the seventy-eight-year-old male incumbent was a young(ish) woman.

Her first Sunday service had been sparsely attended, the majority of the regular congregation – not over-large in the first place – had deserted the church in protest at having a female vicar foisted on them. Rev. Florrie, however, just ignored the lack of communicants and started on a relentless round of parish visits to try to tempt back the regulars and bulk up the congregation with younger members.

Although she was unable to find many young residents in the village, she worked with what she had and had increased attendance significantly; this being, in her opinion, for the village to have the opportunity either to blacken her name still further, or from sheer curiosity at how she would perform. Her visits carried on until she had more than doubled the attendance since she had arrived, and was still involved in a charm offensive on those she had not yet won over.

'All things wise and wonderful ...' she sang, as she shot two trays of fairy cakes into the oven and began to make the mixture for a chocolate sponge cake. She had always been an optimist, to the point that her glass was not merely half-full, but was brimming over with the intoxicating wine of enthusiasm and hope. She'd break them in the end, she just knew she would.

The next day would witness her first venture into a parish 'occasion', as she had decided that a parish party was the best way to get to know people better. It was much more efficient than visiting parishioners individually in their homes. Get them all together in one place, and she could make enormous inroads with enthusing them for her mission, as she too had been enthused, with the charming village and the pretty old church.

She had churned out over a hundred leaflets advertising the event on the old Roneo machine in the little office of the village hall, and personally put one through every letterbox in the vicinity. She had put one in the shop, the pub, the hairdresser's, and on the parish noticeboard, and exhorted all her regular worshippers to work on their friends and neighbours, particularly those who never came to the church, to meet the vicar and have a good time to boot.

Her leaflet had advertised it not just as an opportunity to meet their new incumbent, but as a 'Feed the Five Thousand' party, with a briefly worded explanation underneath, to advise people that it would not be fully catered, but that the intention was that everybody brought something to eat and drink with them, and so, between all of them, they would have a spectacular offering of refreshments.

'We plough the fields and scatter ...' she growled as she removed the fairy cakes from the oven, shot in the two cake tins of chocolate sponge to replace them, then rinsed her bowl in preparation for making butter drop biscuits, simultaneously

4

thinking it odd that she should have picked a harvest hymn when spring was in the air.

It must be the rural setting, she decided, as she put the butter on to melt and weighed the flour. She'd spent all her life, up till now, in an urban or semi-urban environment, and she was delighted to find herself deep in the countryside, and working with a completely new rhythm of life. How lucky could a person get? And tomorrow was party day!

She wasn't completely naïve, and had already obtained a special license to sell alcoholic drinks on the premises, the bar being run by the publican's wife. No party, in the circumstances, could go with a swing without a tot or two to get people relaxed and talking, and she'd also had an offer from the two sons of a parishioner to DJ for the event. She had even persuaded grim old Lettice Keighley-Armstrong to come along, provided Rev. Florrie picked her up in her ancient car and brought her home afterwards. Now that really was progress!

'All we like sheep, have gone astray-ay-ay-ay-ay-ay-ay-ay …' her tortured voice now offered to an audience of only her cat, a dumb creature with no cognizance of the fact that she had now shifted her performance to a snippet from the *Messiah*.

Becoming aware of what she was lustily roaring out made her think that it must be the rural situation of her new home that had brought that one to the surface. There were sheep everywhere surrounding the village, their lambs leaping and pirouetting in the sunshine, glad to be alive, and unaware of how short that life was going to be before they graced someone's Sunday dining table.

Out with the two halves of the chocolate sponge, and onto the cooling trays, then in with the biscuits. These offerings, along with a couple of bottles of sherry, one sweet and one dry, should be sufficient for her contribution to the party. Now, she'd have to see about putting up some bunting in the hall and inflating as many balloons as she could manage before running out of puff.

A quick glance in the mirror in the hall convinced her that she had need of a quick trip to the bathroom as she had chocolate sponge-mix stigmata on her chin and forehead, and she thundered joyously up the staircase, now whistling, in her enthusiasm for life.

She left The Rectory five minutes later, to make the short trip through the graveyard to the village hall, her short thick curls being tossed by the playful spring breeze. Rev. Florrie was of medium height and just a bit on the chubby side, but had a kind face and lively hazel eyes that held those of anyone who spoke to her, and somehow communicated her caring nature and genuine interest in others and their problems.

As she approached the hall, a stray gust of wind lifted her cassock and wrapped her head in the folds of its inky blackness, and she pulled it away from her face with a chuckle. She wore the ungainly garment with pride, and eschewed civvies whenever she could, so proud was she to have the right to be thus enrobed. She was going to enjoy decorating the hall for their forthcoming celebration, and the liveliness of the wind had merely put her in a more playful mood.

In Carpe Diem, Coopers Lane, Gwendolyn Galton was packing bibelots in newsprint in preparation for her Sunday foray into the antiques world. She was a dealer in small collectables, and made her way from fair to fair every weekend with her booty, spending her weekdays searching for new stock and cleaning and repairing her finds.

As she wrapped a particularly ugly but rare Toby jug, she sighed with pleasure, and decided that when she had filled the box she was currently working on, it would not be indecently early to stop for a cup of coffee.

Gwendolyn was a slim woman with long snow-white hair, passable features, and pale blue eyes. About fifty, she had never been married and never felt the need for a life companion. She was comfortable in her own company and only sought that of others if she was in one of her rare sociable moods. Her solitary existence bothered her not a whit, as her profession was all-consuming, and she loved what she did.

When she tripped off to the kitchen to put on the kettle, the

6

reason for packing early recurred to her, and she decided that she really must make something for the party the following evening, immediately setting her mind to decide what would have the most impact, with the least effort.

Trifle! That was it; she'd make a trifle. Everyone loved it and, since the advent of tinned custard, its assembly couldn't have been easier. It was really only a case of waiting for the jelly to set before adding the other layers.

Placing a large glass bowl and a jug on her work surface, she reached into her food cupboard and extracted two sachets of strawberry jelly crystals and a tin of fruit cocktail. A quick look in her cake tin revealed the remains of an angel cake and a raspberry Swiss roll. They would do admirably, and that would leave only the custard and whipped cream to add, with a few hundreds and thousands sprinkled on at the last minute, so that the colour hadn't bled by the time she handed it over.

She could use the water from the kettle to melt the jellies, and it could boil again for her coffee, while she arranged slices of stale cake, covered them with drained fruit, added the syrup to the jelly mix, and poured it over, although it would have to be covered and put in the fridge out of harm's way. Although she lived alone, her ginger cat, Marmalade, had esoteric tastes, and she wouldn't put it past him to develop an over-riding passion for unset strawberry jelly.

Finally pouring water over a teaspoonful of coffee granules and adding a splash of milk, she returned to contemplate what other little trifles of the collectable kind she should include for her stall on Sunday. It would be an early start, so she wouldn't stay over-long at the party; just long enough to have a little chat with her friends and acquaintances, and then head off for an early night.

Tossing her snowy locks over her shoulders, she settled down, kneeling on the floor to survey her treasures, hoping that the weather would be as fair as today when she went out touting her wares. There really was nothing worse than paying what she considered a small fortune for a pitch at a big fair, then having the turnout ruined by torrential rain, high winds, or a

7

combination of both.

In Sweet Dreams on The Green, Krystal Yaxley's fraternal twins, Kevin and Keith, entered the kitchen, to find that most of their view was taken up by their mother's wide buttocks sticking out of a cupboard door as she knelt on the floor rummaging in the back of the shelves. 'What the hell are you doing, Ma?' asked Kevin, the oldest by twenty-three minutes.

'You look like a hippo foraging in a skip,' added Keith, oblivious to how sensitive his mother was about how big she had got in the months since her husband had walked out on her.

'If you must know,' she replied, her voice muffled, as she made no effort to remove her head from the inside of the cupboard, 'I'm looking for something I can take along to that damned party without having to shell out for anything. I can't just be throwing money around, as well you know.'

'But we need some petrol money for the weekend,' Kevin informed her, a wheedling whine entering his voice.

'Look in the usual place then,' she suggested and, when Keith asked them where that might be, informed them that the best place was down the back of the sofa or the armchairs. 'Never know what treasure you're going to come up with down there,' she added, switching her attention back to what she had in her store cupboard that would not only solve the problem, but which might also be nearly out of date, thus using up something she might otherwise have to throw away if she didn't find it soon.

'Mother!' exclaimed Kevin with disgust. 'Don't you have any real money? I'm fed up going to the shop for a newspaper with a handful of coins from the small change jar.'

At this, another of life's little stings, Krystal swiftly removed her head from inside the cupboard, incautiously banging it in her haste, and raised her voice, to inform her two needy teenaged sons, 'I haven't had a penny from your father since he left. I'm well into my overdraft, even though it's only the beginning of the month, and I have no other means of getting my hands on hard cash. What do you want to do? Send me out onto the streets and pimp me?

'Why don't you get in touch with your father instead of whining at me, as if I were some sort of cash-point. I'm potless! Don't you understand the situation? He's done a bunk and taken his nice regular salary with him. Go and whinge at him, if you think it'll do you any good. If not, it's the sofa or nothing.

'And if you're bored, the lawns need mowing, the flower beds need weeding, and you could do a lot more around the house to help me, instead of just lying in bed half the day then playing your damned music for the rest of it while stuffing your faces as if you were constantly starving.'

'Bor-ing!' both lads chorused in unison.

'Boring it might be, but it's all got to be done, and I don't see why I should have to be the only one who does it when there are three of us living in this house. If you want money, go and see if you can get some bar work; wash cars, ask people if they want any gardening done. The Bank of Mum and Dad has closed down until further notice, and you'll just have to find a different source of cash. This cash-cow is milked dry. The end.'

Kevin and Keith slouched off back into the living room with sneers on their faces. So much for this being the house of their dreams: nightmares more like, the way things were going from bad to worse.

Krystal put her head back into the depths of the cupboard, thinking how spoilt the twins had been in the past. Ken had had a six-figure salary, and they'd never wanted for anything. Now he'd gone, she had no idea how on earth she was going to find the wherewithal just to keep the house going, never mind pay next term's tuition fees for them both. At least they'd be out of mischief tomorrow night DJ-ing the music for the parish party.

With a muffled yell of glee, she laid hands on two boxes of cake mix and a packet that promised a perfect lemon meringue pie; and both of them were nearly out of date. Perfect! Six months ago she could never have imagined that such meagre finds could instil her with so much triumph, but she was learning to adapt. She had no other choice.

For a few guilty seconds she remembered the appointment she had made with Wanda Warwick for the next day, and what

9

that would cost her but, in the long run, she considered that it could prove to be money well-spent, if she could get some guidance as to the right path to take in her straitened circumstances.

A similarly desperate situation was going on in the house of Jasper and Belinda Haygarth. They lived in a detached house, situated at the junction of the Downsway Road with The Green, then surrounded still further by a narrow lane that joined the aforementioned roads, creating a triangle, and it was in this triangle that their house was perched, isolated from other residences and aptly named "Three-Ways House".

They had started a textiles business when times were booming, and had made a fair bit of money from it; enough, certainly, to relocate to this postcard-pretty village, away from the urban sprawl that they had so hated. Times had changed, however, and the business was now struggling to break even, let alone make a profit, and was in a state where they had to decide if it was possible to revitalise it, or just walk away from it and cut their losses.

Belinda had had the temerity to start making a shopping list, and ask Jasper if there was anything he needed, at a point where he was contemplating the yawning financial abyss, and thus drawing out of him an unexpected tirade about her spendthrift ways, and how she was going to have to learn to live a more frugal life for the foreseeable future.

'That's all you ever do; spend, spend, spend! How on earth do you think we're going to cope with virtually no income, when you just let it run through your fingers like sand?' he yelled, quite unreasonably, in Belinda's opinion.

'I'm going out to get some *food*!' she stated, more loudly than she had intended. 'If I don't buy any, what do you propose to live on? Cockroach stew and cobwebs? You know I'll get as many things on special offer or reduced as I can find, and we don't exactly live high on the hog these days, do we?'

His reply was unreasonable and illogical, but he couldn't help himself. 'Why the hell are you always buying food? How on earth do we manage to get through so much of the stuff when there's only the two of us?'

'I go once a week to the supermarket, and always when I know they're going to be reducing things, and the reason I'm 'always buying food', as you put it, is because eating is a daily occurrence, and I emptied my emergency store cupboard some time ago. We don't have any food stockpiled like we used to. And anyway, you eat like a horse. I honestly believe you've got hollow legs. I've never known anyone to pack away as much as you do; and three times a day to boot.

'You spend little enough time on the business these days. Why don't you get up off your well-fed arse and dig up that back garden? That way, we could at least grow some of our own stuff. And no, it won't be ready for some time, but later is better than never.' With that sobering suggestion, that he actually do something practical, instead of moaning all the time, his wife flounced out of the house, just in time to miss his indignant protest at the size of his backside, and the voraciousness of his appetite.

Belinda's mind was more concerned with how she could take something appetising to the hall tomorrow for next to no outlay. If she could find a pack of bacon offcuts, maybe she could make an egg and bacon quiche. That always went down well and wouldn't cost her much, if she bought own brand eggs (hopefully near their sell-by date and reduced to clear) and flour, and bought a pack of bacon off-cuts, which may even be reduced too. It was certainly the right time of day for the supermarket employees to be swanning round the store with their price-guns. She just might strike lucky.

She drove off, determined to do her best to spend as little as possible, and to prod her husband to make a start on growing their own food. The latter was not an instant solution, but if he never started, the idea would never come to fruition.

In the house anachronistically named Khartoum, Maude Asquith was also going through her own store cupboards, to gather together the ingredients she would need for the jam tarts and madeleines she intended to bake on Saturday morning, fresh for the party later in the day.

She was an elderly spinster who still lived in the house she had been born in, and in which her father had also first drawn breath, as had his father before him, his widow naming the house in memory of his honourable death in the ill-fated massacre of the Anglo-Egyptian Garrison in 1884-5.

The furniture bore witness to the lack of change that had locked the house in a time-warp in the latter years of Queen Victoria's reign, the family never having been wealthy, and believing that if an object was still functioning there was no need whatsoever to change it. Thus horsehair sofas still adorned her sitting room, and her dining room furniture was of the sturdy style that would probably withstand a nuclear attack.

The bedrooms were similarly furnished, with brass bedsteads, mahogany dressing tables and wardrobes, all lovingly polished by their current owner, and cherished in her memory as a sign of stability in the unchanging tenor of her life.

Not for Maude the fitted carpets and leather furniture of the modern sitting room; no chrome and glass dining table with chrome and leather chairs. It was not that she wouldn't have entertained the idea, had she been sufficiently well-off to consider such a vast change, more a case of always having to survive on limited resources, especially since her parents had died. The loss of their pensions to the household's running costs had been a major blow, as they had died within six months of each other, and she had found it hard to make ends meet ever since.

She soldiered on though, as she had been raised to, making do and mend; taking care of the good quality clothes that she had owned for years, and appearing to care not a fig for fashion, even if it was all an enormous bluff. Sometimes she used to sit and daydream about having untold riches and planning what she would do if she were ever in control of a fortune.

Fortunately, such idle and unrealistic daydreams did not occur too often, but were part of the reason that she, over the last year or two, had launched such a charm offensive on Lettice

Keighley-Armstrong.

She had known Lettice slightly over the years and never really considered it worth wasting her time with such a curmudgeonly old grouse. In more recent times, however, she had begun to realise just how much Lettice was worth, after calling there once with the Christian Aid collecting box as a favour to the dear old vicar, who had been such a sweet old man that one could never say no to him.

On this occasion she had been asked in, to wait while Lettice looked for her purse and as she stood in the drawing room with the old woman pawing through her desk and enormous handbag, she had looked round at the dark furniture, and realised that it was not the same calibre as that which adorned her own home. Lettice's had been fine Georgian pieces, with a few touches of William III. There had even been a couple of medieval coffers placed in the window bays, lurking there darkly and expensively.

She had taken a peek into the dining room while Lettice had been thus occupied, and espied furniture that would fetch untold tens of thousands of pounds in the auction rooms, so rare were they, and of such antiquity.

The floors of both rooms were also covered in huge rugs that looked as if they had been woven from money, and by the time that Miss Keighley-Armstrong had located her battered old pigskin purse and carefully fed three pennies and six two-pence pieces through the slot of the collection box, Maude had decided that she had found a new best friend to cultivate.

The woman was, after all, unmarried, and had no family as far as she understood, and would need a good friend to whom she could leave all her earthly belongings. Why shouldn't that dear and trusted friend be Maude Asquith? She was only seventy-two to Lettice's eighty-five, and had much more time to have a real spree in the autumn of her life, before winter set in.

And so, began Operation Lettice, a charm offensive of such fervour and servility that Miss Keighley-Armstrong wasn't taken in for a minute, much preferring the comfortable old friendship she had with Violet Bingham, a relationship that had existed for what seemed like for ever now, and was in no danger of fading away.

Not realising that she had been rumbled right at the beginning of her plan and didn't have a choc-ice's chance in hell of being mentioned in Lettice's will, Maude put on her light spring coat, adjusted her hat in the hall mirror, and left home to make the short trek down Church Lane to 'Manor Gate' to ingratiate herself, once more, with the old woman.

As she crossed The Green, she noticed Wanda Warwick shaking a duster out of her front window, and waved to her, happy that she was on her way to a visit that might help her feather her own nest with some very fine down.

Wanda Warwick had been having a bit of a clean-up, and noticed the sprightly elderly woman crossing the road, her cream coat and fawn hat catching the brightness of the spring sunshine. At least she didn't seem to be on her way to see her, she thought as she waved with one hand and shook her duster furiously with the other. Company like that she could do without.

She simply didn't have the time for inane gossip and chatter. There were more important things going on in her life; like getting her small cottage clean and tidy for her appointment the next day with Krystal Yaxley. Then, on Sunday, she had a booth at a spring fair, which should bring in some much-needed funds, as her resources were running low. It had been a bad winter in her field of expertise, and she hoped the brightly optimistic weather would prompt people to seek her services now that winter was over and they could feel more positive about life, and optimistic about the future.

Closing the window, she surveyed her small sitting room, trying to adopt the eyes of a stranger to the little property. What impression did it give to an outsider? she wondered. Were there a tad too many dream-catchers hanging at the windows? Were the signs of the zodiac on the ceiling a bit over the top?

Remembering the state her kitchen was still in from the

night before, she muttered, 'To hell with it! It's my home, and it should reflect my lifestyle, otherwise I might as well be living with someone, and spend most of my life compromising. This is how I like it, and if she doesn't like it, she can do one!'

Wanda was a white witch, or follower of Wicca, and lived her life accordingly. Nature must have picked up on this important thread running through her life, for as she turned fifty her features had become more prominent than in the earlier decades of her life, and her nose, with its hooked shape had lengthened, and her chin grown until, now, the unwary would immediately think of a witch on first sight of her, their impression only enhanced by the fact that she dyed her hair an unbecoming and unlikely jet black.

Her clothes were, by habit, black; her complexion pallid in the extreme, and she wore too much make-up, also a relic of her youth. She was quite an intimidating looking woman to anyone who did not know her, and had taken some time to be accepted into village life. After a few years, however, the other residents were used to her, and barely noticed how bizarre she looked when she went out in one of her black cloaks, looking for all the world as if she was off to either a Hallowe'en party or a Black Mass.

An hour later, having tackled the squalor awaiting her in the kitchen, she returned to the sitting room, mug of herbal tea in hand, to sort through her tarot cards and just get the feel of them again for her appointment tomorrow, for reading these cards was another of her eccentricities. She had not done a reading for at least three months, and felt that she needed to get to know her cards again by handling them so that they would fall right for her the next day.

As she sat shuffling, dealing, and laying out her tarot cards, wafts of lavender and herbs drifted down from tied bunches hanging from hooks on the central beam to tease her nostrils. Sitting thus in quiet contemplation, she let her mind wander to the reading she would do the next day. She knew very little about Krystal Yaxley, having had little to do with her since she and her family had settled in the village.

The first time she had spared a thought for her was when the news got out that her husband had walked out on her and their teenaged twin sons on New Year's Day, as if he had made a resolution to do so and not lost his nerve at the last minute. Both boys, she knew, were at university somewhere in the north of the country, and she imagined that Wanda's comfortable, almost charmed life had been absolutely shattered by the sudden departure of her husband and the family's only wage-earner.

Dealing the cards one more time, she tried to capture the right frame of mind for divination. The woman would need advice and help, and a little guidance from the cards would not go amiss in pointing out the right path to follow for the best outcome for her in the future.

In Manor Gate, once a rather grand gate house to the now demolished Georgian country house it had at one time, served Lettice Keighley-Armstrong sipped a cup of Darjeeling tea, relishing the spring-like weather, her French windows wide open, letting in the delicious fragrance of freshly mown grass. Lettice sniffed greedily as she heard the mower buzzing away in what she assumed was Colin Twentymen's rear garden. Very particular, he was, about the state of his garden; she often heard him at work in it, mowing, strimming, and trimming his hedges.

She relished days like today particularly, because she comprehended that she didn't have too many of them left. At eighty-five, she had no real health problems, but sometimes health was only skin-deep. Who knew what lay under the surface, gathering its strength to make an ambush? Many a friend of hers had died from an unexpected heart attack or a stroke. Even cancer camouflaged itself well until it was ready to reveal itself, ugly and gloating, as it spread to other parts of the body that had virtually no effective weapons to deal with it long term.

Every morning when she woke up she decided it was definitely a good day, simply because she had woken up at all, and though she showed most people the rough side of her tongue when dealing with them, it was not out of any innate bad temper; merely that she relished her own company, solitude being a friend that had never let her down. It was just part of her nature to be alone, and only the visits of her old friend Violet Bingham filled her with pleasure these days.

Her chair was turned towards the open French windows, so that she could watch the birds feasting at the feeders she had hung from the trees, within easy view of her armchair, this being one of her pleasures in life. With a sigh, she realised that spring was probably her favourite season, and mourned the fact that this one may be the last one she saw. This thought made her more determined than ever to enjoy every minute of it and not waste her time shut away with the doors all locked and the windows closed.

As she watched the birds and listened to their shrill exchange of opinions, her hands played idly with a string of dull stones that hung from her neck; an odd contrast with the quality of her old silk blouse. At each wrist were strings of the same dull stones, which had the look of childhood acquisitions, if not that of cheap holiday souvenirs, but she seemed inordinately fond of them and they must have held some special memory for her, for she was never seen without them.

Many who knew her had speculated about why she was so attached to such dreary baubles, when her mother had possessed such fine jewellery, made up especially from stones her husband had purchased during his years in South Africa, but none could come up with any explanation that would explain this fondness for such tawdry ornaments.

Her old black and white cat, previously taking a nap on the sofa, awoke, stretched luxuriously, then jumped to the floor and made his way over to the open doors. 'Well, hello to you, Mischief. Finally woke up, did you?'

The cat stared at her as she spoke to it, then turned to take a look out into the garden. Ignoring the birds – he was much too old even to think he could catch one nowadays, he turned back towards his mistress and made a brave attempt to jump into her lap.

Picking him up and plonking him on his goal, her hand automatically started to stroke his head, and she smiled at the loudness of his purr. He was getting on a bit, she thought, but he had been good company, and a much needed distraction when Daddy had finally died, and she was left totally on her own in the world. Maybe they'd both go to sleep one night and slip away together in the same night. That would be perfect, but very unlikely.

Turning her mind towards their new lady vicar, she smiled at how horrified she had been at the woman's appointment, being one of the first to get up and leave during the Induction service. But, give her her due: the woman had made a point of visiting her, to discuss any worries that might exist in her public disapproval, and had carried on visiting ever since.

Lettice's second thoughts had led her to thoroughly approve of Rev. Florrie. She now considered her a bright and enthusiastic girl to whose visits she now looked forward, and thought that she would do a lot of good in her calling, especially for women who had real problems.

Her persistence was the real reason she had agreed to go to the parish party, her insistence on a lift there and home again, just her way of letting Rev. Florrie know who was still in charge, and that she hadn't broken the old woman's spirit with her weekly visits that were becoming more and more of a pleasure, much to Lettice's surprise.

Heck! She wasn't getting soft in her extreme old age, was she? That would never do! As she came to this decision, she heard the tinkle of the old-fashioned pull doorbell, and pulled herself to her feet to answer it, rather hoping that it would be Rev. Florrie, for she felt a little of that young lady's company would be good for her, while she was still in such a good mood, herself.

'Hello, Maude!' she greeted her visitor with a grimace, her feelings of goodwill to all the world suddenly evaporating. 'I can't ask you in, I'm afraid; I'm very busy today with some paperwork from my solicitor. Unless it's something urgent, do you think you could call back another time?'

18

Maude Asquith smiled sycophantically at the old woman, and said that it didn't matter a jot. She was only a few minutes' walk away, and could pop over anytime without any inconvenience whatsoever. That said, she made an involuntary movement that resembled nothing more than a semi-curtsy, and turned from the door to return home.

'Thank the good Lord for that,' muttered Lettice under her breath as her visitor departed, having no idea how her off-the-cuff excuse had excited the spurned caller.

Maude hurried off back home, her stomach churning with excitement. Two years ago next month, it would be, since she had started to court the old woman. This talk of paperwork from a solicitor could mean she had achieved her objective. Never even contemplating that it might have been an out-and-out lie just to get rid of her, she had visions of Lettice drawing up a new will in her favour, and her mouth almost watered at the appetising thought of so much money.

While Colin Twentymen cultivated his garden at the rear of Carters Cottage, two other village residents sat at a table in the beer garden at the rear of The Druid's Head, stretching out their pints as long as they could. Both retired and both able to comprehend the attraction of each other's former professions, they spent as much time as they could in each other's company to avoid, what they referred to as, 'being stalked by all the old tabbies'. There was safety in numbers, they believed, and they were much more vulnerable to attack when they were alone.

Today being such a glorious and unseasonably warm day, they had met in The Druid's Head after a scratch lunch in their own homes. Money for a pint was one thing; money for a pub lunch was quite another, and completely out of the question financially. They were both pragmatic where money was concerned, and hated to waste it on unnecessary expenses like eating in the pub.

At the moment they were discussing their finances. Julius Twelvetrees, who resided at Bijou, The Green, and Toby Lattimer of Tresore in Coopers Lane, also retired and an avid collector of small but beautiful things, had found their pensions shrink in value over the years, and the current financial situation had more or less wiped out interest from savings which had made up part of their incomes in the past.

'There was a time when I could count on nine per cent on my savings, and some good dividends from my shares,' moaned Toby Lattimer, 'but the way things are at the moment, with everything seeming to get more expensive by the day, I've a real job just getting by on what my pension buys these days.'

'I know how you feel, but at least you could sell some of your bibelots, and you've got a load of antique furniture. I know they're mostly small pieces, but some of them are quite exquisite.'

'Perish the thought!' his compatriot in complaint exclaimed. 'And what about you? You're a retired jeweller, for heaven's sake. Surely you've got some old stock from your shop that you could hock to bring in a bob or two?'

'All gone, I'm afraid. I've been doing that for some time now, and I sold the very last bit just before Christmas. And I've still got that great pile of a house in Carsfold. That'll have to go. I can't keep that on any longer. It costs far too much to run; the heating bill alone would turn your stomach if I showed it to you.'

'Have you got any idea how a couple of old codgers like us could make a bob or two just to fill the larder?' asked Julius hopefully.

'Well, yes, I have had an idea occur to me, but a bit less of the 'old codgers' if you don't mind. Me, I'm in my prime, even if you are over the hill.' Toby was, in fact, sixty-six and Julius sixty-eight years of age.

'Come on, man, spit it out, and don't keep me in suspenders, as they say. I mean, apart from winning the Lottery or having a rich relative die and leave you the lot, what other chance is there of coming into a large sum of money?'

Toby merely tapped the side of his nose with an index finger and winked at his eager companion. 'All in good time, Julius, old chap. All in good time. What I will tell you is that it involves a bit of stake money, involves the currency market, and isn't entirely without risk.'

'You can forget that, then. Firstly, I haven't got any stake money and, secondly, if I had, I couldn't afford to risk it. Whatever it is, you'll have to go it alone, and maybe I'll join you, if it proves to be a success.' Julius was definitely out.

'Just sounding you out, old man: just sounding you out, that's all.'

From the little detached house next to the church, there was neither sound nor movement. Bonnie Fletcher fled the village each weekday morning in her little Peugeot, swearing that today would be the day that she missed her train, and returned every evening at about seven-thirty, tired and exasperated, after yet another day spent in the city.

Most weekends she spent in Market Darley where there was a little more nightlife than that provided by The Druid's Head, usually cadging sofas or a spare room from her old school-friends, with whom she socialised. There was no point in going out if she couldn't have a drink, and if she had to drive home, she might as well not go out at all.

Some residents wondered why she didn't just sell up and move to Market Darley, for that was where she spent two days of the week; the other five she commuted from there, so there seemed little point in her living in such an out of the way place as Shepford St Bernard. And this she wouldn't have done, unless her grandmother hadn't left her the cottage, after spending her last ten years in a nursing home.

Property prices were still falling in some areas, and this was definitely not the time to put a piece of prime real estate, such as her pretty village cottage, on to the market. She would put up with her rushed life, as it was only until the market picked up, and she could ask a fair price for a very desirable residence. Bonnie Fletcher considered that she had her head screwed on the right way, and could run her life with the maximum precision, if she just trusted her instincts.

Chapter Two

Friday morning – Market Darley

The door of the CID office in Market Darley was flung open with so much enthusiasm that it rebounded off the inside wall of the room, and DC Chris Roberts bounded in booming an enthusiastic, 'Morning, Guv. Morning Our Davey.'

The two men already in the office both looked up at him with disapproving expressions. 'That's "Sir" or "Inspector" to you, Roberts, as well you know,' this from DI Harry Falconer, the senior plain clothes officer who was almost at the end of his tether with this relative newcomer's inability to understand that he hated being called 'Guv'.

The extra-large man at the other desk patiently waited his turn to complain, and advised the new arrival, 'I'd prefer it if you'd call me Carmichael. Davey's only for family and very close friends.' DS Carmichael was similarly not enamoured of Roberts' informal manner of address.

DI Falconer and DS Carmichael had been working together for some time now, Falconer having joined the Force fresh from some years in the army, after completing a university degree. DS Carmichael had joined as a rookie in uniform, working his way up to his current position more by luck than by judgement.

DC Roberts had arrived on secondment the previous autumn, having secured a temporary transfer from Manchester to help his mother, who had suffered a stroke, and needed some assistance in her daily life while recuperating. His first assignment had been to go undercover as a mature student at the local college but, after an unfortunate incident that hospitalised him for some time, followed by a long period of convalescence, he had been preparing to return to work in the early February.

Unfortunately, a few days before he was due to resume his duties, his mother had suffered another and more catastrophic stroke, and had not survived. That had necessitated him seeking compassionate leave to deal with the paperwork, always a part of any death and, during this period, he had requested a permanent transfer to Market Darley, as he had inherited the family home on his mother's demise, and now needed time to go back to Manchester to give notice on his old digs and tidy up his affairs that end.

Thus, on this beautiful early March morning, he had re-entered their lives with his habitual breezy brashness. 'I'm back!' he announced unnecessarily, as if his returning presence was the most wonderful present they could ever receive, headed for the empty desk that had been prepared for him, and slumped down in the office chair as if he had only been gone for ten minutes.

'Doing anything special this weekend, then, Davey boy?' he asked Carmichael, his good natured face split with a broad, good-humoured grin.

'Please call me Carmichael,' replied the sergeant, making no attempt to answer the question.

'OK! Keep your hair on! I only asked if you've got anything planned for the weekend.'

As Carmichael composed his answer in his head, Falconer muttered, 'Sounds like a ruddy barber,' under his breath.

'As it happens, I am doing something rather special this weekend; tomorrow night, in fact,' Carmichael replied, his face lighting up as he remembered his plans for later.

'What's that then, my little sergeant?' asked Roberts, drawing a scowl from Falconer, and the admonition to show a little more respect for his senior officers.

'I'm going out with my family for the very belated wetting of two babies' heads,' he informed the DC, his expression daring him to ask for more details.

'Oh yes, I remember now. Someone told me you'd become a father, and that *Detective Inspector Falconer* – I bet that was fun for all concerned – had delivered the new arrival.

24

Congratulations to both of you. But whose is the other baby?'

Falconer didn't rise to the bait, and left it to Carmichael to provide any detail that the DC thought was his due. Carmichael obliged willingly, to avoid the topic of little Harriet's birth, simply announcing, 'My new little brother,' then buttoning his lip, as if there were a draught in the room, and he needed to keep his teeth warm.

With a widening of his eyes, Roberts let his mouth fall open and, before he gave himself time to think, asked, 'Good God! How old is your mother, for heaven's sake?' then, seeing the vast body of the DS start to rise from his chair, carried on without a break, with, 'All right! All right! I realise that was out of order. I was just surprised, that's all. What's his name?'

'Harry,' he replied, knowing exactly what was coming next.

'And your little one? A girl, I heard.'

'Harriet,' announced Carmichael, adopting an aggressive manner that dared Roberts to challenge anything he had just learnt.

Roberts, however, had the hide of a rhinoceros and commented, one index finger on his bottom lip, 'Oooh! Has the inspector been making house-calls then, or is all this just a coincidence, Inspector, *sir*?'

Falconer looked daggers at his newly returned DC, and explained that Carmichael had named his daughter after him because of the circumstances that had resulted in him delivering the baby. 'About Mrs Carmichael Senior's choice of name, I have no knowledge whatsoever, although I thought she usually favoured Shakespearean names. What's the story there, Sergeant?'

'Same old thing, sir, except this time she didn't go for a character. She was all caught up with that speech about ... I dunno, something about "Cry God for Harry". There's no point in asking me. I don't read a lot of Shakespeare, but Mum's always been hooked in a strange sort of "watching the films" way.'

'But you said she'd named you 'Ralph', and only gave you a Shakespearean middle name.' Falconer had forgotten why this was. Roberts merely sat with his mouth open as this esoteric conversation unravelled before his very ears.

'I thought I told you she had a thing about Sir Ralph Richardson at the time, only she always pronounced it 'Raif'. God only knows why! And that's why I like to be known as Davey. *If* I've given my permission, that is,' he finished, with a glower at Roberts.

'What the hell are the rest of your family called, for goodness sake?' Roberts was, by now, fascinated, and wanted to follow through to the bitter end.

Taking this in good part, Carmichael began to enumerate his six siblings, quite enjoying the experience of somebody actually being interested in anything concerning him. 'The oldest is Romeo, but he's just known as Rome and he's a builder. Next there's Hamlet: known as Ham, and he works on a farm. Third is Mercutio, just called Merc, and he's a 'man with a van' – does all kinds of stuff.

'I'm next, then the two girls. Juliet's the eldest, and she's a hairdresser and beautician, and Imogen's a librarian. Now we've got little Harry to add to the mob as well.' As Carmichael finished, he smiled at the thought of his siblings, having long ago got over the initial embarrassment he had felt at his mother having another baby at her age.

'Blimey! What a tribe! Have you got any brother or sisters, Guv?'

'Sir,' Falconer corrected him.

'Sorry! Have you got any brothers and sisters, SIR?'

'No,' replied the inspector, with a note of finality in his voice. 'Now, if we could get on with a little work before lunchtime, I'd be very grateful. Here, Roberts, I've got some crime figures in this folder for you to collate. Just hand them in to Bob Bryant on the desk when they're done. Thank you.'

As DC Roberts accepted the file handed to him and dipped his head towards his work, Falconer asked Carmichael what his exact plans were for this delayed celebration. Carmichael's expression of familial pride was a joy to see, and he explained, 'Merc's arranged a minibus taxi for them all to come over to

Castle Farthing, and we're going to spend the evening in The Fisherman's Flies. Dad's babysitting – unheard of in the past – and Ma's coming with them all, as part of it is to celebrate Harry's birth. It should be a riot.'

'Not as much of a riot as your crazy wedding was, I hope.' Falconer still shuddered when he remembered the state the Carmichaels had got him into at that.

'Dunno, sir, but it should be a blast, and I'm not rostered to work on Sunday, so I can get over whatever happens at my own pace.'

'Can I come?' asked Roberts.

'No!' said Carmichael emphatically. 'It's family only,' and turned back to the paperwork on his desk.

Falconer sighed with relief, having, for a moment, wondered if the sergeant was going to extend an invitation to him as he had delivered young Harriet.

28

Chapter Three

Saturday morning – Shepford St Bernard

In The Rectory in Shepford St Bernard, Rev. Florrie woke early, as usual, her mind already seething with all the duties and chores she had to get through that day. She would start with morning prayers in the church, a part of her duty that she usually carried out in utter solitude, as no one ever bothered to show up for them, then she would get back to the hall and blow up some more balloons.

Her efforts the previous day had seemed pretty good to her. Sixty balloons had taken a lot of puff, but when she tied them together in threes and hung them from various points along the wall near the ceiling, they had suddenly looked pathetic, and she had resolved to return there on the morrow and redouble her efforts. There were also some paper chains that she had managed to recover from a box in the attic and these she would also hang, just to give the place a less bare and more festive air.

She had a couple of visits to make to parishioners just outside the village itself and thought that, by then, she'd probably be ready for her lunch. In the afternoon, she'd have to get the tables and chairs set out ready for the food and the party-goers later, and she'd have to be there to receive the twins with their equipment for the evening's music, then she'd have to remember to pick up Lettice before people arrived so that she could greet everyone personally. It was going to be a busy day.

In the shower, she boomed out a loop of the *Hallelujah Chorus*. Unable to progress through the piece, she was quite happy just to make a joyous circle of it, while she soaped and rinsed and shampooed and conditioned. Dried and dressed in her everyday chasuble, she descended the stairs and threw together a huge heap of scrambled eggs to accompany the three slices of toast that she had just removed from the grill. A girl with such a busy life needed a hearty breakfast, she thought, and a hearty lunch, and an equally hearty supper.

The weather was as fair today as it had been the day before, as she trotted off to St Bernard's, a stout canvas bag in her right hand; a suitable receptacle for un-inflated balloons and paper streamers. There was no need to take her ancient car on such a glorious day and with such a short distance between the two buildings, and walking was certainly a lot healthier than driving.

As expected, the church was devoid of other human habitation, and she settled to her prayers in solitary state, as she had expected to. Although it made her feel a little guilty, this lack of company did mean she could gabble the words a bit, and gain a few more minutes in the day than she would have had had someone else turned up, and for this she was grateful.

A little later, as she entered the hall, she concurred with her own opinion of the day before. The balloons did look pathetic, as if only a half-hearted attempt had been made to brighten the place up, and that would never do. She was happy in her work and wanted to show her happiness to her parishioners with as much of a show as she could.

The stepladder was where she had left it the day before, and she settled herself on one of the stacking chairs and began to huff and puff to increase the festive look as much as possible. Every now and again she took a rest and put up some paper streamers, to relieve her labouring lungs, then returned to the balloons again.

Not a soul turned up to see if she needed any help, but then that would probably not have crossed their minds, as the previous elderly incumbent was too feeble even to attempt any parish activity like this, and they were unused to being asked to contribute a little time and effort in preparation for anything of the sort.

By a quarter to eleven, she knew that she had done all she

could to brighten up the place, and strolled back to The Rectory to collect her travelling communion set, in preparation for her morning visits. Neither of the two elderly people she was visiting was 'high' enough to consider fasting before the wafer and wine had been received, so she need feel no guilt that they would waste away at her late arrival.

At twelve-thirty, Toby Lattimer emerged from the bar of The Druid's Head into the pub garden, a pint pot in one hand and a carrier bag in the other, to see his friend and neighbour Julius Twelvetrees already sitting out there at the table they had frequented the previous day. At his feet sat two carrier bags; one with a well-known supermarket chain's logo on it, the other plain.

'Ah, I see you and I had the same idea, then: buy something for this blessed party rather than have to rustle up something,' chortled Toby, settling himself at the table and unburdening himself of the full carrier bag. 'I got my lot in the general store – such a Godsend they have a licence to sell alcohol, I always think. So handy if one runs out of anything outside regular opening hours, and they are open all hours; that's one thing that can be said for them.'

'I split my bit of shopping,' replied Julius. 'Got some cheap hooch in the "general" then popped over to the other one, where I know the snacks are a bit cheaper. How on earth we didn't run into each other I don't know.'

'Accident of timing, I expect,' mused Toby, 'rather like one of those old-fashioned Whitehall farce thingies: people going in and out of doors and all over the place, but never bumping into any of the others.'

'That's the ticket,' agreed Julius and took a long swallow of his beer. 'So we've both been conscripted to turn up to this 'do' tonight, then?'

'Looks like it. I shan't stay late, myself; just pop in, deliver the goodies, as it were, then get off home about an hour later.'

'Couldn't agree more. Don't intend to make a late night of it, either. Just look in for form's sake, speak to a few people, then back to my armchair and a bit of telly.'

'Get you another one, old man?' queried Toby who had already drained his glass. 'Hot day and all that.'

'Delighted, sir. You are a gentleman,' accepted Julius, passing his glass across the table and smiling happily at not being the first one to get in a round. It must be his lucky day. Good thing he'd got here first and had only to buy his own pint, and he'd get himself off after this one, and avoid having to put his hand in his own pocket for any drinks other than his first. And he'd saved a bit by buying his snacks at the garage shop. No point in paying more for anything if one didn't have to, was there?

In several of the other houses in Shepford St Bernard there were preparations being made for the party. Krystal Yaxley, in particular, was in a bit of a tizzy, with so many things to fit into just one day. She had her lemon meringue and Victoria sponge to make in the morning, then her appointment with Wanda in the afternoon, followed by an early start for the party. The vicar had decided that it would commence at six o'clock, to allow those with young children to come along without worrying about bedtime.

Although Wanda felt stressed, she did spare a thought for Rev. Florrie. These things needed a lot of thankless arranging and work, and her decision to make such an early start proved that she recognised the fact that any children attending and therefore going to bed late would not be expected by their parents to be up with the lark on Sunday, as no doubt very few of them would be contemplating the early service that the vicar had to conduct, whether there were any others present or not.

The thought didn't last long, however, as her mind was drawn inexorably to what would happen when she kept her appointment with Wanda. Would she have anything promising to tell her? Was the future all doom and gloom? Or was there something brighter on the horizon for her, after her family's disastrous start to the year? She didn't really know whether she believed in divination, but was willing to give it a try, and just

32

hoped the twins had no inkling that her sixty minute session was going to cost her forty pounds when she'd been so hard on them when they'd asked her for money.

What on earth was she doing, anyway, blowing forty pounds on the dubious reputation of a white witch and tarot reader? She could have put some petrol in the car, got in a bit of food, and treated herself to a cheap bottle of wine for that amount of money. Still, she'd always been one for her facials, manicures, and pedicures before Kenneth left. This was just a little treat for her, and might even yield some sound advice. She needed something to cheer her up, after all she'd been through in the last couple of months.

Slipping the lemon meringue pie into the oven and leaving the ready-filled sponge-tins on the side to go in next, her ears were suddenly assaulted by the familiar 'thump, thump, thump' from her sons, trying out their equipment for later, before they transported it over to the hall and, as usual, the strip light in the kitchen began to vibrate against the ceiling.

The noise had always irritated her in the past, but at least it probably meant that the boys were adjusting better than she was, to their new and unwelcome deserted way of life. If only Kenneth would get in touch, or put some money into the bank account. If nothing else, it would at least prove that he hadn't disappeared off the face of the earth and was still living and breathing, even if it wasn't in what she had always considered their dream house.

She had convinced him to change the name to 'Sweet Dreams' when they had first moved in, considering that it was the perfect house for them to finish raising the boys then settle down to growing old together, and now here she was, suddenly a single parent – her dreams for the future completely shattered, her financial position uncomfortably precarious. For a moment, a wave of utter despair rolled over her, but she fought to free herself from it, biting back bitter tears of self-pity and resentment.

With a shake of her head at these negative thoughts, she put on the oven timer to alert her when the pie was ready, and went off to the bedroom to start getting ready for her reading. She needed to keep up appearances at all costs, and her nails badly needed doing, even if she wasn't used to doing them herself, her hair could do with some attention, and she didn't have even a lick of make-up on her face.

As she sat, totally absorbed in the creation of the camouflage with which she faced the outside world, in the bedroom across the landing Kevin and Keith were compiling the music they intended to offer the party-goers later that day.

They realised that they would have to use a lot of stuff that they considered should have been consigned to the musical dustbin thirty or more years ago, but there were a couple of numbers that they were going to slip in towards the end of the evening, when the old folks were a little more relaxed and had had a drink or two. 'The Real Slim Shady' was one of them, and Keith was still not sure whether or not this particular track would get them in hot water.

'Look, bro,' Kevin said, with a determined stare at his twin, 'if we're going to be spinning the tunes, then let's at least put something in that'll make some people prick up their ears; then, as it's such old hat now, we can claim that we chose it at random and didn't know what it was like till we started playing it. That way we can have a giggle *and* shock the old dears, without being busted for it. Mum's been a pushover since Dad left, and we might as well take advantage of that.'

'And you don't think that's taking the piss?' queried Keith.

'No way, bro. We've got to get our fun somewhere, and there's precious little of it in this house at the moment. Just think of their faces, as the words start to sink in.'

'OK, you've convinced me,' agreed Keith, always the weaker of the two. 'But if we get grounded, I'm going to tell Mum it was your idea and you bullied me into it.'

'Wuss!' replied his brother, not taking his gaze off the music he was putting in order for later.

Maude Asquith was in Khartoum's antiquated kitchen, the jam tarts already cooling on a large wire cooling tray, the madeleines now taking up her attention as she prepared to construct the outer coating, as her mother had taught her when she was young. None of those tiddly little French biscuits for her.

To her, a madeleine was a little tower of sponge cake, covered in apricot jam, then rolled in coconut. On the table, beside the tray of already cool cakes, were a bowl of warmed apricot jam and her baking slab, a small area of which was covered in desiccated coconut. No one had ever failed to be delighted with these little cakes when she had produced them, and there was another batch in the oven already, for she needed to bring enough to satisfy all-comers.

As she coated and rolled, she turned her thoughts to dear Lettice, and how she had been sucking up to her recently – not that she put it quite that way, herself. The two of them had been united in their disapproval of their new lady vicar, but the young woman hadn't given up, and had visited Lettice at least once a week since she arrived – as Lettice had, at that point, stopped attending Sunday service, as had Maude. Maude herself had rebuffed the young woman's advances on her first visit to Khartoum, and requested that she didn't waste any more time in calling again.

For a week or two, Maude had tried to revert Lettice's opinion back to disapproval, but something about the young cleric must have moved her, and suddenly she was back in her usual pew on a Sunday morning, joining in with a fervour she hadn't shown for years, as some of the congregation had been only too eager to tell Maude.

What else could she do but capitulate, and start going again herself, making sure that when she schmoozed the vicar, she did it in Lettice's full sight. There was no point in going out of her way to suck up to somebody she disapproved of so much, and not have the object of her real attention not notice what she was doing.

Rev. Florrie really brought out the worst in her, and she'd happily have spat in her face, had circumstances been different, but she just had to keep in with Lettice. An elderly spinster in

35

possession of her own property and a fortune in jewellery and stones, which she had inherited from her mother, was not someone to get on the wrong side of, and there was always hope that she would be mentioned in the will. She'd certainly worked hard enough at smarming her way into at least a small inheritance.

God knows, she could do with an injection of capital. The interest she received from her investments was pitiful, but she daren't liquidate any of them, in case interest rates rose again and left her under-invested. Yes, a little bit of bunce would be very nice indeed, and Lettice couldn't last for ever. The last time she'd worked it out, she had decided that Lettice was eighty-five if she was a day. She had to go some time and, when she did, it would be nice to receive a little of her largesse; posthumously, as it would have to be.

She'd go to the party tonight and be as nice as pie to the two of them, even though she had nothing but contempt for Lettice, who had so much and did nothing with it, and for the vicar, just because she was a woman in what Maude considered was a man's territory. There seemed to be no end, these days, to the amount of hypocrisy a person had to go through, just to get a little injection of liquid assets.

In Carters Cottage on The Green, Colin Twentymen looked smugly at the three dozen golden scones he had just baked, and wondered what the reaction of his neighbours would be when he turned up with them this evening. He'd seen Lattimer and Twelvetrees stocking up in the village shops, and knew all they would contribute would be crisps, pretzels, and other similar pre-packaged offerings.

He had kept himself very much to himself since he had moved into his present home, and would continue to do so, staying for only a short while tonight. That he was going along at all surprised him, but the vicar had seemed so determined that he, as a relative newcomer, should come along and meet many of his neighbours that, in the end, he hadn't had the heart to refuse her pleadings.

He'd hand over his scones, looking out for the surprised glances that he hoped they would draw, have a drink, listen to whatever was on offer musically for half an hour or so, nip outside to smoke a pipe, then go back in for another drink – and to say goodnight to everyone, claiming that he had been working so hard in the garden, with the glorious weather, that he needed an early night.

Let 'em carry on guessing, he thought. Whatever he had done in his past, was concerned with in the present, and planned to do in the future, was nobody's business but his own, and he intended for things to stay that way.

Chapter Four

Saturday afternoon – Shepford St Bernard

At two o'clock, as Krystal Yaxley was knocking nervously at the door of Wanda Warwick's cottage, the raised voices of Belinda and Jasper Haygarth were making the walls of Three-Ways House ring with their argument. 'You paid how much for that bacon?' yelled Jasper, in despair at his wife's spend-thrift ways.

'You know damned well I only bought a packet of off-cuts. There simply isn't anything cheaper,' shouted back Belinda, in her own defence.

'And why are you making such a huge quiche? Wouldn't a little one do?'

'Don't be so ridiculous! We'll get enough to eat there, so there'll be no need for me to cook a meal tonight. One this size is the least that I could bring along, taking that into consideration.'

'Well, I'd have made a much smaller one and be done with it,' her husband stated, his eyes now bulging out of his head with anger.

'Yes, you would, wouldn't you?' replied Belinda, turning away from him in disgust. They were in difficulties with the way the business was going, but she didn't see how making a quiche of whatever size was going to save their bacon, she thought, then smiled at her unintentional pun. It was bacon that had started this petty disagreement in the first place.

'I've a good mind not to go at all,' stated Jasper spitefully.

'Oh, good idea, Clever Clogs! So you're going to stay here tonight and do without? Well, make sure you do do without, for there's no spare food for a meal for you if you're going to spurn the free food on offer at the hall. Just think about that for a second, will you? If you can't abide the thought of me taking over such a big quiche, however are you going to get a chance to eat most of it if you don't even turn up?'

There were a few seconds of silence before he capitulated. 'You're perfectly right,' he agreed. 'I'm just so damned sensitive about anything to do with spending at the moment. Of course I'll come, and I'll stuff my face as heartily as I can. Truce?'

'Truce,' replied Belinda, glad of the opportunity to finish what she had been doing before she had been so abruptly and rudely interrupted.

In Robin's Perch, Bonnie Fletcher was probably the only village resident with her thoughts anywhere but the forthcoming party. She was off out tonight, and she had high hopes of a very good time indeed.

She intended to spend all afternoon on her make-up, nails, and hair, and then in choosing which of her going-out outfits would be the most flattering. It would make a change not to go into Market Darley just to meet up with the girls, and she was looking forward to it eagerly.

She wouldn't even have to get herself anything to eat before she went out, as she was being taken out to dinner, and she was impatient for eight o'clock, when she would be picked up from her own door instead of having to drive herself into the market town. She wouldn't even have to bed down on a sofa or floor tonight, because she would be dropped back right to her own doorstep, with no uncomfortable night to look forward to.

In fact, if things worked out well enough, she might even have a very good night to look forward to. It had been a long time since she had spent the night with anyone but her teddy bear, and her stomach gave a little flip of anticipation as she imagined how romantically the evening might end.

Tutting with impatience, she tripped upstairs eagerly to begin her toilette, and transform herself from a weekday office girl into a luscious night-time temptress, giggling with glee at the thought.

At roughly the same hour, Rev. Florrie was back at the church hall, lugging trestle tables off a stack at the back of the room and assembling them in an oblong horseshoe shape, so that people could get to the food from both sides. As usual, no one had volunteered to help her, but if she did a good enough job motivating this parish and increasing her congregation over the coming year, maybe this would be the only time she had to cope single-handed.

As she hauled and erected, she imagined what things would be like in the future, with many willing volunteers on hand to help out, all happy to be working together and looking forward to the reward that their efforts would bring. Rev. Florrie was an eternal optimist, and always looked for the best in people.

Look at the way she had won over old Miss Keighley-Armstrong at Manor Gate. The old girl had walked out of her Induction service and refused to set foot in the church ever again, until she had started including her on her parish visiting rounds. It really hadn't taken long to talk her into coming back to services, as it was obvious that she missed them, and was only cutting off her own nose to spite her face. And that had soon lured back that vinegar-faced Asquith woman.

She'd even persuaded Lettice to attend this little soirée, provided she was chauffeured there and back, which was no real imposition on Florrie's time, and would, in fact, give her a breather from being assaulted from all sides with different conversations. As she moved on to setting out the folding chairs in sociable little groups, she sent up a silent prayer that everything would go well, and maybe change some people's opinions of women vicars.

As she came to the end of her task, Kevin and Keith Yaxley arrived, a noisy collection of gangling teenaged limbs, speakers, turntables, and enough loud chatter to herald a small crowd of people entering the hall. 'Hello, you two,' she hailed them over the hubbub. 'Do you want to set up on the stage?'

'Thanks, Vicar,' they chanted in unison, and turned their heavily burdened way towards the small flight of wooden steps that let up to the small stage, at the other end of the hall.

'I'll leave you to it, if you like. I've just about finished here, and I know you'll want to make a load of sound checks just to make sure that everything's in working order for later.'

'Nice one, Vicar.' They really were uncanny, the way they so often spoke together: and they were only fraternal twins after all, she thought, not identical ones.

'If I leave the key with you, will you promise to lock up behind you, and put the key through The Rectory letterbox?' she asked.

'No problem, Vicar.' There they were, at it again. It was quite unnerving, and she'd be glad to get out of here, not least because she didn't want to be subjected to the sort of noise they were bound to make before declaring themselves satisfied.

'See you later then, lads,' she called, walking through the door into the sunshine.

'Laters,' in unison, floated out after her, as the twins confirmed her parting comment, and she gave a tiny shudder at their uncanny connection.

Gwendolyn Galton removed a large bowl from her fridge and looked at it in assessment. Yes, it looked like the jelly had set properly, encasing, as it did, chunks of fruit and slices of cake. That would just leave the custard, cream, and hundreds and thousands.

The custard she could deal with straight away, as it only involved opening four cans – it was to be a very large trifle – and pouring their contents over the bright red surface. The cream she would whip afterwards, putting it in the fridge for a while before she added it. The hundreds and thousands could wait.

The trifle was the least of her worries at the moment. Tomorrow was her big day. She'd already loaded her car, stuffing it to maximum capacity with all her carefully packed stock, and would have to leave at about five the next morning so as not to be too late to get a good pitch. This was one of the biggest antiques fairs in the area, and they were only held every quarter.

She attended all of the not-too-distant fairs in the area, but these quarterly fairs were enormous and, if she was lucky, she could make as much in a day at one of those as she could in the rest of the quarter with the smaller ones, so they were very important to her general financial situation.

At this relatively early point in the year, the local ones were just beginning to appear again, November to the end of January being almost blank as far as opportunities for her to sell were concerned. For one thing, the weather was usually inclement, and for another, people were more concerned with preparations for and physically recovering from Christmas.

The previous year had not been a good one, buyers pulling in their horns because of the general economic downturn, and she sincerely hoped that there would be an easing in the near future, as she'd already had to raid what meagre savings she had accrued over the summer months just to keep her head above water, what with the utility bills going up so much, and the bitterly cold and prolonged winter the country had just endured.

Wearing her usual 'rough' clothes of jeans and an Aran sweater so venerable that it was matted, in places from wear, her long silver-white hair held back with a 'scrunchie', she transferred box after box to the boot of her car, thanking her lucky stars that she hadn't chosen to deal in something inconveniently unwieldy, like furniture. The thought of having to transport antique tables, chairs, sideboards, and beds around was too grim to contemplate, working, as she did, alone.

Wanda Warwick must have been standing just the other side of her front door, thought Krystal Yaxley, with the speed with which she had answered her knock. Krystal had made a great effort with her appearance, as she had let the way she presented herself slip since Kenneth had up and left them, and felt glad that Wanda appeared to have done the same.

43

The tarot card reader was dressed all in black, her pale complexion emphasised with face powder, her eye-shadow dark and smoky and her lips coated with a dark plum lipstick. She had little clips in her hair with stars and moons on them, and her fingers dripped with chunky silver and semi-precious stoned rings.

'Do come in and make yourself comfortable, Krystal,' intoned the hostess. 'You don't mind my informality in calling you Krystal, do you?'

'Not at all,' concurred Krystal, surprised to hear her voice somewhat shaky had hesitant.

'And you must call me Wanda,' she was exhorted. 'We need a relaxed atmosphere to let things flow, otherwise my communion with the cards will be patchy, and I might get mixed messages.'

It all sounded very esoteric to Krystal, and she stepped over the threshold with trepidation. What had she got herself into? Did she really want to give this weird woman forty quid of what little funds she still possessed? And why was it necessary to burn so many candles when there was bright sunshine outside? There must have been twenty of them scattered around the little room, flickering in vain contest with the sunlight that streamed in through the windows.

Wanda gave her no more time for thought, and immediately ushered her to an armchair in front of a tiny grate, which glowed red with the comfort of a real fire. 'Always so relaxing and homely, don't you think, a real fire?' she asked rhetorically, then continued, 'And, of course, fire being one of the elements, it should help in communing with whatever is out there, as assistance.

'You'll probably notice during our time together that on the mantel is a bowl of earth and a bowl of water. What with the draught that creeps in under the front door, that gives us all the elements: earth, air, fire, and water – very necessary for a good reading. Now, make yourself comfortable, and just try to relax.'

Krystal sat bunched up in the chair, a ball of tension. She was out of her comfort zone here, and believed that relaxation was completely out of the question but, when Wanda said she always did a reading with a glass of home-made wine, she felt a little happier.

Pouring a dark fluid into two glasses, Wanda informed her that this was a blackberry and elderberry concoction that she had made just over a year ago. 'The two fruits aren't in season together, so I froze the elderberries until the blackberries were ripe. I thought the combination of the two seasons might make a difference to its psychic potency,' she finished, passing a glass to Krystal.

Taking a sip, Krystal thought it might have made a difference to the physical potency as well. It was like fruity firewater and by the time she was only halfway down the glass, her muscles could not keep up the unequal struggle anymore, and she began to unknot herself.

When both glasses had been drained, Wanda went to a low cupboard to the left of the hearth and extracted a wooden box covered with symbols that meant nothing to Krystal, but impressed her nonetheless. The cards proved to be wrapped in a piece of black velvet cloth when Wanda removed them, and she then proceeded to shuffle them a few times, fondling them as she did so as if she were caressing an old friend.

Seeing Krystal watching her intently, she smiled and explained, 'I need to keep them within my influence, so I need to handle them often. It's a bit like charging a battery, to give it an everyday analogy. They need to know that they're still mine, otherwise they won't respond properly.

When the cards had been spread out in a large half-circle on the table, Krystal chose the number requested of her, then handed them to Wanda without looking at them, as she had been instructed. 'Sorry about that,' Wanda explained, 'but you could unsuspectingly imbue them with your own personality, and they would become confused.

As she spoke, she dealt the chosen cards into a cross shape, with a few other small piles above, below, and to left and right in groups of three, still face down. She then riffled through the remaining cards and extracted one, placing it in the middle of the shape. 'As I thought,' she stated. 'The card that I had decided would work best as your significator was still in the pack of unchosen cards, so I shall place it here, to represent you.

'We're now going to take a look at the first four sets of cards. These represent,' she intoned, 'what is behind you.' Here, she indicated the group of three cards to the left. Pointing to the three to the right of the grouping, she added, 'and what is before you.' Moving her indicating finger to the three topmost cards, she said, 'These cards represent what has influence over you, and this group here,' moving her hand to the bottom three, 'are what's below you, meaning that these are things that you can have influence over. I'll explain the other groups as we go along.'

Krystal was now thoroughly relaxed, partly because of the singsong, soothing character that Wanda's voice had taken on, partly to do with the half-full second glass of home-made wine that sat by her right hand. She had a feeling that this was exactly what she should be doing at this difficult point in her life, and was more than half-hypnotised by the atmosphere and the scent from two incense sticks that Wanda had lit, just before she had removed the cards from their home in the cupboard.

The next half hour passed peacefully, as Wanda turned over trios of cards, considered each one on its own, then the three together, to get a group meaning. She listened as Wanda outlined the present difficulties in her life, exclaiming that there were very few cards in the suit of cups, which meant her burdens would not disappear in the near future, but with ingenuity and hard work, she would eventually arrive on the other side of this problematic phase, a better person.

When it came to turning over the final three cards, which represented the probable outcome of things, Krystal, who was almost drifting off, heard a sharp intake of breath, and sat up straight to see Wanda's hand frozen above the cards, a look of incomprehension on her face.

'What's the matter?' she asked, as Wanda's face described a mask of surprise.

46

'I don't know,' she replied, honestly puzzled.

'Well, what do they mean?' Krystal was completely alert now.

'I don't know! These cards can't be yours! Something must have interfered with the atmosphere when you were choosing.'

Krystal looked at the three cards in question: one showed a tower with two people tumbling from it, the second, a skeleton holding a long-handled shovel, the third, a large sword which stretched the whole length of the card. 'Are they bad?' she asked, a little catch in her voice.

'Individually, no; but grouped together like this … I simply don't understand it. These cards shouldn't be together. The choice must have been contaminated.'

'Well, what are they, and what do they mean?' Krystal was now feeling a little worried.

'I'll tell you, but these cards were definitely not meant for you. In a minute I'll get you to draw three others, for these three don't coalesce with the others you chose. This one,' she almost whispered, pointing to the first of the three, 'is called The Tower, and usually indicates either some sort of tremendous upheaval in the subject's life, or even their downfall.'

Pointing to the middle card, she continued, 'And this card is Death, but does not usually represent its literal meaning. It usually indicates a profound change – a complete turnaround in the subject's life. Together with the Ace of Swords, though.' Here, she pointed to the third and final card. 'I just don't know. I've never had that combination before in all the years I've been reading. It seems to indicate something really calamitous, but I know these cards don't indicate anything in *your* life. Choose three more cards.'

Rising shakily from her chair, Krystal refused as politely as she could manage, rummaged in her bag for the two twenty-pound notes that represented her payment for the reading, and left as hastily as possible. That'd teach her to have faith in some damned charlatan who just wanted to get her hands on other people's money. She'd just have to find herself a job: it didn't matter what. She just needed something to keep the larder ticking over while she rallied her resources.

At least this afternoon had taught her something: a fool and his or her money are soon parted. Walking across the road to her own home, her steps were determined. No one but she could get her little family back on its feet. There would be no divine intervention, no matter how much she longed for some.

Back in the sitting room of her little cottage, appropriately named 'The Ace of Cups', Wanda was still sitting in her seat at the table she used for readings. She was totally nonplussed. The cards simply shouldn't have come out like that. Something was very awry.

Suddenly the scent of the incense smelled cloying and overpowering, as if it would curdle her mind if it managed to get into her head. Jumping to her feet, she extinguished the little that was left of them, and the candles, and opened both the windows and the front door to clear away the smell, suddenly sickened by it.

She felt decidedly wobbly, and a tiny susurration of fear fluttered at her heart and in her stomach, as she whispered to herself, 'Something wicked this way comes.' There was definitely evil in the air, but even she, a Wiccan and tarot reader, had no inkling of what was to come in the near future, and what an effect it would have on her business.

Wrapping her arms around her body as if she were cold, Wanda made off to the kitchen to throw together a large bowl of salad as her offering for the evening. That and a couple of French sticks she had bought that morning were the simplest things to take along, and should be welcome enough, as she suspected that most people would bring sweet things.

Chapter Five

Saturday evening – Castle Farthing

A minibus taxi drew up outside The Fisherman's Flies at seven o'clock precisely, and the driver gave three sharp toots on the horn, as instructed by the passenger who had sat in front with him. 'Back at closing time as arranged,' the passenger said, and the minibus disgorged its cargo of six assorted Carmichaels.

The first to get out was Merc, almost as tall as his younger brother Davey and equally as broad. Next out was Ham, a midget in comparison at five feet nine, joined immediately by Rome; a man of just over six feet in height, but slimly built: at a distance, and in a bad light, he looked rather like a human string bean. The girls emerged next, first Juliet, tall for a woman, and impeccably turned out as her profession demanded, then Imogen, a squat dumpy figure who didn't give a fig what she looked like, as long as she had her books and her job.

The Carmichaels senior were totally disparate in appearance, Mr Carmichael being a tiny man of below-average height, who had fallen instantly in love with his wife when he first set eyes on her Valkyrie-like stature. She was very nearly six feet herself, and generously built, four of their children taking after her, two after her husband. Of the seventh, there was no judgement as of yet, he being so young. Ma Carmichael alone was present with her offspring, her husband having nobly stayed at home to babysit little Harry.

At the sound of the horn, a door opened on the other side of the village green, and the long arm of the law, in the form of DC Carmichael, came loping across it, almost forgetting about the pond in his eagerness to join his family. Tonight, the

Carmichaels were *en fete* to celebrate the births of two new family members, an occasion postponed for far too long. The regulars of The Fisherman's Flies wouldn't know what had hit them when this ill-assorted gaggle invaded its normally peaceful atmosphere.

Carmichael – the Davey element of the family – had informed George Covington, the landlord, in advance of the onslaught, so that he wouldn't be caught out and think that the performers of a travelling circus had turned up out of the blue. Mrs Carmichael senior – Daisy by name, although no one could have looked less like a daisy than Ma Carmichael – was particularly excited about going out with her family.

It was a long time since they had all been together and, due to her unplanned surprise pregnancy which had resulted in baby Harry, she had not really been out for a long time, and she felt like she had been newly released from prison.

Her detective son joined them, engulfing her in a bear hug, as he did with his sisters, and shaking hands and slapping the backs of his brothers in good-natured welcome. Daisy had brought them up well. Although they still lived in a council house in Market Darley, her boys knew their manners, and none of them had ever been in any trouble with the police: just as well really, as the prospect of one of their own brothers arresting them was not a happy or comfortable thought.

What Falconer had considered a chaotic household before Carmichael had moved out was, in fact, a well-oiled machine that functioned efficiently, although some parts of the machine were a little oversized. Creating a solid block of humanity, they burst in through the doors to have George Covington shout out a welcome to them, his wife Paula already at the pumps, ready to fulfil their order, having dispatched their barmaid to attend to serving at the hall, so intrigued was she at the thought of seeing the Carmichaels *en famille*.

'Seven pints of your best bitter, please,' called Merc over the babble of his family's voices, for all the other customers in the pub had fallen silent at this onslaught of giants, and it was only the smiling faces of the Covingtons and the jolly way they bantered with the members of this group of newcomers that earthed the electricity in the air, and let the other customers know that there would be no trouble, and there was nothing to worry about, for Carmichaels, *en masse,* can be quite intimidating.

As Paula filled pint glasses and George handed them over the bar, the buzz of quiet conversation soon resumed, and Imogen went in search of a couple of tables that they could pull together so that they could all sit and chat without any of them being separated. There was so much news to catch up on.

Rome had finally found himself a girlfriend, Juliet a boyfriend, and Merc's business was really doing well, people in general not having the money these days to use removal companies for anything that would fit in a Luton, and so much furniture was now being bought second-hand.

Their ma also had some photos of little Harry, and there was the likelihood that Davey would finally tell them what had really happened when Harriet had been born, for they had been told nothing about the birth, her son informing her that he wanted to wait until they were all together before he told the tale to save him having to tell it six times.

They made a noisy group in the corner furthest from the door, loudly exchanging news and ribbing each other mercilessly at what they heard. Only one customer left in protest, that being the old man who lived in Ivy Cottage, in the same terrace as Carmichael, and he had only given them five minutes grace before draining his half-pint glass, and taking hold of the walking sticks that he had finally been persuaded to use after the iciness that had prevailed underfoot for so long over Christmas and the New Year.

George Covington noticed his exit, but thought that his custom would be no loss. Sometimes the old man managed to string out one half of mild for the whole evening, so his takings weren't about to go down noticeably. On the contrary, he was looking forward to a bumper evening, with the lively crowd of Carmichaels all on good form.

At ten o'clock, Carmichael announced that it really was

about time he got back to 'Cherry and the kildren', but Merc persuaded him that he ought to have another pint, as it was two babies' heads they were wetting, then, when he had drunk that, Rome appeared at his shoulder with a tray containing shots, his excuse being, 'Gotta get them properly soaked, haven't we – the babies' heads, I mean.'

By this time, Carmichael's resistance was low, and he took one of the glasses, a thimble in his huge hand, and tossed it back with enthusiasm. 'Gotta get 'em a'solutely dren-hic!-ched!' he declared with the hammy seriousness of the inebriated.

A lot of toasts followed, and quite a few more drinks, and when Carmichael reached the 'loving' stage of drunkenness and began to hug his siblings and tell them how much he loved them all, Merv appeared at his side and nodded to Ham. Each of them took an arm, and helped their brother to his feet, Ham informing him that it was time they got him back to the bosom of his other family, as the minibus was due to collect them in ten minutes.

With a last loving embrace of his mother, he was steered out through the door and across the green in a wavering line that would have done credit to any self-respecting snail. Kerry heard them coming and had the door already open so that they could deposit him on the sofa, before going back to the pub for their ride home.

Kerry took one look at her husband, sprawled the full length of the sofa with his legs dangling over the edge, his head tipped backwards over the other end and, as he began to snore, went to the linen cupboard and grabbed a spare duvet. Arranging this as best she could along his enormous figure, she locked up and went upstairs to bed.

The boys had been asleep for hours, and she had already fed the baby. Now, she needed sleep herself, as her day would start tomorrow at six o'clock, never mind that it was Sunday. Babies didn't understand Sundays, any more than they understood their parents' need for a full night's sleep, and didn't have the energy to play for an hour at three a.m. if the babies awoke and were full of energy and feeling a tad bored.

Saturday evening – Shepford St Bernard

Rev. Florrie arrived at the hall at half past five, just to check that everything that could be done had been done, and was joined shortly by the Yaxley twins, who had decided that they ought to make just one final check of their equipment before dazzling the party-goers with their innovative DJ-ing technique.

It seemed no time at all after that until the first of the guests began to arrive, first those with young children as expected, a few of them from the Sunday school, others, out of sheer curiosity and in reaction to the leaflet that had been stuffed through their letterboxes.

Florrie greeted them all with equal warmth whether she had met them before or not, and began to introduce people and get them talking and helping themselves to food and liquid refreshment. The older guests whom she already knew started coming through the door shortly after half past six, and the tables steadily filled with food, both sweet and savoury, the table set aside for drinks rapidly to expand its range of choices.

By seven o'clock the Yaxleys had got the music in full swing, and a party atmosphere was really beginning to develop. Apart from one panicky moment, when a six-year-old had been discovered to be draining beer cans of any leftover fluid they possessed, everything was running smoothly, the hum of chatter rising to a level that was equal to that produced by the mixing decks.

Jasper and Belinda Haygarth had seated themselves really close to the food tables, and made frequent forays to it to refill their plates. Toby Lattimer and Gwendolyn Galton were in their element, talking antiques next to the bar, and Maude, Violet, and Lettice made a trio that would have graced any production of *Macbeth*, holding court as far away from the speakers as they could get.

In the middle of the hall, Julius Twelvetrees was doing his best to make conversation with Colin Twentymen, and not appearing to get much change for all the effort he was putting in. Colin managed to field every probing question effortlessly and politely and after about ten minutes excused himself, as he said he was going outside for a smoke of his pipe. Everything was going exactly as he had envisaged it earlier when he had finished his baking, with the exception of one bewildering comment that he still did not fully understand.

Krystal Yaxley and Wanda Warwick were the only two in the hall who couldn't seem to settle, both wandering from group to group without becoming immersed in any sustained conversation, and avoiding each other in a rather obvious way should their paths cross. Neither had got over the rather odd occurrence that afternoon, and each wanted to be left in peace to consider what they believed had really happened.

The main entertainment of the evening came from an unexpected source. The three Scottish play witches, Lettice, Maude Asquith, and Violet Bingham, had underestimated the strength of the punch that Rev. Florrie had thrown together in her rather haphazard way, and a number of people present there that evening would wake up with dry mouths and headaches the next morning, so innocuous did it taste to the uninitiated.

The volume of the conversation from this trio suddenly rose in volume, and was accompanied by gusts of wheezy laughter. Florrie eventually visited their corner, intrigued by what could be amusing them so much, but was none the wiser after listening for a while.

Lettice suddenly got to her feet and began to circulate, chatting with all and sundry, a very different Lettice from the everyday one, who was invariably rude to anyone who tried to make conversation with her. Her two friends gazed on, perplexed, then sank another glass of punch and forgot all about the change in her character, as they too felt the urge to be uncharacteristically sociable.

Both those who knew the three ladies, and those who had never met them before, were regaled variously with tales of Maude Asquith's late grandfather's heroics in the Siege of Khartoum, Violet Bingham's long friendship with Lettice and, most surprising of all, Lettice's tales of her father's life in South Africa and all the gems he had had made into fabulous pieces of jewellery for her mother. This latter was something that Lettice hardly ever mentioned, being quite close-mouthed about her childhood and her parents, and astonished Violet and Maude when they overheard her.

Taking the opportunity to intervene by grabbing her arm in passing, Maude hissed at her that she should keep quiet about the valuable pieces that her mother had left her, but Lettice just laughed, and said she didn't often feel like opening up about her life, and to leave her alone as she was enjoying herself. Toby Lattimer also approached her and whispered something in her ear, but she shook her head at him and laughed. She was having a good time, and was going to let no one put a stop to her enjoyment.

By the time that Rev. Florrie took her by the arm about nine-thirty, she must have spoken to just about everyone who was there. Fortunately, by that time, the majority of people had left to go home, this not being the sort of 'do' that would be likely to continue into the early hours, and the vicar asked the Yaxley boys to keep an eye on the last few stragglers while she ran Lettice home.

She'd already slipped out to position her car just outside the hall's door, and took Lettice firmly by the arm, to help support her in her rather squiffy state, and inserted her bulky body into the passenger seat.

'Oh, I did enjoy that, Vicar,' she said, squirming to get herself comfortable. 'I haven't had so much fun in years. It did my heart good to get out and talk to other people, instead of just having that sour-faced old Asquith biddy coming round all the time, sucking up to me like a leech, and peppering her conversation with the most spiteful gossip I've heard in years.'

'Don't be so ungrateful, Miss Keighley-Armstrong. At least she comes round to visit you,' Florrie admonished her.

'As do you, my dear, but your motives are much more charitable. Maude only comes round to lick my,' she whispered the next word, 'arse,' then blushed, 'because she's hoping I'll leave her something in my will. Oh, don't you object, Vicar. I know very well what she's up to, you can be assured of that.'

'Let's get you off home, so that you can have a good night's sleep,' Florrie advised, as she pulled up outside the front door of Manor Gate. 'Come on; let me give you a hand out. I'll see you safely to your sitting room before I go back to clear up.'

'I'm perfectly capable of going in by myself, you know. I'm not senile,' retorted the older woman.

'Of course you're not,' replied Florrie, 'but you are just a little bit tiddly, and I'd never forgive myself if you went in and tripped over the cat, or something silly like that, and ended up hurting yourself after such a splendid evening.'

'It was rather good, wasn't it? I must say that I haven't enjoyed myself so much for a long time. Thank you very much, my dear, for doing something positive about this parish. I didn't realise how it had stagnated, but since you've been here, it's begun to wake up again.'

'Well, thank you kindly. There you are,' Florrie fussed, settling Lettice in her favourite chair, and poking the fire and adding another log before she left. 'Is there anything else I can do before I go?'

'No, you get back and say goodnight to your last guests. There'll be plenty of clearing up to do, and I know how early you have to rise in the morning for early communion.'

Leaving the old lady comfortably settled, an uncharacteristic smile on her face, her cat The Bishop settling himself on her lap, the vicar drove back to the church hall to get stuck into restoring the place to the state it had been in before she started hanging her balloons and streamers.

The weather had turned during the evening, and the clouds that had gathered after sunset now began to shed their load of rain, already turning heavy, and a flash of lightning in the distance was followed by a rumble of thunder. How lucky they'd been, that the wet weather had held off until after the party.

The storm grew in violence, rain lashing the village, driven by strong winds and even more ferocious squalls. Gutters gurgled as rivulets ran downhill, to disappear down drains in the vain hope of reaching the sea, and spring flowers that had shown their heads too early in the season, coaxed out by the unseasonal sunshine and warmth, were battered and beaten down.

No one heard the shrill scream of alarm, muffled as it was, not just by the storm, but by the thick walls of the old building. No one heard the pitiful cries for help either, and by midnight, the only audible sounds were those of nature, playing untamed in the environs of the small community, amusing itself by seeing how many branches it could detach from trees before it blew itself out.

No one slept well that night, except for one. That 'one' slept the sleep of the dead, and for very good reason.

Chapter Six

Sunday morning – Shepford St Bernard

The rain was still falling like stair-rods when Rev. Florrie left for early communion, so she took the car, even though she could have reached the church much more directly on foot by cutting through the graveyard. She had no intention of standing in the chilly church in a soaking-wet cassock, and treated herself to this unplanned use of her rackety old vehicle.

When she had finished her lonely task, she decided to visit Lettice, as she knew she had been having some trouble with the tiles on her roof, but would be unlikely to seek the expertise of a builder if left to her own devices. A streak of meanness ran right through her like the writing inside a stick of rock, a trait, she claimed, she had inherited from her mother, who was always scandalised when her father presented her with yet another piece of fine jewellery.

The unmade-up cul-de-sac past the back of St Bernard's was a sea of water-filled potholes and ruts. Whereas it had been merely a rough drive the evening before, when she had collected and returned Lettice, today it was treacherously slippery, and she drove with care as she approached Manor Gate at the end of it.

Getting out of her car, she made a dash for the porch, and was immediately alerted to the fact the something was out of kilter, as the door, sheltered as it was by the porch, swung gently on its hinges, open, and inviting unwelcome attention to anyone with an eye for the main chance.

Entering the house cautiously, she was immediately greeted by the elderly black and white cat, which meowed piteously at her, and tried to lead her towards the kitchen, where its food bowls lived. Rev. Florrie took this as a sign that there was no one in the house who shouldn't be there. Had that been the case, the animal would have hidden itself and kept quiet.

Still feeling slightly cautious, she examined the ground floor rooms, calling quietly, 'Lettice, are you there? It's only me, Florrie. Are you all right?' but answer came there none. She paused in the kitchen to pour some dried food into the cat's bowl and refill its water, then slowly mounted the stairs, her level of anxiety increasing with every step.

I do hope I don't find her dead in bed, she thought, as she made her way along the landing. Bracing herself, she flung open the first door, and found herself looking into a bathroom that wouldn't have looked out of place in a 1930s advertisement. Lady Luck was toying with her today, and the next door she opened, a little more calmly this time, was a store room filled with boxes, a sagging old brass-framed bed in the dead centre of it.

As it turned out, she found no one on the first floor, and was perplexed as to where a woman of Lettice's age could have got to during the hours of darkness, on such a fearful night, weather-wise.

She felt under the doormat in the porch, as she felt for a key which, inevitably, proved to be there, sighing with exasperation at the fact that she had had no joy in dissuading Lettice from this dangerous practise. A quick prayer that she hadn't fallen victim to an unwelcome visitor formed in her head, even as she spotted the humped shape just a few steps away, where the headstones of the graveyard joined the shallow frontage of Manor Gate.

At one time, long after the Georgian manor had been reduced to rubble through the ravages of time and a calamitous fire, the house had been used for a curate (the parish being largely rural, and church attendance being the norm rather than the exception), and no wall had ever divided the two.

Reluctantly, and as slowly as if she were walking in treacle, she braved the weather conditions and approached what, at first sight, appeared to be a pile of old clothes that had been carelessly tossed away.

As she got closer, she was able to make out the humped shape of a body, and another step identified that body as Lettice Keighley-Armstrong, lying in the mud, drowned and motionless. She looked pathetically abandoned, her clothes a sodden mass, her hair running with rain, her face splashed with the mud that had been disturbed, as the ferocity of the falling water had rebounded and bounced upwards to besmear her features.

Moaning, 'Oh, no! Lettice!' Rev. Florrie knelt in the sodden ground, heedless of the mess it was making of her cassock, and leaned closer to the old woman, hoping vainly that she had just fallen and was merely unconscious. One look at her face annihilated this faint hope, for the wound at her temple may have been washed by the cleansing rain, but the blue-black depression at this spot told the true story. Lettice was stone dead.

Her immediate reaction was to give her a blessing to speed her soul on its way, but she realised that time was of the essence. She had to get in touch with the police as soon as possible, and, as she had not taken her mobile phone to church with her, that would mean getting back to The Rectory as soon as possible, and leaving Lettice's body out here in the open for the crows to peck at.

With a shudder of disgust, she retrieved an old raincoat she kept on the back seat of the car, and placed it over the lifeless form's head and shoulders. That should keep the disgusting creatures away until she returned. She didn't think she had the stomach to face an eye-less corpse.

She had covered the body tenderly, as if covering a sick parishioner on one of her visits for, although she knew, intellectually, that Lettice was gone, her heart wouldn't accept it, seeing her lying there so peacefully. Checking that she had closed the front door firmly, the key in the pocket of her cassock, she got back into her car and drove the short distance to The Rectory to dial 999.

At Market Darley police station, Bob Bryant took the call, impressed with the conciseness of the information and the calm voice in which the details were imparted, although he would never know how much courage it had taken the caller to sound so. Rev. Florrie was inured to, if still not entirely comfortable with the dead, and this was someone whom she had considered she knew quite well. Still steeling herself to sound perfectly in control, she informed Sergeant Bryant that she would return to the scene and wait there for assistance.

Now, who was out on patrol today? he thought, ending the call. A quick check of the staff rota revealed that PC Merv Green and PC Starr were out in one of the cars, doing the rounds of the villages, rather than keeping an eye out for trouble in the town, and he radioed a message straight to them to attend the scene and let him know what the situation was so that he could alert a team if it turned out not to be a natural death but a suspicious one.

Twenty minutes later, he received a reply stating that it looked like 'a rum 'un', in Merv's own words, and that they would be needing the necessary personnel in attendance. Promising to erect crime tape, Merv signed off, leaving Bob Bryant to sort out who should be disturbed on a Sunday morning. He'd have to get a SOCO team mustered, get in touch with Doc Christmas, and give Harry Falconer a ring, as he would be the senior investigating officer.

Let him choose whom he wanted to rouse from weekend late slumbers. Bob had enough on his plate, with the thought that he had a responsibility to let Superintendent 'Jelly' Chivers know what was going on. That was not a task he had the appetite for carrying out immediately, and decided to shelve this final call until the man would be decently awake and, hopefully, not behaving like a bear with a sore head, after a night out at the golf club the evening before.

It was still only nine o'clock when the telephone in Falconer's house shrilled, but he answered its summons immediately. 'Hello, Bob. What's brewing?' he asked with a wry smile. He'd bet himself a bottle of Chablis that he wouldn't get an undisturbed day off, especially at the weekend, and it looked like he'd won the wine.

'You're up, then,' he greeted the inspector. 'I thought you might be catching a lie-in at this time of a Sunday morning.'

'No chance. That's something I forgot how to do in the army. I'm up the same time every morning. The only exception I can think of was the day after Carmichael's wedding, when I didn't even know if I was alive or dead when I woke up the morning after. What have you got for me, then, that's so urgent?'

'Dead body found out at Shepford St Bernard,' Bob informed him. 'Old lady. It sounds like she's lain outside all night in the rain. Vicar found her – a Rev. Feldman. Victim's name is Miss Lettice Keighley-Armstrong. Eighty-five years old. Not known to be in ill health, apart from the usual stuff at that age. The vicar will meet you at the scene.'

'Which is?' enquired Falconer with a sigh.

'Into the village, crossing the Downsway Road, all the way past the green, then there's a sign opposite the shop on the right that points to the church ...'

'Surely not in the church, Bob; not on a Sunday?'

'No. When you get to the church, the road carries on for a bit, unmade-up, and you'll come to the house, which is called Manor Gate. The body's outside, just within the boundaries of the graveyard. The vicar will be waiting outside the house.'

'What about the rest of the cavalry?' asked the inspector, hoping that he was not expected to rally his own troops.

'I'm just about to get the SOCO team alerted, I've already spoken to Doc Christmas, and I'll leave you to choose your own company. I know how Roberts gets up your nose, cheeky young devil, but I also know that Carmichael was having some sort of 'do' last night with his family. It's up to you. Just spare a thought for me, having to tell Chivers, when I know he will probably not have got in until the early hours as they had something on at the golf club.'

'Oh, God! I'll take a stiff any day over Chivers with a hangover. Good luck. And, just for your information, in case the old dragon asks, I'm going to plump for Carmichael. He's not known for his alcohol consumption, and I don't think I could stand Roberts wittering on all the time while I'm trying to think.'

'Pragmatic choice, Harry. Let me know as soon as you know anything, so that I can keep the Jelly up to date.'

'Rather you, than me,' replied Falconer, shuddering at the mere thought.

It was Kerry, Carmichael's wife, who answered the phone, sounding a little sheepish when Falconer asked to speak to her husband. 'I'm awfully sorry, but he's not awake yet. I think he rather pushed the boat out last night, but I'm sure I can return him to the land of the living if you need him. I don't think he'll be fit to drive, though. I'd bet anything that he's still a bit over the limit.'

'I'll pick him up, then. No problem,' offered Falconer rashly, not really thinking it through.

'How long have I got?'

'Make it half an hour, and make sure you get him into the shower and set it on cool. I shall need him awake and functioning, not dozing off all the time, which I know for a fact he can do standing up.'

'I'll do my best, but I can't promise a miracle.'

'Good girl. I'm grateful to you. Right, see you in about thirty minutes,' he finished and hung up.

That was odd. It wasn't like Carmichael to have more than a couple of halves at the most. It must've been his family's bad influence over him, if he'd had one over the eight. Still, a cool shower and the thought of a new case should brighten him up no end,' thought the inspector, without a trace of comprehension at how naïve he was being.

Sunday morning – Castle Farthing

Harriet hadn't woken for a feed yet, so Kerry left the boys in the living room playing quietly while she mounted the stairs with trepidation. He had managed to crawl up the stairs in the early hours, like a desperate homing pigeon seeking its roost, then had collapsed into bed and the sleep of the magnificently intoxicated.

She had no idea how she was going to rouse her comatose husband, get him through a shower, and dressed and ready for work within the confines of only thirty short minutes, and estimated that it would take her that long just to get him to his feet, let alone all the rest of getting him ready. He'd had a real skinful the night before, and she'd never seen him like that before, in all the time she'd known him.

When she entered the bedroom she could just see a huge lump, the duvet wrapped round it like a cocoon, and from which monumental snores rent the air. 'Come on, my love. Get yourself awake. You've got to go to work.' She shook his body violently as she spoke, and part of a face emerged from beneath the duvet, and one bloodshot eye half-opened and squinted at her, suffering from the intrusion of daylight upon its dark and peaceful world.

'Whaaa …?' came floating out to her, as the rest of the head appeared.

'Come on, Davey. The inspector's just been on the phone. Something's come up, and he's going to be picking you up in … oh, probably only about twenty-five minutes, now. You've got to get out of bed and get ready.'

'Go 'way,' muttered the head, diving under the duvet once more, hands pulling it more closely around its face.

'I'm not joking, Davey. You've got to get up. Inspector Falconer's on his way here this very minute.'

The lump on the bed wriggled itself more comfortably under its covering and Kerry knew it was time to get tough. Going into the bathroom, she soaked a face cloth in cold water, then returned to the bedroom, pulled the duvet away from her husband's head, and pushed the icy flannel at him, covering as much of his face as she could get at. That had a more positive effect.

'What're you doing? Leave me alone? I feel like death!'

'You've got to go to work. Didn't you hear me before? Falconer's on his way over to pick you up. I told him you weren't fit to drive, so he's coming here, and he expects you to be ready to go when he arrives.'

'You've got to be kidding me!' Carmichael was now sitting bolt upright in the bed, his red-rimmed and bloodshot eyes wide open in disbelief. 'Tell me this is just a joke. Tell me it's a dream. Just don't tell me that this is real,' he pleaded.

'Oh, it's for real all right,' replied Kerry, tugging at the duvet, to encourage him to get out of the bed. 'Come on, DS Carmichael. Time for your walk. See if you can get as far as the bathroom, and I'll put the shower on for you.'

'Couldn't you just tell him that I'd died in the night?'

'I could, but it wouldn't be true, would it?'

'Almost.'

'Get out of that bed this minute, and try to get a grip, before I lose my temper. You wouldn't like me when I'm angry. I go all green and turn into a monster.'

'Hard to tell the difference, then,' Carmichael replied, recovering just a little, and ducking with just sufficient speed to avoid the slap she had aimed at his head.

When Falconer pulled up in front of Jasmine Cottage, he gave a double beep on the horn, surprised that his sergeant wasn't already waiting outside the door, and hoped that his hangover wasn't bad enough to keep him from his work.

As he considered this unedifying prospect, and the alternative of working with Roberts, the door of the cottage opened and a sorry pair exited, Kerry first, leading what looked to be a punch-drunk and pathetic figure. Once outside, the formidable figure of Carmichael put an arm around the smaller figure, and this unmatched combination began to stagger slowly towards the Boxster, looking like David and Goliath going off to A&E after the contest.

Leaning over and opening the passenger door, the inspector took a quick look in the glove compartment, seemed to be satisfied with what he saw, and closed it again firmly. Like a boy scout, he was always prepared.

Carmichael, with the complexion of a pistachio nut, folded himself into the passenger seat with infinite slowness, then groaned as he reached for the seat belt. 'Sometimes I wish I didn't have family,' he croaked, his mouth and throat still suffering from dehydration.

'You managed to wet the babies' heads, then?' Falconer asked rhetorically. 'I'm just glad I wasn't there as chief midwife.'

'I did mean to invite you, sir.'

'Then thank heaven for forgetfulness. I do know how you feel, though. You look exactly how I felt after your wedding reception, and I decided there and then that I never wanted to feel like that again.'

'It was all Merc's fault! I said I didn't want any more to drink, but he just kept them coming.'

'Then, I suppose, you got to the state where another bucket-load wouldn't matter.'

'Exactly, sir. I felt like a murder victim when I woke up this morning.'

'How lucky, as that's probably exactly what's waiting for you in Shepford St Bernard. You're right, though. You do look like a corpse. The only thing out of kilter is that you're still walking and talking. Did you manage any breakfast?'

'!' Carmichael gave him a look of mute appeal, and began breathing shallow breaths of desperation.

Without a word, Falconer pressed the button to open the passenger window and pushed Carmichael's head outside, from whence came the stomach-churning noises of someone blowing their chunks.

When the sound ceased and Carmichael began to withdraw his head, Falconer leaned over again, popped the catch on the glove compartment, removed a sick bag he had pilfered from the last time he had flown, and a packet of tissues.

'Well done, Sergeant!' he congratulated his passenger, while passing over his finds. 'You managed to miss the cyclist, but only just and, if what I believe to be true is accurate, the side of my car probably looks like it's trying to grow a pizza. You can wash that when we get back to your place, later. You'll find mints in the door pocket if you want to freshen your mouth.'

'Mmmf!' replied Carmichael, who was cleaning himself up as best as he could. He did look a little less grass-tinged now, and the addition of a Polo mint should help with his breath while they were incarcerated together in the same tin can. Even Porsches didn't come with instant passenger fresheners.

'Thanks, sir,' said the sergeant, his voice a little closer to its normal bass boom. 'That was very efficient of you.'

'Be prepared!' Falconer replied, with no mention of boy scouts, and leaving Carmichael a bit puzzled, but too weak to ask for an explanation.

With both windows half-open, a clean, clear breeze blowing past both of them, Carmichael was feeling rather better when they arrived at Shepford St Bernard, and he attempted to exit the car, but with more than his usual difficulty of being so big and broad. Today, with the added handicap of suffering from a severe hangover, he lacked sufficient coordination to complete the complicated manoeuvre, and he fought weakly to reach the outside world. He now had, however, a fresher complexion, the green tinge having disappeared, and his cheeks were rosy with the blast of air they had received on the journey over.

The rain had ceased just before Falconer reached Castle Farthing, but it was still drizzly here, just a few miles away. Following instructions, Falconer took the un-adopted and rough road just to the south of the church, and pulled up outside Manor Gate to see one other solitary car, parked just outside the front porch.

There was no sign of a waiting vicar, so Falconer got out of his car, surveying with distaste the un-commissioned decoration down the passenger side of his pride and joy, and approached the other solitary vehicle, knocking discretely on the driver's window. When the window was wound down he caught sight of the occupant, a pleasant-looking woman in her late thirties, and spoke.

'I wonder if you could help me,' he asked, surmising that this was probably the vicar's wife. 'I'm Detective Inspector Falconer of the Market Darley CID, and I'm looking for the Rev. Feldman. Do you, perhaps, know his present whereabouts?'

To his furious embarrassment, she replied, 'You've found her, Inspector. Did the duty officer not tell you I was female?'

'No, he didn't,' said Falconer, through clenched teeth. 'I do apologise, and I shall have that officer's guts for garters when I get back to the station. Probably his idea of setting me up. I hope I didn't upset you.'

'Happens all the time,' replied Rev. Florrie with a rueful smile. 'Sometimes I even find myself apologising for not being male. Not to worry, though. No harm done.'

Turning towards the car and back to the woman again, he said, 'I'd like to introduce you to Detective Sergeant Carmichael, but he seems to be having some difficulty getting out of the car. Would you excuse me for a moment? He's not feeling in top form today.' And, so saying, he went to the passenger door of the Boxster, grabbed one of Carmichael's enormous paws, noticing that he'd only managed to get one leg out so far, and pulled for all he was worth.

Slowly the Kraken emerged, a dishevelled heap of suffering, and shambled over to introduce himself to the woman, who had exited her own car, and was seen to be wearing a cassock. She was in clerical uniform because this was Sunday, assumed by the less well-informed, to be the busiest day of the week for the clergy.

He extended a slightly tremulous hand and bade her good morning, while Falconer waited impatiently to be apprised of the exact location of the body. Finally, 'Miss Keighley-Armstrong's body is over by that nearest gravestone. It almost looks as if she were reaching out to grab it, doesn't it?'

Falconer squelched across the unmade-up roadway and espied the body in that exact position, there being no fence, wall, or other barrier between the boundary of the road and the graveyard. He was turning, rather unwarily, given the conditions underfoot, to summon his sergeant, when he slipped and did a very good *Riverdance* impression before regaining his balance, if not his dignity. 'Come along Carmichael,' he said, rather sharply, 'We've got work to do,' ignoring the sergeant's snicker, as he rallied a little, and his *sotto voce* comment of,

'Didn't know you knew any Irish dancing, sir,' as inappropriate in the given circumstances.

Lettice's mortal remains were as Florrie had found them, the face slightly cleaner, now that the rain was just a drizzle, and not violent enough to make dirty splashes on her features. The softer rain had cleansed her face and at her left temple and clearly visible was a clean-washed depression, her wispy, wet hair fanned across the wound. She had no outdoor clothes on, and her arms did seem to be reaching out for the rough surface of the old, weather-worn grave stone.

'It's almost as if she were trying to leave us a message, isn't it,' asked the vicar, her forehead creased into a frown. 'I wonder if she was actually trying to tell us something.'

'It is a thought,' agreed Falconer, as the sound of other vehicles became discernible, approaching them up the muddy access road, then added, 'Here comes the cavalry. By the look of it, that's Doc Christmas' car, with the SOCO van just behind. I'll just have a quick word with them, and perhaps we could go inside the house and take a look round. Something must have alarmed the old lady considerably, for her to rush out in last night's weather with no coat, hat, or umbrella.'

'And was she attacked inside or outside the house?' The voice of Carmichael startled Falconer as if the living dead had spoken.

'You're back in the land of the living, then, are you?'

'I think so, sir.'

'I apologise for my sergeant, but he was sick on the journey over,' he explained for the benefit of Florrie, who was looking puzzled as to why a man in this condition should be on active duty.

'Oh, you poor man! I'll just nip back to The Rectory and make you a sandwich and a flask. There's nothing worse than trying to work on an empty stomach, especially if you've actually been sick. Perhaps it was something he ate,' she concluded, getting back into her car and looking for somewhere to turn round, hoping that she could squeeze past the other three vehicles on the road.

'Or something he drank,' muttered Falconer, giving Carmichael a murderous glance. If his sergeant wasn't fully recovered in the time it took for them to take a look round the premises, and possibly get the names of some of the residents for interview, he'd have to call in Roberts, and then his day would be completely spoilt. It wasn't that he resented working on his day off, rather that he'd prefer not to have an impudent young pup bouncing round his ankles, continually barking and whining – and that's exactly what Roberts reminded him of.

Once inside the rather gloomy hall, Carmichael's voice sounded in a sepulchral tone, echoing slightly in the uncarpeted space. 'Do you think I might sit down somewhere, sir? Now I'm standing up, I feel rather dizzy.' One look at him revealed him to be now rather whey-faced, and Falconer permitted him to sit down on the stairs. There was no way he was going to let him sit on a chair, or any other item of furniture, till the SOCO team had been over the whole place.

'You stay there a moment, while I see if I can get through to Roberts. You're in no fit state to be out of bed. Kerry never said you were *this* bad.'

He eventually got a signal by standing out in the back garden of the property: not a good one, but good enough to indicate to DC Roberts that he was needed at the scene of the crime. He hadn't dared use the house's landline, in case there was any sort of forensic evidence to be gathered from it which he would have destroyed or contaminated just by lifting the receiver, for the victim still had a venerable telephone with a dial, and no removable handset.

Roberts did, indeed, sound as eager as a puppy that has just been let off the leash for a run, and Falconer ended the call with a heartfelt sigh. He'd love to have booked Roberts in for some canine obedience classes, but he didn't think they accepted human pupils.

When he got back to the hall, Doc Christmas was just entering, the inevitable blue disposable 'nappies' over his shoes, so as not to transfer anything alien and compromise the integrity of the scene. 'Good day to you, Philip. How goes it?' called Falconer, pleased to see someone official who was competent and sober, and might be able to convey positive information to him.

'Hello there, Harry, and you, Davey. One of us doesn't look too bright. Not going to be needing my services again, later in the day, are you?' he asked, catching sight of Carmichael's miserable figure hunched on the stairs.

'I don't think it's terminal. Just a bit of a hangover after wetting two babies' heads last night, with his family. The man's a lightweight like myself, not being much of a drinker, and he fell afoul of those brothers of his, out for a night of merrymaking.'

'And Imogen,' Carmichael confirmed. 'She could drink any bloke I know under the table. And Juliet's nearly as bad.'

'What a charming family you must have,' commented Christmas, more eager to pass on his finding than to indulge in small talk. 'I've had a look at our stiff, and the wound was definitely inflicted ante-mortem, so somewhere, there's some blood to be found, which will tell us roughly where she was when she was hit.

'Trauma with a blunt instrument – the usual story. This blow didn't kill, however, and must just have stunned her temporarily, although I'm surprised she could get herself all the way out here. Must have been a very determined old lady.

'Come on; let's have a little look round for where it happened. I've got nothing official on after this, and the wife's mother's staying, so I've got no reason to rush back. I wouldn't mind spending a bit of time gumshoeing around in these delicious disposable paper slippers.'

'You can stand in for Carmichael, then. I don't think he's going anywhere fast. He perked up in the car when I opened the windows, but since he got himself upright, he's definitely gone downhill again.'

'Been Uncle Dick, has he?'

'Enviable diagnostic skills, Philip,' replied Falconer, only to have his compliment pricked with the reply,

'I didn't suppose you usually appeared in public with such a mess down the side of your car. I then see the sergeant looking like Banquo's ghost and, QED, the lad's obviously been fighting a losing battle with his insides. Pushed his head out of the window, did you?'

'Of course,' agreed Falconer, with a slight smirk at his own ingenuity, 'Got it in one, Doc! You take the dining room, which I believe,' he stated, pushing a door to his left open, 'is in here, and I'll go stake out the living room.'

It wasn't long before Falconer called out to the doctor that he'd discovered where the blow had been delivered. There was blood on the back and arm of Lettice's favourite armchair, and then a thin trail led out through the French windows. Any evidence outside had been washed away by the rain, but at least they knew where she had exited the house.

'Can't see anything she could have fallen and hit her head on, and been able to get back into her chair,' commented the doctor, slightly nonplussed as a cat began to insinuate itself round his ankles.

His head behind the chair, Falconer called, 'Bingo!' and returned himself to an upright position with a bronze statuette in one gloved hand. 'This looks like what the blow was delivered with; blood and hair still there for our convenience. Whoever did it didn't think to take the weapon with them.'

'And at least we know there was someone else here, and she hadn't just fallen somewhere, got back to her chair, then decided she ought to get some help,' Doc Christmas gave as his opinion.

'Surely she'd have made for the phone first, if that had been the case,' said Falconer, following logic.

'Not necessarily,' replied the doctor. 'When someone's been knocked silly, there's no end to the daft things they'll do, like crawling outdoors on a filthy night to try to find help. Lucky you found that statuette. It's the right weight to have done the job, and it's got 'leftovers' on it. Good job, Harry!'

'I'll get it bagged, then the SOCOs can come in and get this photographed, and take their samples. I'll give them a shout, and we can wait in the hall until that vicar returns, so that we can find out something about the victim.'

Outside, there was a screech of brakes and a slight crunching sound, followed by a word that Falconer would never use himself and, a minute or so later, Roberts bounced into the hallway, feet properly covered, and the statement, 'Just had a bit of a bish with the SOCO wagon, but I'm sure that can all be sorted out without any fuss. What's going down, guv?'

'Inspector!' thundered Falconer.

'What, there are two of you here?' Roberts chirped back, still smiling.

'You'll call me Inspector or sir. I don't mind which, but I will *not* be called guv. *Do* you understand me, DC Roberts?'

'Perfectly – Inspector – and there's no need to shout. *You* can call *me* Chris, if you like.'

'I should prefer to call you DC Roberts, for the time being, and don't be insubordinate.'

'I wouldn't even know how to spell that – sir,' he replied, still with an irrepressible grin on his face. 'How's tricks, Doc? Turned any lately?'

'Roberts!'

'Sorry, Inspector. Just being sociable.' Falconer found Roberts a bit of a trial, and was now feeling rather sulky that he'd had the man's company thrust on him today by circumstances completely beyond his control.

'Go and wait in your car until I've got something definite for you to do. And don't speak to anyone else. I've got enough on my plate without having to deal with complaints about your manner of address. And don't say anything about your address being in Market Darley, either. I'm learning how to read you. Back to your car, and don't get out again until I come to get you.'

Thus dismissed, DC Roberts exited the house and sauntered

over to his car, whistling, irrepressible as usual. He had recovered very well from a bad beating he had suffered on his first case at Market Darley, even though he had been left for dead at the roadside in freezing temperatures overnight, and he was just glad to be alive and back on the job.

He had had little contact with either Falconer or Carmichael before he was sent undercover, but now had the chance to acquaint them with his unique and unquenchable approach to life. He'd bring them round to his way of thinking, eventually. DC Roberts was an eternal optimist.

Shortly after his departure, the vicar returned bearing a plastic sandwich box and a medium-sized vacuum flask with a spare plastic cup. Brandishing this latter at Falconer, she said, 'I thought you might be in need of a bit of internal warmth, as well. I don't know if either of you takes sugar, but I've got some sachets in my pocket, which I always take, as my right as a paying customer, whenever I have tea or coffee out.'

That was just as well, thought the inspector, as Carmichael took six sugars in his drinks, but out loud, thanked her for her kindness, and watched as Carmichael sniffed the contents of the plastic box suspiciously. 'Only cheese and pickle,' Rev. Florrie informed him. 'Nothing too adventurous for an upset stomach.'

Carmichael must have been feeling a bit better, for he set about the sandwiches like a man who hadn't eaten for a week. While he ate, Falconer drew her to one side and asked her if she had any idea if Miss Keighley-Armstrong had had any company the previous evening.

'I'll say she had. We had a parish party, for which I picked her up and dropped her home afterwards but, in between, she must have conversed with half the village. She had a jolly good time, and I'm heartbroken that she should have ended up like this, after such a lovely evening.'

'At least she had the lovely evening beforehand. She might have stayed in alone, and just been knocked off without a last happy memory.' Falconer knew this was sentimental tosh, but it seemed to cheer the vicar up a mite.

'That's true,' she agreed. 'I suppose you want me to tell you the names of everybody she spoke to, now, just in case she upset someone, and they came after her, no matter how impossible and bizarre that sounds.'

'Good woman. That's exactly what I'd like you to do, and the names of anyone she might have been on bad terms with,' he replied, getting out his own notebook, slightly thrown off kilter by the fact that Carmichael wasn't by his side doing this part for him, and Roberts had been confined to his basket until it was safe to let him off the leash again.

'Can we do it a bit later?' she requested. 'I'd like to go back to The Rectory, and get away from all this official business. I knew Lettice well, and it's rather upsetting to see her being treated as just another victim.'

'You get off,' agreed Falconer, 'and we'll call round to see you when we've finished here. And thanks for the coffee and sandwiches; that was very kind of you.'

Carmichael must have been feeling better, for there was a call from him, from behind a door Falconer had not yet investigated, due to Doc Christmas', the SOCO team's, and Roberts' arrival. 'In here, sir. I think this must have been an office or study, at some time or other.'

Falconer followed the sound of his sergeant's voice, and found himself in a smallish but business-like room, lined with bookshelves, a desk to the left-hand side of it and, on the right, the gaping door of a safe, miscellaneous papers scattered all over the floor, these proving, on inspection, to be share certificates and property deeds, with a copy of the deceased's will. 'Hang on a minute,' he exhorted Carmichael, and raced from the room to call back the vicar.

When he caught up with her at her car, he asked immediately, 'We've just gone into what looks like a study, and there's a safe in there, door wide open. Did you know about it, and what might it have contained, that might be of sufficient value for someone to do that to an elderly woman who had no way to defend herself?'

'I'd forgotten all about that, because I'd only been told about it, not actually seen it – it was her father's study – but it's easy to explain. Lettice – Miss Keighley-Armstrong – had a collection of very valuable jewellery pieces in there. They had belonged to her mother, for whom they were commissioned by her father, who was a gem dealer in South Africa when she was a child. She didn't come to England until she was a teenager.'

Falconer whistled softly. 'So that proves motive, and a very profitable one at that. There was no sign whatsoever of jewellery in the safe. Just a lot of paperwork scattered on the floor. Did a lot of people know about what her father did?'

'Poor Lettice, knowing she was being robbed of her inheritance, and not being able to do anything about it,' she mused. 'She may have been a bit reclusive herself, but her parents moved here with her, donkey's years ago, so even if she never mentioned it, her mother or her father might have been a bit free with the information. Anyway, that's a moot point, as I heard her myself telling all and sundry about it at the party.'

'That blows the field wide open, then,' retorted Falconer with gloom in his voice. 'Never mind: I'll just have to do CRB checks on the lot of them. Thanks for the information. It should prove very helpful.'

Chapter Seven

Sunday afternoon – Shepford St Bernard

An hour later found the three detectives in The Druid's Head, Carmichael's stomach having been sufficiently settled by the sandwiches to allow him to tolerate the smell of stale ale and pub grub. In fact, so recovered was he that, although they only ordered three coffees to drink, lunch was to consist of three ploughman's. His appetite had recovered, taken the sandwiches to represent breakfast, and was now clamouring for lunch, the hour being past noon.

After a succinct summing up of the information he had obtained from the vicar, Falconer concluded his monologue with, 'So, we need to check the village's residents for any criminal record for jewel theft, receiving or handling stolen goods, or fencing of same. There's no telling who someone living here might have passed that information on to, or who might have overheard her talking about it.

'It could be a long-term resident who's fallen on hard times, and decided to do something positive with their knowledge, either personally, or using an accomplice. It could be a newcomer who had decided to take advantage of newly acquired knowledge, and net a nice little profit for themselves. Whoever is responsible for this crime, it's possible we'll need to do a great deal of digging, and maybe in some very grubby places.'

'What have you got for us to deal with for now, *sir*?' asked Roberts, placing great emphasis on the last word.

'A list of names to be divided up between us for initial interviews,' he replied, hoping that Roberts wasn't expecting a doggy treat for his unusual cooperation with mode of address.

Two notebooks appeared from pockets, and two eager faces gazed at him across the table. Things were looking up; Carmichael appeared to be back to his normal self and Roberts wasn't playing the clown for once.

'Do you mind interviewing on your own, Roberts?' he asked, 'Only Carmichael and I are in the habit of working in tandem.'

'Not at all, *Inspector*,' the DC replied. 'We didn't always have the luxury of sufficient officers where I come from, so it was necessary to do lot of stuff without a partner.'

Not quite finished playing the goat, then. He'd heard that emphasis on the word 'inspector'. Ignoring it, he continued, 'I'd like you to take the east side of the village. You can start with the landlord here, then go on to,' he proceeded, using a comprehensive list he had obtained from Rev. Feldman, 'Coopers Lane, where you will find a Ms Gwendolyn Galton at 'Carpe Diem', a Mr Toby Lattimer at 'Tresore' and a Miss Maude Asquith at a place called 'Khartoum'.

Roberts made as if to speak, but Falconer held up a hand. 'Then you can go on to 'Sweet Dreams', here on The Green; family by the name of Yaxley, and finally, on to see Mr and Mrs Jasper Haygarth at 'Three-Ways House' on the junction of The Green with the Downsway Road. When you've finished that lot, we'll meet you back at the office.'

'Sometime tomorrow morning, I presume,' replied Roberts, looking put-upon.

'Sometime later today, Constable. And make sure you find out everything you can about the householders in question, as well as what they can tell you about the victim, and what social contact they had with her yesterday evening. Got that?'

'Got it, *sir*,' replied Roberts ruefully, getting up and heading for the bar to speak to the landlord.

'Who are we going to interview?' asked Carmichael, with the everyday eagerness that Falconer had been taking for granted for some time, and had only missed this morning, when it was not present.

'We're taking the west side of the village, from the first house, right round to The Rectory. I shall need an official statement from the vicar, and I also want to access a house key again, for the insurance company will need to be contacted, not just for their information, but so that we can check whether they have photographs of the jewellery for identification purposes.'

'Let's ride them dogies then, sir,' replied Carmichael, apparently speaking a foreign language. 'I'm back on ma horse.'

Falconer and Carmichael left the pub premises before Roberts, he being in deep, note-taking conversation with the landlord before moving on to Coopers Lane. Their first port of call was 'Robin's Perch', the occupant of which had been named as a Miss Bonnie Fletcher. After a lot of ringing of the doorbell, enthusiastic use of the doorknocker, a few calls of, 'Miss Fletcher, are you in there?' and a quick look round the back of the property, they decided that she was either deaf or not in, and moved on to their next target.

'Bijou' was also a detached cottage, but in need of a lick of paint to its door and windows. Their knock was quickly answered by a man in his sixties, dressed casually in a cardigan and open shirt collar – no sign of a tie, but then it was Sunday.

Falconer gave their names and, the two of them displayed their warrant cards, for confirmation that they were kosher, and the man gave his name as Julius Twelvetrees, and invited them in, the three of them eventually settling in a sitting room that looked rather like the set for a dated sitcom – too cottagey to be real.

'I heard all the hoo-ha with cars and whatnot, this morning. What's been going on? Something up at old Lettice's place? Forgotten to pay her TV licence; something like that?' He spoke light-heartedly, but there was a tremor in his voice that belied his words.

'I'm sorry to inform you that Miss Keighley-Armstrong is now deceased, and that we are treating her death as suspicious,' Falconer informed him, as Carmichael made himself as

81

comfortable as was possible, given his build, in a chintz armchair that was scaled to the size of the room – dinky – and took out his notebook.

'Good God!' the man replied, with what seemed like genuine surprise. 'Whatever happened to her?'

'It would seem that someone gained admittance to her house, hit her with a bronze statuette, then broke into the safe, and cleared it of anything worth stealing. Do you personally have any knowledge of what was in that safe?'

There was a moment of silence before Twelvetrees spoke, during which he looked as if he were screwing himself up to an unpleasant admission. Which he was. 'As a matter of fact I do. She showed me what was in there; just the once, you understand, and several years ago, at that,' he admitted, colouring as he spoke, although whether this was from guilt, or genuine embarrassment, it was impossible to tell.

'And why would she do that, I wonder,' queried Falconer, 'when I'd heard she was a bit of a recluse.'

'It was just a reaction to my profession at the time. I suppose she wanted to show off her pieces to someone who would really appreciate them.'

'And what profession would that be, Mr Twelvetrees?'

'I used to be a jeweller – retail, that is,' he informed them. 'Had a little shop in Market Darley. Maybe you remember it? It was in one of the roads that lead off the market square. 'Bijouterie', it was called.'

'No, but then I don't buy jewellery,' replied Falconer, only to be outdone by Carmichael, who piped up with, 'I bought my wife's engagement and wedding rings there.'

'Do you know, I think I remember you, now. Such an unforgettable build,' Twelvetrees batted back at him with a small smile.

This was all getting a bit too pally for Falconer's liking, and he steered the interview back to the subject in hand. 'Did you attend the parish party last night at the hall?'

'I did indeed. I didn't stay to the end, but it was better than I thought it was going to be. Damned good job that lady vicar

82

made of it, I thought.'

'Did you speak to Miss Keighley-Armstrong at all during the evening?'

'Not as I recall. I spent most of my time there nattering to old Toby Lattimer about this and that. I did try to speak to my relatively new next-door neighbour, but he seems to be an uncommonly uncommunicative fellow, and I got myself snubbed, if you want to know.'

'I shouldn't let that worry you, sir. We'll be speaking to him soon, and he won't be able to snub us: we're unsnubbable, and have got the badges to prove it,' replied the inspector, making a rare joke.

'Ha ha! Very good, Inspector Falconer,' Twelvetrees applauded his efforts.

'When did you last see or speak to Miss Keighley-Armstrong, sir?'

'I haven't spoken to her since after church last Sunday, and I haven't seen her since the party last night. Is that what you wanted to know?'

'Thank you for your cooperation, sir. Now, are you aware of anyone who might hold a grudge against the deceased, or who is desperate enough for money that they would risk breaking in and stealing what was in the safe?'

'How'd anyone get the combination out of her in the first place?' asked Twelvetrees, genuinely interested.

'Intimidation and violence are the usual methods, sir. Now, if you wouldn't mind answering my last question.'

Twelvetrees sat in silence for a moment, as he wracked his brains for anything that might be of interest to his two unexpected guests.

DC Roberts' first call was to Carpe Diem, a Georgian house which was well enough maintained so that a first impression of it didn't mark it down as scruffy, but closer inspection revealed a rather lackadaisical attitude towards upkeep. The lawn was not shaggy, but the flowerbeds were empty, and although fairly weed-free, no spring flowers poked their heads out of the soil. The paintwork wasn't neglected, but a more thorough look revealed the window frames were beginning to flake.

At the front door, he noticed that the varnish had worn thin in places, with the onslaught of the weather, and the brass knocker was dull and unpolished. Ms Gwendolyn Galton, he thought, was either losing heart, or had more pressing calls on her cash.

Seizing the knocker, which was a lion's head, firmly in his hand, he applied it three times, surprised at just how much noise it made. After a minute or so, he knocked again, then made his way round the property, to see if the owner was in the back garden. Finding this not to be so, he cupped his hands round his eyes, and sneaked a peek through the downstairs windows.

Not a very tidy person, he decided, noting that what appeared to be the dining room had sheets of newspaper everywhere, and some small ornamental items scattered across the table, not displayed proudly on units or shelves, as he would have expected them to be. Deciding that there was definitely no one at home, he trailed round to the front again, wrote a brief message on one of his cards for the owner to phone him, slipped it through the letterbox, and moved on to the next property, galled at this inauspicious start to his first case back on duty.

I hope I have a bit more luck with the rest of them, he thought, otherwise the guv's going to think I'm a right slacker. And here's me, raring to go, hoping that I'm going to be the one who spots the vital clue which brings the murderer to justice.

Falconer and Carmichael, in the meantime, having finished with Julius Twelvetrees, now stood at the door of Carters Cottage, hoping that Colin Twentymen was at home. They didn't have long to wait to have their hopes realised, as the door swung open within a few seconds of the bell ringing, and a man of medium height, with greying blond hair and a beard and moustache showing just a touch of faint red, stood before them.

He ushered them inside without a word and, still silently, motioned them into the kitchen and into wheel-backed chairs in the larger than expected room. 'Mr Twentymen?' enquired Falconer, somewhat nonplussed by this rural English Marcel

Marceau.

''S right,' he replied. 'You're police.' His attitude was curt to the point of insolence, but that may be explained by the rare occurrence of finding policemen on his doorstep.

'We're here about Miss Keighley-Armstrong,' Falconer continued, refusing to be intimidated by the man's brusque manner. 'She's dead, I'm afraid – sometime last night, we believe – and we're asking people when they last saw or spoke to her. At the moment, we're treating the death as suspicious.'

'Didn't know her. Not been here long,' replied Twentymen, giving them no information whatsoever.

'Did you attend the party at the hall yesterday evening?'

'Yep.'

'Did you see or talk to Miss Keighley-Armstrong?'

'Saw her. Didn't speak to her.'

This was like pulling teeth, or getting blood out of a stone. Did the man not know how to construct a full sentence, or was he always like this? 'Miss Keighley-Armstrong also had a valuable collection of jewellery stolen from her safe. Did you know about this collection?'

'Nope.'

'Have you any idea who, in this village, might have had a grudge against Miss Keighley-Armstrong, or a score to settle with her?' Falconer silently bet himself a tenner that Twentymen would not use a proper sentence to answer this question, nor provide them with anything they didn't already know.

'Nope. I don't indulge in idle gossip, and keep myself to myself.'

Damn, he'd lost his bet, and was glad he hadn't had the opportunity to make the wager with Carmichael, or he'd be ten pounds out of pocket, and still none the wiser. He gave it one last shot. 'Is there anything you can tell me that might be helpful to the case?'

'Nope. Sorry.' At least he had a trace of manners, somewhere, in that he offered this cursory apology.

'We'll be on our way, then. Thank you for your time.' They

could hardly thank him for his help, for they were leaving empty-handed, with not even a jot of new information.

Outside the door again, Carmichael heaved a huge sigh and commented, 'Doesn't waste his words, does he?'

'Nope,' replied Falconer, unconsciously echoing Twentymen.

At the house next door, a tiled Victorian pile of a building, the garden neat in an almost military fashion, with bulbs showing their shoots in serried ranks and the outdated name of Khartoum, Roberts found the owner at home, and anxious to get him off the doorstep, once he had revealed himself as a detective.

'Get inside quickly, young man,' she ordered him. 'I don't want any of the neighbours to know I've had a visit from the police, after which she hurried him into a sitting room straight from a *fin de siècle* television period drama, and indicated that he should sit on a hideous horsehair-stuffed sofa.

'What do you want?' she asked without preamble, sitting bolt upright opposite him in a similarly uncomfortable armchair, and glaring at him with injured innocence at the thought that she should have such an unwelcome visitor.

'I'm here to try to gather any information you may have, that might help me find the murderer of a Miss Keighley-Armstrong of Manor Gate,' Roberts stated baldly.

He got no further, as she gave a shrill scream, her hands flying to her face. 'No,' she shrieked. 'Dear Lettice can't be dead. You must be mistaken. Oh, what a wicked trick to play on an old woman. Who put you up to this, young man?'

Roberts held out his warrant card to her, as asking to see it was a precaution she had not taken, in her haste to get him out of general view. 'I can assure you that I'm deadly serious, Madam,' he replied.

'Miss,' she corrected him automatically. 'But I only saw her last night. When did this happen? Oh, poor, dear Lettice. She was my best friend, you know, and I shall miss her so.'

She may have sounded heartbroken, but he could see her

peeping surreptitiously between her fingers as she spoke, in an effort to gauge his reaction to her distress. 'I'm sorry if I've caused you any distress,' he apologised, determined to take the line of least resistance. 'Perhaps you could answer a few questions, and then tell me something about your friend.'

'Certainly, Inspector.' Either her eyesight wasn't up to much, or she was trying to charm him. Either way, he didn't feel like putting her right, as being addressed as Inspector was unexpectedly pleasant.

'Did you see Miss Keighley-Armstrong at all, yesterday?' he asked, feeling quite puffed up with importance at his unexpected promotion.

'Of course. I saw her at the party in the church hall. I spent quite a bit of the evening sitting with her and chatting.'

'What sort of mood was she in? Did she seem worried about anything, or mention anything that was causing her anxiety?'

'Absolutely not. She seemed in fine form, and had a jolly good time. I do remember, though, that she talked a lot, and quite loudly about her jewellery, and I did suggest to her that this wasn't a wise thing to do.'

'And why did you advise that, Miss Asquith?'

'Because you never knew who was listening and taking note of it all. She could have been robbed.'

'She has been robbed. It's all gone. Every last piece. And she's been murdered, into the bargain.' He informed her, with a 'what do you think of that, then?' expression on his face.

'Oh my good Lord! All of that beautiful jewellery gone – just like that,' the woman exclaimed, a look of profound loss on her face, this expression completely genuine.

'Had you seen the pieces, then?' asked Roberts, anxious to have them described to him.

'Not actually seen them, but dear Lettice did talk about them sometimes, and they sounded fabulous. Like a treasure from the Arabian Nights. Did she …? Do you know if she …? Did you find her will?' There it was, then; the old biddy had been hoping to be mentioned in the will, and was desperate to know whether or not she'd been left something.

'I'm sorry, but I can't disclose any information on what was actually found when the house was searched. I can only tell you what was not.' Roberts could see the sort of woman he was dealing with, now, and was not willing to offer her any comfort at all. He'd keep the knowledge gained from the insurance papers to himself, as well. No point in letting her off the hook she'd been caught on any earlier than he had to.

'One final question: did you see Miss Keighley-Armstrong again after the party?'

'Of course I didn't, young man. What exactly are you implying?' She was so indignant that a red spot appeared on each of her cheeks, and she began puffing and blowing with the grossness of what she perceived as a grave insult.

'I'm implying nothing at all, Miss Asquith. For all I know, you could have gone round to see her after the party for a milky drink and a good gossip about how the party had gone.'

Somewhat mollified, Maude satisfied her honour by replying, 'I most certainly did not, young man, and I shall expect to be kept informed about any progress on the case, being her best friend. Also, I've not been at all happy with your attitude towards me this afternoon, and I shall certainly be speaking to your superior about it, Constable. It's simply not good enough!'

So, all that 'Inspector' business had been so much B-S, to try to get more details out of him. Roberts left Khartoum with no new information, but the impression that he had just spent some time in the company of a leech. Mean old bat didn't even offer him a cup of tea.

Falconer and Carmichael had, by that time, arrived outside the second of a terrace of three cottages, this one being name 'Ace of Cups', a name that perplexed them both, this phrase meaning nothing to either of them.

To their surprise, the door was answered by what looked like a middle-aged witch, straight from the pages of the Grimms' fairytales. The woman was dressed from head to toe in black, and her long hair was also dyed the colour of jet. She was adorned by various silver charms and unrecognisable symbols, strung on chains and hanging from her neck and both her wrists, and positively jingling as she came to rest with one hand on the door.

Both men were struck dumb by this unexpected apparition, and it was the witch who was the first to speak. 'Were you perhaps hoping for a reading? Speak up and don't be shy; I don't bite.'

There was a silence of perhaps five seconds before Falconer regained his voice. 'Miss Wanda Warwick?' he enquired, tentatively.

'That is I,' she replied. 'How can I help you? I can fit you in this afternoon if you'd like.'

'I think we might be at cross purposes here, Miss Warwick,' explained Falconer. 'We are from Market Darley CID, investigating the death of Miss Keighley-Armstrong of Manor Gate, and wondered if we might have a short word with you about the deceased.'

Wanda's already pale face turned even paler, and she gasped, before gabbling, 'I knew there was something dreadful about to happen when I turned over those last cards yesterday, and now I've been proved right. How did it happen?' Reaching the back of one hand to her forehead, she made a fair facsimile of a woman about to swoon, and Carmichael shot forward to catch her, before she fell.

As the sergeant helped her indoors and into a chair, Falconer trailed in behind them, thinking, naïve boy, to fall for so obvious an act. The inspector wasn't fooled for a minute. She put on a fair performance of being profoundly shocked at something, but whatever this was, there would be some sort of glory in it for her, or he was a Dutchman.

'I was supposed to be doing readings at a fair today, but I simply couldn't face it.'

'So, was it the weather that put you off? It can't be much fun out in this rain for a whole day, getting soaking wet and not being able to dry off.'

'Oh, is it raining? I can't say that I even noticed. I'm still too spooked about what happened yesterday afternoon.'

'Would you like to explain what upset you so much, Miss Warwick?' he asked, settling himself into another chair.

'Oh, please call me Wanda,' she requested, then continued, 'I did a tarot reading for Mrs Yaxley across The Green yesterday, and the last three cards didn't seem to fit in at all with all of the others. They predicted calamity and death; something I fluffed over, and said there must be some mistake. There obviously wasn't, though, and I didn't get in quickly enough with reassuring Mrs Yaxley either, because she went off with the jitters a short while later. But I was right, wasn't I? I was right?'

'Indeed you were, Ms ... Wanda. So you're a tarot card reader, are you?' Falconer asked, quite curious to know exactly what this weird woman did.

'I'm actually a white witch, but I read the cards, and also have a certain amount of psychic ability. I'm sure it was a warning and my unconscious influence that made those particular cards turn up yesterday. They just didn't gel with any of the other groups of cards. I was being given a warning from beyond the veil, of a tragedy about to occur, and failed to recognise it for what it was.'

Carmichael looked impressed, but Falconer could see her milking this one for all it was worth, especially if she'd spooked her client, as well. The word would soon get round the village grapevine, and maybe she'd even get a piece in the local paper, with her looking her psychic best, and utterly witchy.

'What happened to the poor old lady?' she asked, still pale, but her eyes alight with excitement.

'It would appear that someone got into the house – we don't know how yet – got the combination of her safe out of her, banged her on the head, then made off with her collection of jewellery.'

'How awful. And where was she found? In her chair? On the floor?'

'I'm afraid I can't go into further detail at the moment, Ms ... Wanda, for procedural reasons.' The woman was obviously fishing for details, so that she could tell people that she'd envisaged the whole scene: that it was revealed, from 'the other side', in great detail, to her psychic mind.

'I'm sure you understand,' Falconer apologised, but noted the thwarted look in her eyes. She wouldn't get quite as much mileage out of this as she had, at first, supposed, now that she couldn't describe the scene of the death with some detail, and it would be in the local rag before she got her hands on exactly where the death had occurred.

'I understand,' she said rather sharply, then continued, 'Everybody hereabouts knew about them, you know, but only a very few have ever seen them. I haven't. That being so, how can I help you, if I can't tempt you to have a little glance into the future?'

Falconer quelled Carmichael with a glance. He was looking just a little too like an eager puppy who has been offered an unexpected walk. 'We'd like to ask you about the last time you saw or spoke to the deceased, and whether you are aware of anyone who bore the old lady a grudge.'

Realising the inspector had rumbled her, she informed them that she had seen Lettice at the party, and had had a brief word with her. (No luck there, then, concluded Falconer.) She had not seen Miss Keighley-Armstrong again, after she had left the party in the company of Rev. Florrie, who had volunteered to run her home in her car.

'Did you hear anything from the direction of Manor Gate later in the evening, when you'd returned home?'

'By the time I got home, it was raining stair-rods, and the thunder was almost deafening. I don't think I'd have heard a brass band over the racket that made.'

'Do you know of anyone local with whom Miss Keighley-Armstrong was on, let's say, bad terms?'

'I don't know about bad terms, but she had a down on that woman from Coopers Lane, Sour-Puss Asquith. She was always visiting Lettice, sucking up to her and schmoozing her.'

'Miss Keighley-Armstrong told you this?'

'No, but it was as plain as the nose on your face. I saw them talking together last night, and the hostile vibes that were coming off Lettice were almost visible.'

Yeah, sure! 'Anything else, Wanda?' Falconer had got used to the feel of her forename in his mouth now, and used it with more ease.

'Not that I can think of, but if you leave your card with me, I'll give it some thought.'

When they were out of the cottage, Falconer declared, 'What a fraud! I'll bet she pulls that trick of weird cards influenced by the ether at least once a quarter, in the hope that something will happen just after it which she can attribute to her psychic ability. Psychic ability, my big fat hairy arse!'

'It doesn't look that big, sir,' replied Carmichael with a straight face, then let a smile break out, to let the inspector know he was only kidding. 'Shall we take a short break in The Druid's Head for a coffee, sir?'

'Good idea, Carmichael. Let's get over there.'

'And I thought she was scary.'

'Scary, she might have been. Genuine, she ain't,' replied Falconer, firmly closing the matter for the time being.

In Coopers Lane, Roberts had arrived at Tresore and was at that moment receiving an effusive welcome from Toby Lattimer. 'Do come in,' he invited when Roberts had introduced himself. 'I thought something was going on, and now you've arrived to satisfy my curiosity. Sit yourself down and I'll put on the kettle, so we can have a nice pot of Darjeeling and a good old gossip, and you can give me every little detail about what's happened.'

This was more like it, thought Roberts, heading for the comfiest-looking chair and eyeing the plethora of ornaments and cabinets of bits and bobs that filled the room. Bit overcrowded, he considered, but it looked like there was some good stuff in here.

When Lattimer returned, bearing a tray, Roberts was not surprised to see that it bore a silver tea service, and that the cups and saucers were porcelain, giving him a moment of nerves that he might drop and break his cup. He could be a tad clumsy when he was nervous, and anything valuable and breakable always made him break out in a sweat. Deciding that, no matter how bad-mannered it looked, he'd have to cradle the delicate vessel in both hands, with no extended pinkie, to avoid disaster, he took out his notebook.

'Right, first question,' he stated, as Lattimer poured the pale amber liquid into his second best china. 'Were you at the party at the hall, last night?'

'Indeed I was, young man, and Lettice – Miss Keighley-Armstrong, that is – got quite tiddly on the punch, and made a bit of an exhibition of herself, in my opinion. What has she done? Streaked down The Green, or something similarly shaming?' he asked, his eyes like slits.

'She's dead,' declared Roberts, without a thought for the man's feelings. The stream of amber liquid wavered, as the information was assimilated, and Lattimer put down the teapot and just stared at his guest.

'Dead? She can't be! I only saw her last night. Don't be so cruel.'

'I'm not, sir. She really is dead – and murdered, by the looks of it.'

'Do take a cup,' said Lattimer, on automatic pilot with courtesy, because of the jolt the detective's words had given him. Recovering himself slightly, he asked, 'How? When? Who? Why? I want to know everything you've discovered.'

Golly, the man really was a gossip hound. 'That's the reason I'm here, sir, to try to find out anything I can about what may have happened, and who may be responsible for what happened. Just a few questions, if you wouldn't mind.'

'Fire away, then, but I don't see how I can help you.' Toby Lattimer had almost recovered his aplomb and was determined to milk this exciting visit for all it was worth.

'You've already stated that you attended the parish party last night, so did you speak to Miss Keighley-Armstrong during the course of the evening?'

'Yes, to that particular question. I stayed a couple of hours, fascinated by Lettice, as she was well away, swigging the punch, and I did speak to her. She had become a little too free, talking about her mother's jewellery, and I spoke to her about her indiscretion. You never know who might be listening, or who they might pass the information on to, in all innocence.

'She didn't give a fig, though: said she'd had precious little joy from the inheritance because she never wore any of it. The least she could do was to be able to talk about it, and make a few people feel envious,' Lattimer ventured, a wicked twinkle in his eyes.

'Do you think she had anyone in particular in mind when she made that last comment?' asked Roberts, his pen at the ready.

'Looking back, I seem to remember that she shot that Asquith woman a bit of a venomous glance. That's Maude Asquith: lives next door in a monstrosity of a house with the ridiculous name of Khartoum.'

'We've just met,' declared Roberts unhappily, then added indignantly, 'She said she was Miss Keighley-Armstrong's best friend.'

'What a load of old codswallop. She wishes! She sucked up to Lettice at every opportunity that presented itself, and she was always calling round on the off-chance that the old lady needed some shopping, but it was really to try and endear herself to her. No chance! What a bum-suck!'

Roberts laughed, before he had time to stop himself. 'Well, she is,' stated Lattimer, before the detective had had the chance to apologise. 'There's just no other word for it. Her behaviour would make a cat sick.'

'I certainly didn't find her very welcoming, Mr Lattimer.'

'The only people that old biddy would welcome into her home would be the Queen or the Governor of the Bank of England.'

'That excludes me, then,' said Roberts, chuckling. This interview seemed to be going better than the last one.

'And me,' agreed Lattimer. 'I never went round there unless I absolutely had to. Now, what else can I tell you about our small but far from happy community?'

'You have gossip?' he asked, naively, but it was taken in

good part.

'Just as I collect little bits and pieces,' – here Toby Lattimer held out his arms and indicated the contents of the room – 'so I collect bits and pieces of gossip, and store them away, in case they ever come in useful.' As he said this last, his eyes flicked from side to side like a wary animal's, on guard in case there was any danger to his hoard.

'Fire away, sir,' invited Roberts, his notebook open, his pen ready to start recording any juicy little titbits.

After forty-five minutes of very interesting information about Shepford St Bernard's inhabitants, Roberts found himself out in the fresh air and craving caffeine. Maybe he'd stop into the pub on his way to Sweet Dreams, and satisfy his craving with a double espresso.

As he came out of the little alleyway that led down the side of Carpe Diem to The Green, he caught sight of Falconer and Carmichael crossing the road, with probably the very same thought in their minds. He'd definitely join them, to see how they were getting on.

Chapter Eight

Shepford St Bernard, Sunday afternoon

The landlord of The Druid's Head didn't usually open on Sunday afternoon but, after sticking his head out of an upstairs window to see who was knocking at the door with such persistence, he came down and let them in, quite happy for them to have a short meeting on his premises so long as they didn't want anything alcoholic served. They didn't.

Within five minutes, Falconer sat sipping a cappuccino, Roberts his desired double espresso, and Carmichael a pint of orange squash – because he was still feeling a bit dehydrated – accompanied by three rounds of sandwiches, which the landlord's wife had whipped up for 'the poor hungry lad'.

'So how did you get on, Roberts?' Falconer asked, receiving the reply,

'Apart from the pub, two and a "not at home".'

'Same as us,' replied Carmichael indistinctly, through a mouthful of ham sandwich

'I met a really unpleasant old woman, though. She was a real nasty piece of work, and she said she was going to make a complaint against me. Given her attitude, I reckon I ought to be able to complain about her. Ignore it, if she says anything nasty about me. The nastiness is all in her head,' said Roberts, pleading his own case before he was even charged.

'Any complaint made about one of my officers will be considered with a completely open mind,' the inspector replied, watching in disbelief as the last mouthful of sandwich entered Carmichael's gaping maw. How did he do it? And feeling the way he had just that morning.

Swallowing furiously, the sergeant said, with a hint of awe in his voice, 'We met a real witch.'

'You never!'

'We did. In that cottage opposite called "Ace of Cups". She all but passed out when we gave her the news of the murder.'

'Oh, Carmichael, you are so naïve sometimes. If I told you I was the Queen of Sheba you'd believe me.'

'No I wouldn't, sir.'

'Why not?'

''Cause you're a man, so you couldn't possibly be a queen of anywhere.'

'Fair point, and well-reasoned,' was Falconer's response, adding, for Roberts' benefit, 'She claimed to be a white witch; a follower of Wiccan, whatever that means, and, please, don't either of you start explaining it to me, because I'm not in the least interested. I just know that she's a charlatan, and we'll leave it at that, shall we?'

The other two looked at him rather sharply. This woman had obviously upset him, but neither of them was about to ask how.

'Now, if you've finished, let's get on with the job at hand, and we'll meet back at the station when we're finished. OK?'

A unison 'OK,' agreed with him, and they went their separate ways again for the rest of the afternoon.

Falconer and Carmichael's first call of round two was at 'Tootelon Down' – ugh! What a twee name – which was at the northern end of the terrace of three, just opposite The Druid's Head. This was the home of Violet Bingham, a widow who revealed herself, when she opened the door to them, to be somewhere in her mid-seventies. Her eyes were red-rimmed and puffy, tears still wet her cheeks, and her free hand held a wet and crumpled old-fashioned linen handkerchief.

She bade them enter, and apologised for her distraught state. 'I had a call from dear Rev. Florrie,' she told them. 'She thought she ought to let me know, as Lettice and I have been best friends for years now. I met her when my children were quite young, and we just clicked. I'm completely devastated at what has happened, and I shall help in any way that will assist in catching whatever evil person has done this.'

By now they were in her sitting room on comfy chairs, the room a sea of rich red and white with touches of gold. It was surprisingly luxuriously decorated and furnished, in comparison to the other residences they had visited, and a bright log fire burnt in the hearth, making the room even more cosy and comfortable.

'What a lovely room, Miss Bingham,' Falconer could not help but state.

'Thank you, Inspector. I think so, too, but it isn't to everybody's taste. There's a mort of chintz in the interiors of this village, but I just can't take to it. I like plain colours, well-coordinated, with just the hint of a highlight.'

After this statement, she stopped abruptly, and her tears returned. 'I really don't understand how I can talk quite calmly about interior design, when my heart is breaking. Poor, poor Lettice! I do hope she didn't suffer. Who could do such a thing to an old woman like that?'

'That's what we're here to find out, Miss Bingham. We have a few questions we'd like you to answer, then we'll leave you in peace,' Falconer assured her.

'Oh, don't rush on my account. At least company distracts my mind from the awful visions I've been imagining. Let me get you some refreshment. Would you like some tea, perhaps?'

'That would be very kind of you. Thank you,' agreed Falconer, aware that they had only just had coffee, but recognising that the woman needed company more than she needed solitude and, if she had, indeed, been Miss Keighley-Armstrong's friend for so long, she might be able to fill in the details about the victim's character, and provide the names of anyone who may have had reason to dislike her.

Carmichael, he noticed, was as happy as a pig in poo. The chairs were man-sized, and he knew that his sergeant would welcome any fluid offered after his stint of carousing the evening before.

Once settled, Violet, with innate intuition having provided

Carmichael with a large mug, rather than the dainty china cup and saucer she provided for herself and Falconer, and proceeded to unburden herself of anything that might prove useful to them.

'As I said, I met Lettice a long time ago, and we were friends while my two were growing up. When my husband died, we became even closer, spending a part of most days together, usually at her house. She wasn't much of a one for going out, and preferred people to come to her – a bit reclusive, really. Her only regular trip out was to church every Sunday, and even that stopped when Rev. Florrie arrived. But she soon got over herself on that one. Rev. Florrie can be very persuasive when she puts her mind to it.'

'How did she manage about her shopping and suchlike?' asked Carmichael in the silence between answer and next question, and ever practical.

'She had it delivered from the village. Neither shopkeeper minded bringing it up to her, as she was sort of semi-gentry. Her parents had always been the most affluent residents before they died, and their reputation just transferred itself to Lettice.

'If she wanted anything a bit more exotic than they stocked, I would pick it up for her when I went to the supermarket. I didn't mind at all: we were good friends.'

'Had she fallen out with anyone in the recent past?' asked Falconer, Carmichael sitting eagerly with his pen to the ready, hoping for some meaty stuff.

'Not really, except for with the vicar, before she got to know her properly. She could be a bit sharp-tongued, but then she didn't see that many people, so she couldn't get herself into hot water.'

'What about Miss Asquith, who also claimed to be a good friend of hers?' enquired Falconer, not realising he had really thrown the cat among the pigeons.

'Huh! Dear old Maudie?' Violet's face had coloured, and she seemed to be getting her dander up about something. 'If you'll just cover your sergeant's ears, Inspector, I'll tell you all about dear Maudie. She was what my husband would have called an "arse-licker". Not a pretty epithet, but she sucked up

100

to Lettice shamelessly.

'She was one person whom Lettice did actively dislike,' she continued, as Carmichael giggled quietly at such an ugly expression coming out of such a respectable, elderly mouth. 'She was always calling round on the off-chance that Lettice might need something from the shops or the supermarket, then insinuating herself into the house, and – excuse the expression – "bumming" a cup of tea and a nasty little chat.

'Lettice declared that there was nothing like a "nice" little chat with that woman. She's a bag of hot air filled with gossip and spite and, recently, Lettice had taken to hiding in the walk-in larder, to avoid her snooping through the windows. She'd stayed firmly in her armchair once, in revolt to answering the door to her, but the cheeky old besom had gone round the house, looking through the windows. Lettice had to pretend to have been taking a nap, once she was busted.'

'She sounds a thoroughly unpleasant woman,' Falconer opined. 'Our colleague called on her earlier, and found her in rather robust form, even threatening to complain about his behaviour.'

'He won't have been charmed, I can assure you,' she stated, with emphasis.

'Can you tell me about last night and the party – I assume you attended?'

'Of course I did. One has to do everything within one's power to help Rev. Florrie in her bid to revitalise the parish and build up the congregation.'

'What was Miss Keighley-Armstrong's mood at the party? Did she seem as if anything was on her mind, or that she was worrying about anything?'

'Quite the opposite. She was in fine form, slugging down the punch as if there were no tomorrow ...' Here, she broke off. 'Of course, for her, there really *was* no tomorrow. Maybe she had some sort of premonition.'

'You don't believe in all that supernatural stuff, do you?' Falconer was surprised that this may be so.

'Of course not, but I did hear about that reading Wanda –

that's our local witch – did yesterday, and how upset she was at the last three cards she turned up. Nothing stays private for long in a village, and I did hear that Krystal Yaxley was badly shaken by Wanda's reaction.'

That was an interesting idea, Falconer suddenly thought. Maybe the cards had been rigged so that Wanda could get at the victim, while claiming that the information had been in the cards earlier that day, and she wasn't responsible for which cards turned up. At best, she was possibly going for a bit of publicity about her powers: at worst, she was setting the scene for a dreadful act shortly after she had predicted it. Ms Warwick was certainly worth another look.

'Back to the party, Mrs Bingham, if you'd be so good.'

'Yes, the party; Lettice was in one of her very rare outgoing moods, and told all and sundry about her father's work in South Africa, and about all the stones he had collected, and the fabulous pieces of jewellery he had had made for her mother. Anyone could have heard her, and I tried to get her to keep quiet about it, but she simply ignored me. All gone, now, I suppose.'

'All gone, I'm afraid,' Falconer confirmed.

'Poor Lettice. Those stones cost her her life. Nothing material was ever worth that.'

'When we found her, she had managed to get herself outside, maybe to call for help, and she was lying with her arms outstretched just about touching one of the old gravestones,' Falconer informed her. 'Do you think that may have meant something?' The thought had only just recurred to him.

'Maybe she was just trying to show that it was her stones that had gone, and that they had been the cause of her injuries,' offered Mrs Bingham, speculating wildly.

'That certainly is food for thought,' said Falconer, thinking it imaginative but unlikely, but filing it away at the back of his mind, in case it came in handy at any time during the investigation. 'Thank you very much for your time and the tea. We'll get back in touch with you if we need to. Before we go, though, do you know who her next of kin is? We'll need somebody to officially identify the body.'

'She was all alone in the world, I'm afraid. Her last cousin died two years ago.' Seeing Falconer's desolate expression, she added, 'I suppose I could do it. Heaven knows, I've known her long enough. I might as well be the one to see her off on her final journey.' And she gave a deep sigh.

'That's very generous-spirited of you, Mrs Bingham. I'll be in touch about day and time.'

'What a nice old lady,' stated Carmichael sincerely, after she had closed the door on them, and they made their way towards The Rectory.

Meanwhile, Roberts took the few steps necessary, having turned left on exiting the pub, to his next destination at Sweet Dreams. Krystal Yaxley answered the door to him after a short delay, still shouting to her sons upstairs to turn their bloody music down before she went mad, finishing with, 'And you should have asked a fee for last night. We could have done with the money, no matter how little.'

Turning towards her caller, she apologised, and asked how she could help him. 'DC Roberts from Market Darley,' he introduced himself, and a fleeting look of fear crossed her face.

'What's happened?' she asked, suddenly wondering if this visitor had come to tell her that something had happened to her runaway husband. If it had, though, maybe the insurance would get her out of her financial mess, and the mortgage would be automatically paid off. The fear was replaced by a look of hopeful anticipation, this only to be wiped off her face when Roberts informed her that he was pursuing the investigation of the death of Miss Keighley-Armstrong.

'The old lady's dead?' she asked, and the colour drained slowly from her face.

'Did you know her?' asked Roberts, intrigued by this reaction.

'No, no, I'm just surprised, that's all,' she said, and remained standing where she was, a slight tremor developing in the hands that hung at her sides.

'Do you think I might come in?' enquired the DC, beginning to feel like a door-to-door salesman who had forgotten his case of brushes, and rather conspicuous.

'Of course. I'm sorry. You just knocked me off kilter for a moment.' Her voice had strong traces of a Lancashire accent, and he knew at once that she wasn't a long-term inhabitant in these parts. 'Come on in and sit yourself down. Can I get you anything to drink? I feel in need of a gin and tonic myself.'

'Not while I'm on duty, Mrs Yaxley, but thanks for asking.' Had Falconer not been in the vicinity, he would have agreed with alacrity, for he saw no harm in one drink, if one was driving. He didn't fancy his chances of escaping without a wigging, however, if he ran into the inspector and breathed gin fumes all over him.

Once settled, and after a' large swig from her tumbler, Krystal asked exactly what had happened, and why he thought she could help him.

'I'm sorry to have to tell you that Miss Keighley-Armstrong died last night, after a burglary. Her safe was found to be open, and her valuable collection of jewellery gone. Had you ever seen her jewellery?'

'No, but I had heard about it. I think everyone in the village knew about it, but very few people were allowed to feast their eyes on it. And she was on such good form last night. Have you any idea who is responsible?'

'Not so far, but our enquiries are progressing. Now, I know you said you didn't know her, but could you tell me anything you remember about her behaviour yesterday evening? I assume you were at the party.'

'Oh, yes. I had to be. My boys were DJ-ing. As it was, I had to get them to turn off one of the songs they played. They only went and put on Eminem's "The Real Slim Shady". Not suitable at all for a church gig. They're such little tinkers.

'Anyway, Miss Keighley-Armstrong seemed to be in her element. She was necking down punch, and telling all and sundry about her beautiful jewels, and how her father had been a gem dealer in South Africa, and how she'd lived there throughout her childhood. I don't think there was a person in the hall that didn't get the gist of her story,' Krystal told him, draining her glass, then falling into introspection.

In the silence that followed, Roberts noticed that her hands had started to shake again. 'Is there anything worrying you, Mrs Yaxley? You seem a bit nervous, if you don't mind me mentioning it.' He was on his best behaviour, but if she started to get slippery and avoid the issue, he'd revert to his usual, more robust approach.

Rising from her chair, she said, 'Yes, there is, but I'll need another drink before I tell you about it. This little anecdote's a two-slug dose of Dutch courage,' and she wandered off to the sideboard to refill her glass: two-thirds gin and a much smaller splash of tonic this time, he noticed.

Re-seating herself, she took a long swallow from her glass, and began, 'It's something that happened yesterday afternoon, but I'd better begin at the beginning. My husband walked out on us recently, and times have been very hard, what with the mortgage and twin sons at university. I've been looking out for work, but nothing suitable seems to be available at the moment.

'Anyway, yesterday I consulted Wanda Warwick, a woman across the road who reads tarot cards, to see if she could see anything positive in my life; just to give me hope, really. Everything was going along swimmingly, until she turned over the last three cards, then she had a hairy fit.

'I asked her what was wrong, and she started going on about it not being possible for those three to turn up like that. It all looked like disaster was looming, but she didn't seem to think it could possibly be related to me. Then you turn up on the doorstep and, for a moment, I thought you'd come to tell me that my husband was dead.

'No such bloody luck! However, something bad has happened, so it looks like her prediction was right, doesn't it? It really spooked me,' she declared, draining her second drink dry.

'Never underestimate the role of coincidence, Mrs Yaxley. I, personally, don't believe in the supernatural. The cards must just have been an unlucky fluke.'

105

'If you say so, but I think you had to be there, to feel the atmosphere of evil that pervaded her sitting room when it happened.'

Ay oop! thought Roberts, his mind imitating the woman's accent in his head. She'd already embroidered the story to make it more interesting. There'd be no chance of shifting her in what she believed had happened, but, thank God, that wasn't really relevant to the enquiry.

'Do you know of anyone who might have had it in for the woman?' He was reverting to type now. No more Mr Nice Guy. 'Someone audacious enough to knock her on the head, get into her safe, and make away with the contents?'

'Sorry,' she replied. 'We've not lived here that long and, what with my husband taking off like that, and my boys having to come home from university to support me in my hour of need, I've kept myself well to myself. I haven't got to know anybody that well. I know a few to pass the time of day with, and Rev. Florrie comes round to make sure I'm bearing up, once a week, but I don't go out much, or have many visitors.'

With a sigh of resignation, Roberts rose from his chair and prepared to leave. 'Thank you for your time, Mrs Yaxley. I hope life gets a little easier for you in the future.' He was back on his best behaviour for departure, and took his leave of her with a smile and a wave.

He hadn't taken the opportunity to speak to the sons, but that could be done later on in the enquiry. If they were away at university most of the time, they'd have had even less time to make friends. And if Inspector ruddy Falconer didn't like it, he could damned well lump it.

He knew the last thought was only bravado on his part, but it made him feel better. For all the noisy music from upstairs and the tell-tale signs of family occupation, such as discarded newspapers and magazines, the house had had an atmosphere of hopelessness. He could taste the despair on his tongue when he was in there, and he didn't want to spend a minute longer than he had to in such a depressing atmosphere.

His final visit was to Three-Ways House, where he was given to understand a Mr and Mrs Haygarth lived. To his surprise, once again, the door was answered by a woman in mid-argument. As the door opened, he caught the words, '… you can do it your bloody self in future. Perhaps that'll satisfy you.' Pause. 'Good afternoon. How can I help you?' The voice had gone from a shrill, harsh shriek, to a normal volume purr within a heartbeat.

'Sorry to bother you, but are you Mrs Haygarth?' Roberts felt suddenly unsure of himself.

'That's right, luv. What's your business?' Dammit! This woman had actually taken him for a salesman.

'I'm Detective Constable Roberts from the Market Darley CID,' he explained, holding out his warrant card, so there could be no mistake and that he'd suddenly whip a suitcase from behind his legs and try to sell her brushes and cleaning cloths. 'I'm here to talk to you about the death of Mrs Keighley-Armstrong of Manor Gate, the house at the back of the church.'

'I know where she lives … lived, I suppose it should be, if you're right. What'd she die of? Exhaustion, after counting all her money?'

He had a right one here, and no mistake, he thought, as he asked if he might come inside. The vision of a suitcase was beginning to materialise on the path behind him, and he would have no truck with that. He was a detective, after all, and being made to stand on the doorstep was not how he was used to being treated.

'Come on inside, then, but don't be expecting tea and biscuits, or anything like that. We're in the poor house, and we can't afford to be giving refreshments to every Tom, Dick, or Harry who turns up out of the blue.'

What a graceless, spiky woman she was, he thought, as she led him into a cheerless sitting room where a man, who was presumably her husband, sat at a desk, his fingers working away at a calculator, his disgusted face staring at a heap of paperwork in front of him.

In an attitude that mirrored his wife's, he grated, 'Who the hell are you? And what do you want? If it's money you're after, we haven't got any. Perhaps we could make a deal for my soul, though, in the absence of any filthy lucre to hand over to you.'

'This is Detective Constable Roberts, come about Miss Keighley-Armstrong. Who appears to be dead,' she added, as her husband's expression grew even blacker and he made as if to speak.

'Dead? That old biddy? I wonder who gets the stash. With the house, and goodness knows what else, it should be a fair few hundred thousand, if not over a million.'

'Jasper!'

'Well, here we are, virtually penniless, and that old cow was loaded.'

'She was murdered sometime last night,' Roberts stated emphatically, in an effort to get the situation on a more professional footing.

'Good! Although I know she won't have left us a penny piece.'

'We didn't know her, Jasper. Why would she leave us anything if she didn't know us from Adam?'

'That's not the point. If we don't halt the business losses, we're going to be getting all our utilities cut off and the bailiffs in, and in less than six months, we'll be repossessed and living on the streets.' The man was working himself up into a real rage.

'Would you please behave yourself, sir? I'm here on a serious matter, and I don't want it side-lined by listening to your tales of woe. I sympathise with you if you're in financial difficulties, but if you could just rein in your temper for half an hour, we can get this over with, and I can leave you in peace to carry on with your tantrum.'

This was bold stuff, and Roberts hoped that it didn't lead to another complaint about him. He just didn't see how else he could manage the situation without having to bail out and come back again the next day.

As he finished speaking, his wife yelled, 'Jasper! Pull yourself together, and try to remember your manners. It's not this poor officer's fault that we're up to our arses in alligators

108

with the business.'

Between the two of them, they seemed to have made Mr Haygarth see sense, and he took several deep breaths, before rising from his chair, crossing the room, and extending his hand to Roberts. 'Sorry! I was just going through this month's figures so far, and they don't paint a very pretty picture. You just happened to arrive at the wrong time. Please accept my apologies. You, too, Belinda. I'm sorry I went off on one.'

'Let's all sit down and find out what Detective Roberts wants, shall we?' his wife suggested, and while they complied with her wishes, Roberts thought, Detective Roberts? I rather like the sound of that. It's a lot better than Constable. More clout.

He cleared his throat to announce he was ready to begin, and told them about exactly what had happened the previous night, emphasising that he was only asking people their impression of the old lady the previous evening, and whether or not they knew of anyone who held anything against her from, perhaps, something that had happened in the past.

'She was well away last night, that I do know, for I saw it with my own eyes, hoovering up all the free drink as if it was her last chance,' Jasper almost spat.

'But it was, as it turned out, Jas. She's dead and will never go to another party, ever. Don't be so unfeeling,' Belinda chastened him.

'True, true. But it's got nothing to do with us. We did what we had to do last night, and that was to get a damned good feed, as it had been necessary to take along some food with us. There was no way we could provide food for other people, then have to come back here and cook a meal. The wallet just won't stretch to that sort of thing anymore. In fact, I think it's finally run out of elasticity altogether. We're at full stretch.'

'So you didn't speak to her at all?'

'We've already said that. Don't you listen?'

'Jasper, shut up!'

'Mr Haygarth, if you intend to continue in this vein I shall have to ask you to accompany me to the station so that we can carry out this interview in more civilised surroundings.'

That seemed to sober the disgruntled, failed businessman, and he calmed down while Roberts asked his last few questions. No, they hadn't seen the woman after she left the party, and no, they'd never seen her precious jewels.

In fact, they'd not really heard about them, or at least the reality of them, till that moment. There had been whispers, but they'd viewed the idea of a woman like that having a priceless collection of jewellery as being fabulous, and viewed them as probably as real as the Loch Ness Monster.

Roberts was very glad to leave Three-Ways House, and relieved to be heading back to the station, all his interviews completed for the day.

Rev. Florrie gave the two detectives a warm welcome at The Rectory, but her eyes still held deep sadness at what had happened. 'I was just about to make a pot of tea,' she declared, 'Will you join me? Oh, and there'll be cake as well. I always find sweet things a source of comfort when I'm feeling miserable. If I can't work out, spiritually, when something dreadful has happened, then I fall back on the earthly comforts of cake, biscuits, and chocolate.

'It doesn't diminish my faith, or compromise it in any way,' she explained, 'It just comforts me until I realise why such a thing could have been in God's plan. And they taste good as well, and aren't actually a sin. I think of it as, when God – temporarily – can't provide, Mr Kipling and Cadbury can.'

'Very logical thinking, Vicar. We'd be delighted to join you, and afterwards, perhaps you could tell us all you know about Miss Keighley-Armstrong, so that my sergeant here can make a note of it, then, exactly what happened when you found her this morning.'

'No problem, and then I shall have to get my skates on to be ready for Evensong, not that I expect anyone else to attend. Quite often it was just Lettice, her friend Violet, and me. Now Lettice is gone, I expect Violet will be too upset to come this evening.'

'Oh, and I'd like to borrow the keys to Manor Gate before we leave. I want to pick up her insurance policies, and find something with her solicitor's address on it, so that I can set the wheels in motion in those quarters. I understand she had no next of kin; no blood ties, as it were.'

'That's right. She was all alone in the world. That, I think, is what made me so fond of her in the first place. She might have been railing about my appointment, but there she was, with nobody to call her own, and yet she still had spirit. She never moaned or complained; just got on with her life, and enjoyed whatever she could from it.'

'By the way,' said Falconer, a thought having just struck him, 'do you know if she kept any cash in her safe? There was no sign of any when we searched the property.'

'I'm not sure, but I rather think she did. I was there once when her groceries were delivered, and she was gone rather a long time. I got up, because I had to leave anyway, and she was still at the door with the delivery man, counting cash out into his hand. Maybe she got it from the safe. It wouldn't have taken her so long to get money from her purse, and I noticed that the study door was open, which it certainly wasn't when I arrived.'

'Thank you very much indeed, Vicar. That's a bit more food for thought.'

When Carmichael had everything down in his notebook, they rose to take their leave, along with the key of Manor Gate. Carmichael hung back looking embarrassed, and eventually said, 'You go on ahead, sir. I need to speak to the vicar about something private.'

Puzzled but compliant, Falconer went outside to wait for his partner in the car. He didn't have long to wait, as Carmichael soon emerged, skipping down The Rectory path with a grin that fair split his face in two. He had the general demeanour of someone who has just been informed that he's won the lottery, and on a rollover week to boot. All in all, he didn't look like the same man who had almost crawled out of his house just that morning.

'What's come over you, Mr Happy?' asked Falconer, as the

sergeant got into the car.

'Are you still up for being godfather for my mob, sir?' he asked.

'Of course I am. I promised, didn't I?'

'Great!' whooped Carmichael. 'I've just had a word with the vicar, and she says she can probably arrange to come over to Castle Farthing and conduct the service there. She doesn't reckon she'll have any trouble getting permission, so it looks like Kerry and me can get on with arranging it now. Isn't that great, sir?'

Omitting to mention that it should be 'Kerry and I', the inspector merely replied, 'Splendid! Super!' and contemplated another thrash involving the entire Carmichael family. He was still recovering from his partner's wedding, and that had been over a year ago now.

At Manor Gate, the necessary documents weren't difficult to find, still lying on the floor in the study. A letter from her solicitor, all the insurance policies they could find, with an envelope of photographs, plus a copy of the victim's will were gathered together, before they headed back to Market Darley to have an information-sharing session with Roberts.

Late afternoon – Market Darley

They found Roberts at his desk, tapping a pencil on its surface in apparent impatience. 'Everything OK?' asked Falconer, as they breezed in.

'Sort of,' Roberts replied, stilling the pencil and putting it down on the desk.

'What do you mean, "sort of"?' asked the inspector.

'It's just that I haven't got a lot of time just at the moment. There's a bit of a surveillance going down tonight, and a few of the uniforms are off with chicken pox – it's that time of year, especially if you've got young kids. I've been asked if I'll come in on night duty, just so that there's an extra body available, and I said I would, because it's all overtime, isn't it?'

'Have you got any time at all now for your *official* work

with plain-clothes?'

'Not much. I want to get my head down for a few hours before I come back on duty, but I could give you a quick run through of what I got noted down today. You can tell me what happened with you tomorrow, if I can stay awake.'

'Fair enough this time, Roberts, but in future please consult me first before agreeing to anything that Bob Bryant tries to talk you into. He might do the rosters, but he has no authority over you, nor any right at all on your services. I suppose you'll be like a wet dish-rag tomorrow, when I need you to be alert?'

'I'll try my best not to be. Sorry,' the constable replied insincerely, just thinking about the overtime payment.

'Go on, then. Spill your guts,' ordered Falconer, glaring.

Roberts spilt.

Falconer got the papers he had collected from the house out of the folder he had slipped them into in the car, and began to go through them, reading to Carmichael as he went. 'Her solicitor's here in Market Darley, so we shouldn't have too much difficulty getting an appointment with him tomorrow. So is her insurance broker, which makes life a bit easier for us.'

Pulling a number of photographs out of a buff envelope, that appeared to be related to the policies, he gave a low whistle, as he looked at the images, one by one. 'Look at this, Carmichael. I believe we have, here, photographs of the infamous collection of jewellery.'

So saying, he began to hand the images to his sergeant one at a time, so that Carmichael could appreciate what had made him whistle. 'My God, sir. These are very upmarket, aren't they? They must be worth a fortune.'

'Indeed. They were not exaggerated in the telling as most things are. These really are the goods. No wonder someone finally broke in and had it on their toes with them. But look at these policies for the house and contents. They can't have been updated in years. And she's not been advised to go for new for old on replacement of any items claimed for. That's ludicrous. Her broker needs a damned good hiding, taking his eye off the ball to that extent.'

'There shouldn't be any trouble getting full value on the jewellery, though, sir. Each sheet has a description of the piece, with the carat of the gold and approximate weight, and a carat value for the stones. Golly, these must have cost a bomb to have commissioned. Her father must have made a mint in South Africa,' offered Carmichael, his eyes wide at the information they were taking in.

'That's the way things used to be in the old days, Sergeant. Now, let's have a look at her will. Phew!' He whistled again, glancing at the final bequest. 'That'll set the cat among the pigeons without a doubt.' At that point neither could identify any other legatees, but he would address this when they could put faces to names, motive, and opportunity.

'What's that, sir?' asked Carmichael, finally dragging his eyes away from the photographs.

'This,' replied the inspector, 'Read the last bequest,' he said, handing the solitary sheet of stiff paper that comprised the old lady's last will and testament.

Carmichael read the line slowly, then replied, 'You're right about that, sir. This'll really set tongues wagging, and teeth gnashing if I'm not mistaken.'

Chapter Nine

Early hours of Monday morning – Market Darley

The call came in just after midnight, and as there were no cars available due to the surveillance, Bob Bryant rang Roberts and alerted him to the fact that there appeared to be a prowler in Shepford St Bernard. The constable had been stood down from the surveillance at the last minute, when one of the officers who'd previously been off sick returned to work, and was lolling about at home, sulking about the missed opportunity to earn a bit more this month.

'It was reported by a Mrs Bingham of Tootelon Down in the main street. Last of a terrace of three houses, apparently, just next to the garage,' the sergeant informed him. 'Says the cat didn't come home till late, and when she opened her back door, she heard a cry of what sounded like pain; as if someone had got their foot down a rabbit hole and twisted their ankle. Then she saw the light of what she presumed was a torch, but when she called out, 'Who's there?' the torch went off, and everything went quiet.

'She didn't want to open the back gate, in case whoever it was went for her, so she called it in. Do you think you could get over there and take a look? It's probably nothing. She'll just be spooked by that other old woman's death, but better safe than sorry, eh?'

'Will do,' agreed Roberts, who had just got his head down on the sofa, and was dropping off the nightly cliff into sleep, downstairs. 'The fresh air will do me good.'

'If you find anything, call it in, and I'll see what I can do with bodies to assist, but I bet you a pair of my best underpants that's it's a false alarm.'

Roberts struggled to his feet, and yawned and stretched. If it was just a twitchy old lady, then he'd be back home within the hour, and could, perhaps, get in a couple of hours' kip. For now, though, he ought to take a trip to the bathroom, and splash his face and the back of his neck with cold water to make sure he was awake enough to drive.

Shepford St Bernard

Damn, damn, damn, a rabbit hole. That hurt, but not too bad. Turn the bloody torch off. Stay absolutely still and try to think of an excuse for being here. Keep completely silent. Don't move. God, she'd shouted now. What to do? Nothing. That was the answer. Do nothing.

That sounded like the back door closing. Good, she'd gone back inside. Now, to carry out the plan. Thought ceased, as further progress was made in the graveyard.

There was the back gate. Positive it was newly oiled. Perfect. No creak whatsoever. And the downstairs lights were on. Couldn't be going better. The back door was unlocked, as expected. Now, get inside and spin the tale. Then it would be time to do what this little visit was all about. Then get the hell out of here, and back to safety.

As he entered Shepford St Bernard, Roberts decided to park in the car park in front of The Druid's Head as the road through the village was so narrow. It might not get a lot of traffic through it at night, but the street lights were unusually dim, and he didn't want someone to clip his motor as they swung through.

As he got out and locked the doors, he heard the revving of another engine, but didn't give it another thought. Probably just someone having difficulty getting their vehicle started. He began to cross the road, then was blinded as headlights were turned on and the engine noise got louder.

His reflexes were not what they would have been after a

good night's sleep, and he was a fraction of a second late in his jump out of the way. This helped a little, but not enough to stop him being caught by the car's wing, and flung to the ground, his head making solid contact with the tarmac. As the lights of the car were turned off again, so were those in Roberts' head, and he lapsed into unconsciousness.

Market Darley

I don't believe it, thought Bob Bryant, as he heard the voice of Violet Bingham for the second time that night. What can the old dear possibly want, now? Someone of a higher rank, perhaps? He couldn't have been more wrong.

'I'm sorry to trouble you again, but there's been an accident opposite my house. I just heard the roar of an engine, then a thud, and when I went out to see if anything had happened, I chanced upon a young man, unconscious, in the front car park of The Druid's Head. I wonder if you could get someone out here and alert an ambulance to collect him?'

'Did you recognise the victim?' asked the sergeant, hopefully.

'Yes, well, that's the thing, isn't it?' she replied. 'It was the young man I saw coming out of the pub after lunch, with the two nice detectives, who were on their way to call on me. I happened to be looking out of the window at the time, and it was definitely the same young man who's now been hit by a car. I assume he was on his way to talk to me about my call about the prowler.'

Bob Bryant swore softly under his breath, then turned his attention back to his caller. 'If you can put a blanket or something over him, I'll get another officer and an ambulance out there as soon as I can. Stay with him, and keep an eye on him, because the paramedics will probably ask you about any change in his condition when they get there.'

'Will do, Officer, and sorry to bother you again so soon after the last call.'

'Think nothing of it, madam. That's what we're here for,'

replied Bryant, furiously thinking about whom he could divert to the village to investigate not only what had happened to Roberts, but also what the original call had been about.

After checking on the surveillance, he got the kiss-off, and his only alternative was to call Falconer. It was one of his officers, after all, so he could hardly complain. He wouldn't be happy about being roused from his bed at one o'clock in the morning, but what could a beleaguered desk sergeant do about it, if there was no one else available?

Harry Falconer was having a delicious dream about Dr Honey Dubois, his 'sort of' girlfriend, with whom he had had a few dinner dates since the New Year, and for whom he had high hopes of getting a lot closer to as the year rolled on.

The intrusive noise was treated by his brain as part of the dream, so as not to rouse him, but, as it continued, the subconscious had to give up and go off for a sulk. It wasn't going to cease, and let the dream continue. Thus, Falconer gradually became aware of the sound of the phone shrilling.

He opened one eye cautiously, and noted the time. One fifteen a.m. Not good. A reluctant hand reached out of the duvet and answered the insistent summons, the owner of the hand struggling to a sitting position and trying to get his thoughts in order. 'Falconer,' he enunciated groggily into the mouthpiece, all the while thinking, this had better be worth it, dragging me away from Serena ... For a split second, his mind froze. No! Not Serena! Honey! It was Honey! Serena was from the past! What on earth had made him think that name?

'Sorry, Bob, I didn't quite catch that,' he said, pulling himself together. 'What? When? Not again? Is that man jinxed?' Pause. 'OK, I understand all the others are tied up. Just give me time to throw on some clothes, and I'll be there. Who reported it?' Pause. 'I'll go straight to her address, then. I'll call in when I've got more information. Thanks a bunch for the early alarm call.'

Reluctantly dragging on the clothes he had taken off only a couple of hours before, he mulled over what Bob Bryant had told him. A prowler reported behind the cottages on The Green. Roberts, not on night duty now, but sent out because of lack of other available personnel. And he'd been hit by a car, on his first case back since he'd been beaten nearly to death in November.

Did he just attract accidents, or was it purely bad luck – being in the wrong place at the wrong time? For all the good it had done the department, he might as well have stayed in Manchester. He seemed constantly to be either in hospital or convalescing. At that point, he quelled these selfish thoughts. Maybe it would have happened to anyone who had answered the call.

But Shepford St Bernard wasn't exactly thronging with traffic during the day. At night, it must be like a grave. How on earth, then, had Roberts managed to get himself run down by a car, when there probably wasn't another vehicle on the road for miles around?

Leaving the house, being careful to close the front door and car door quietly, so as not to disturb the neighbours, he drove away, wondering what he would encounter at the other end of his drive.

Shepford St Bernard

As he approached the road through the village, he could see the still-flashing lights of an ambulance, and hear the crackle of the vehicle's radio. Two paramedics were lifting a gurney into the back of the vehicle, causing him to park as quickly as possible, so that he could check on Roberts' condition, before he was sped away.

'He's not too bad,' one of the paramedic's explained. 'He was conscious when we got here, and he says he did his best to jump out of the way, so he was caught more of a glancing blow than a head-on one. He's going to be black and blue on his right side in the morning, and he's got a head wound from where he hit the tarmac; that's going to need to be stitched, but apart from that he's been lucky.'

119

'I bet he doesn't think so,' replied Falconer, trying to peer into the back of the ambulance.

'Do you want to have a word with him, before we leave for the hospital?' asked the same paramedic. 'We've given him something for the pain, but he's perfectly capable of talking.'

'Thanks. I would, just to see if I can get a clearer picture of what happened,' and Falconer climbed into the back of the vehicle, and hunched down beside his DC.

'What have you got yourself into now, Roberts?' he asked, looking down at a face with tribal paintings in blood on it. 'Can't I trust you to do anything on your own?' He said this in a semi-jocular way, however, not being good at conversing with the sick or injured.

'Sorry, sir. I hadn't even got to Mrs Bingham's house. I just parked up, off the road so that I wouldn't congest it. Then I heard a revving engine, the squeal of tyres, lights suddenly came on, blinding me, and I flung myself to one side; more of an instinctive reaction than a rational one.'

'Then thank God you've got good instincts. I wouldn't like to think you had a death wish. Did Mrs Bingham go back to her house?'

'She left when the paramedics were examining me.'

'Well, I won't delay your arrival at the hospital any longer. I'll take over where you left off, and I'll come and see you tomorrow, when they've got you nicely tucked up in bed with your teddy bear.'

As the ambulance drew away, leaving Falconer holding the blanket that Mrs Bingham had draped over Roberts' prone body, while they waited for the ambulance to arrive, he could see that there was a light on in Tootelon Down, and the curtain at one of the front windows was drawn aside, as Mrs Bingham kept an eye on events from the shelter of her own home. Waving to her, to let her know he had seen her, he crossed to the door, and she opened it as he reached it.

'Come on in, Inspector. Such a dreadful thing to happen, and so soon after what … what happened … to poor, dear Lettice,' she said, a catch in her voice. 'Whatever is this village coming to? It's definitely being stalked by something evil.'

'I couldn't agree more. Here's your blanket, by the way. It was lucky you were awake and realised what had happened, otherwise my DC could have been lying out in the open all night. Now, perhaps you could tell me about your prowler, and then anything you can about DC Roberts' accident.'

'Is he all right? What did the ambulance men say? I feel so guilty, because this never would have happened if I hadn't phoned the police station about someone prowling about out the back.'

'You mustn't blame yourself. This was an act carried out in cold blood, from what Roberts was able to tell me. The car seemed to aim straight for him, with no lights on, then turned them on to dazzle him so they could get a better aim. That has nothing whatsoever to do with your call, so don't let it worry you. Now, tell me what you can about earlier,' Falconer asked, in a reassuring voice.

'I was just letting my cat in. He was a naughty boy, and didn't come back until late tonight, and as I had the door open for him, I heard a noise from the graveyard, as if someone was prowling about out there, and had gone into a rabbit hole or something similar and twisted their ankle. Then I looked in that direction, and there was definitely the light of a torch, probably aimed upwards, as whoever it was regained their balance, and that was what made it possible for me to see it.

'I called out for them to show themselves, but everything went silent and black, and I began to feel a little nervous. That's when I made the first phone call. Then, when I was waiting for someone to arrive, that naughty old cat of mine decided he needed a last tiddle. I let him out of the front door this time, in case the prowler was still about, and that was when I heard a sort of choking yell and a muffled crash, as if something had been knocked over in someone's house.

'At night, this village is as quiet as the graves behind these houses, and sound really travels. Not many of us have the luxury of double glazing. That, along with the fact that I could see lights on at Mr Twelvetrees' house has made me sure that

that was where the noise was coming from.

'It was all so clear in my mind that I could almost picture it, but by then, I was too afraid to go round and see if Mr Twelvetrees was all right. If there was someone in the house trying to harm him, I didn't want to put myself in any danger.'

'That was very sensible of you. At least that leaves you here to tell the tale. Have you heard anything since from that direction?' the inspector asked, not over-anxious to go round to the house and be attacked himself.

'It's been quiet as the grave since just before that poor man was run down,' she replied with conviction.

'In that case, I'm going down to take a look. If I'm not back in ten minutes, or if you hear any sounds that might be a scuffle, ring the station again, for I might need some help.'

'You be careful, young man. I don't want another attack on my conscience,' she warned him.

'I'll take every precaution necessary not to become another victim, Mrs Bingham,' Falconer replied, rather pleased at her description of him as young.

Closing her front door behind him, Falconer walked the short distance to Bijou, knocked sharply on the door, and rang the bell, then tried to see if he could see anything through the windows, but the curtains were closed. He then tried calling through the letterbox, but there was no answer to this summons, either. Think! The downstairs lights were on, the upstairs lights were off. That didn't look too good for Mr Twelvetrees. He'd have to try to gain entrance at the rear of the property.

Tapping softly on the door of Tootelon Down, he went back inside the cottage and asked, 'Is there any back access to these properties?'

'There is; on the boundary of the graveyard. Do you want to go out through my back gate? Otherwise you'll have to walk round there from the road.'

'That would be very convenient, thank you, Mrs Bingham. Again, if I'm not back in ten minutes, sound the alarm.' He was getting a bad feeling about this situation, and a frisson of fear passed through his body, as he hoped against hope that there was no one still lurking in Bijou.

He went out of the rear gate, having borrowed a torch from Violet, his own still in the glove compartment of his car. The gate to the property in question was unbolted, which was convenient, even if it did increase his feeling of unease. The back door was closed but unlocked, which he discovered when the knob turned in his hand, and the door swung open.

The illumination of the house lights was disquieting in the silence of the dwelling, and it was with extreme caution that he crept carefully towards the door of the living room, which had been left ajar. Was there someone behind it, waiting to set upon him? With infinite caution he crept up to it, then gathering his courage, he flung it open and yelled, 'Police! Don't move!'

The merciless silence continued, as he stared at the scene in front of him in horror. There was someone completely ruthless at large in this small community, and they'd struck again. Before him, Julius Twelvetrees lay sprawled in a wing-backed chair, his throat cut, and an apron of gore decorating the front of his body, the blood also having dripped and formed a pool at his feet. As the freshet of red had cascaded from the wound, it had had sufficient force to stain the upper legs of his trousers, completing the image of the man wearing an abattoir apron. Beside the chair, a small table had been overturned, and a glass lay on the floor, its contents now forming a discoloured circle on the carpet.

On the coffee table in front of his chair were scattered an assortment of pieces of jewellery, their brightness twinkling in the overhead light, and mocking the dead man with their beauty and imperviousness. Falconer felt the bile rise in his throat, and returned immediately to the kitchen, where he wouldn't have to stare at the scene of such carnage.

Taking a few moments for his stomach to settle, he took out his mobile and phoned it in, thanking God that he was able to get a signal from this cottage. Damn their night-time surveillance! At the very least, he'd need a SOCO team and Philip Christmas. When he'd finished his call, he turned the key in the back door, pocketed it, then let himself out of the front door, and went back to Violet Bingham's.

He might be responsible for the crime scene until other officers arrived, but he was damned if he was going to stay in that house any longer, with that grisly corpse smiling at him with its neck gaping and bloody. Likewise, the jewels would have to stay in position until they'd been photographed and dusted for prints. He hoped that Mrs Bingham would offer him a cup of strong tea, because, by golly, he could do with one at this particular moment.

Doc Christmas was the first to arrive, Bob Bryant probably still busy rousing people from their beds and waiting for them to arrive, so that they could set off in a group in one of the official SOCO vans.

'One of yours again, Harry?' the doctor asked, as he was admitted to Bijou. 'Are you intent on wiping out rural life in this area? I could've done without being roused from my bed at such an unsociable hour. Lord, that's a messy one, isn't it?'

Falconer concurred silently, with a nod of his head, and the doctor continued, 'That's enough to turn anyone's stomach. Just as well you didn't have Carmichael with you, or he'd probably have blown his guts all over the body.' Again, Falconer nodded. Seeing the man sprawled in the chair, as if enjoying an evening in front of the television, made him feel nauseous again; apparent innocent domesticity demonstrated in the most ugly way.

'This has all the outward appearances of a suicide, but I think that's just for show, and it's an incomplete scene,' Dr Christmas gave as his considered opinion.

'What makes you say that?' asked Falconer, amazed by what appeared to be the doctor's perspicacity.

'You mean apart from the absence of the weapon?' Pointing to a cup and saucer lying on the coffee table that was adorned with jewels, and a newspaper and pen on the lid of the open bureau, he said, 'There's your evidence.'

'I don't get it,' said Falconer, perplexed.

'His throat was cut from left to right, which indicates a right-handed culprit. If you observe the cup and saucer, they lie to the left of the table, and the bureau holds a pen and newspaper, the latter folded to reveal a half-completed crossword. The pen has been left to the left of the paper; ergo, he was left-handed, but whoever cut his throat was in such a hurry, or didn't realise he was a southpaw, for the slash across his throat has been made by a right-handed person, from behind.

'The absence of any weapon either indicates the complete panic the murderer was in, or an inordinately strong attraction to the knife used, and whoever it was couldn't bear to just abandon it. Or maybe if we had found it, it would have immediately identified who was responsible. Have a chew on that baccy for a moment.

'Of course, you're going to have to get the SOCO lads to check out all the knives in the house, but it's my bet that this is a case of "slit-and-run".'

'By golly, you sound just like Holmes astounding Watson,' replied Falconer, genuinely impressed.

'Also,' continued the doctor, 'the glass has been left as if it had fallen from his right hand, whereas all the other evidence in the room suggests that he was left-handed. This is another murder, Harry boy. That's two in not-quite-twenty-four hours, going by the discovery times. Old Chivers is going to get into a right muck sweat. I have known him in the past to refer to you as Dr Death. This double is going to get right up His High-and-Mightiness' nostrils.

'He can hardly hold me responsible for the murderous actions of every resident of the county,' stated Falconer with indignation.

'It might seem unreasonable, but he does. I should stay out of the office as much as possible until these two are wrapped up. Keep a low profile, and he won't get the opportunity to set off any heavyweight salvos.'

A discreet knock at the front door alerted them to the fact that the SOCO team had arrived, and that they could take a break from the oppressiveness of the room, with its dreadful metallic smell of blood.

Chapter Ten

Monday morning – Market Darley

When Carmichael got into the office, a baggy-eyed, grey-skinned Falconer was hard at work at his desk, and appeared to have been there for some time.

'Morning, sir. Golly! You look rough. Just the way I looked yesterday morning. Have you been on a bender?'

'I most certainly have not, Carmichael. I was roused from my innocent slumber about two hours after I got to sleep, and spent some considerable time in Shepford St Bernard, where I had the pleasure of attending another murder scene, and also seeing DC Roberts off in an ambulance. And discovering the missing jewellery. I mustn't leave out that bit.'

'Crikey, sir, you have been busy. Why didn't you give me a bell?'

'Because you looked so awful yesterday that I thought you were in great need of a good night's sleep. And now I look as bad as you did.' At this point Falconer finally looked up from his paperwork and exclaimed, 'Carmichael! What the devil are you wearing, man? I thought you'd got rid of the dressing-up box.'

'Sir!' said Carmichael, looking slightly hurt. 'You know I like bright colours; they cheer me up, and it's such a lovely day today.'

Falconer gazed at his sergeant in disbelief. He was, indeed, back to his old ways, and had on a brightly decorated Hawaiian shirt and canary yellow trousers. 'You're giving me a headache just looking at you.'

'Well, Kerry said I looked good enough to eat,' Carmichael

threw back at him.

'She probably meant you looked like something from a giant pick-and-mix advert – dolly mixtures and those ghastly yellow banana-shaped spongy things. Be it on your own head; we're out and about today, and I want you to walk a few paces behind me. I refuse to be mistaken for your carer.

'Right! We're off to the hospital first, then back to Shepford St Bernard. There were some missed interviews yesterday – I've read through Roberts' notes, so I'm up and running with what he learnt.'

Shepford St Bernard

It was barely nine o'clock when Toby Lattimer knocked on Gwendolyn Galton's front door, and she answered it in her dressing gown, her eyelids still heavy with sleep. 'What do you want this early in the morning, Toby? You know I'm utterly wasted after an all-day fair. As it was, I didn't get back till nine last night, and by the time I'd unloaded the van it was gone ten.'

'I'm sorry, dear Gwen, but I just had to know whether or not you'd sold that divine tortoiseshell box with the inlaid silver. I've been lusting after it since you bought it; should've made you an offer for it before you went off yesterday, but you know how I prevaricate. Have you sold it?'

'If that's all, couldn't you have waited till a more civilised hour? Really, Toby, look at the state of me,' she said, tossing her white tresses over her shoulder, out of the way. She hadn't yet brushed her hair this morning, and it was still tangled from its night on the pillow.

'I couldn't wait a moment longer. Tell me, have you sold it yet? Oh, please tell me you haven't. I shall die if it can't be mine!'

'As a matter of fact, I haven't. So you want to buy it?'

'Oh, I do, very much,' he replied, his face as eager as a puppy's when it expects a treat.

'You'd better come in then, so we can agree a price, but you'll have to make the coffee while I unpack it. It's still in one of the boxes from yesterday.'

'Will do,' agreed her neighbour, then called through to her in the dining room, 'How much do you want for it?'

She wandered back into the kitchen with the exquisite little item in her hands. 'I was asking a hundred and fifty, and I think that's very reasonable,' she declared, as Toby's face creased up in alarm.

'That much?' he asked, his expression suddenly downcast. 'I was going to offer you a hundred for it. I've raided all my little copper pots, and that's how much I came up with. I was sure you'd accept. It seemed such a good price to me.'

'You old fake. You did no such thing. You know damned well it's worth every penny of a hundred and fifty. You're just taking the piss, but as it's you, how about a hundred and twenty-five?'

'Done!' replied Toby, reaching a hand into each of his trouser pockets. From one he drew out five crisp twenty pound notes, and from the other, another twenty and a five. 'Here you are. Now, how do you take your coffee?'

'You old fraud,' she answered him. 'You had the hundred in one pocket, hoping your sob story would work, and put twenty-five in the other, in case I wasn't such a pushover. I'd be willing to bet that you've got another twenty-five in your shirt pocket, in case I was in a hard bargaining mood today.'

'Don't be silly,' Toby replied, but he had the grace to blush at the accuracy of her supposition.

'Hey, Monday isn't pension day. You really have been putting away your pennies for this, haven't you? And don't give me that look. You might not look it, but I know perfectly well how old you are.'

'But you still love me, don't you?' replied Toby with a twinkle. 'Coming round for a glass of wine, tonight?' he asked, surprised at his own boldness.

'Might as well. I've got nothing better to do.'

'How honoured you make me feel. About eight?'

'You're on, but are you sure you're up to staying awake that late? You've got huge bags under your eyes, and you look like you should have stayed in bed.'

'That was the little box. It had me tossing and turning so that I couldn't get off to sleep, but I shall be fine now it's mine. There's something else I wanted to ask you, as well. Have you got any tie clips or lapel pins with gemstones? I have a yen for something like that. Oh, and men's rings set with stones, too? I want to expand my collections, and I don't have much in that line.'

'I might have one or two bits. Tell you what; I'll have a look through when I'm unpacking. Shall I bring anything I find with me when I come round this evening?'

'Please. But if you have nothing, just bring your lovely self, Gwen. You will be feast enough for my eyes.'

'Are you attempting to flirt with me, Toby?' she asked, giving him a wry grin.

'Definitely, O Lovely One!'

After his coffee, Toby went back next door, not only with his beautiful box, but with a sort of date for that evening, and the possibility of some more 'pretties'. Things were looking up in all respects. Fortune really does favour the bold.

Market Darley Hospital

Being policemen gave Falconer and Carmichael the opportunity to charm their way on to the wards outside official visiting hours, and they found Roberts on Carsfold Ward, sheets tucked up to his chin, his head swathed in bandages, and sleeping the sleep of the innocent.

A nurse spied them approaching his bed, and went over to shake him awake gently, having harboured suspicions that his two visitors would not have as delicate a touch as hers.

'Good morning to you, DC Roberts,' Falconer greeted him.

'Been in the wars again?' asked Carmichael. 'This place must be beginning to feel like home to you.'

Roberts opened his eyes, blinked several times, then looked Carmichael up and down and said, 'I see it's non-uniform day again. Did your mummy send you to school with a pound?'

Carmichael gave him a slight frown, putting his manners down to his state of health. Falconer ignored him, but silently marked his card, before asking him how he felt. 'Battered and bruised, guv – sorry, sir – but I'll live.'

'But not for long, if you go on behaving like this. Do you feel up to talking about exactly what happened when you got hit?'

'I can manage, if you'll just put Carmichael on the other side of the bed, where he can't blind me. He looks like Rupert Bear on holiday.'

'Hey, you leave off my clothes. I don't criticise yours, so keep your opinions to yourself,' snapped Carmichael, quite riled now.

'Children, children,' Falconer intervened, 'Play nicely now, or you won't get any cake at teatime. Go on, Roberts.'

'I'd only just got out of the car, and had taken a couple of steps, when I became aware of the revving of an engine; didn't think much of it; just thought someone was having difficulty starting their motor, and there wasn't a car in sight.

'Then the sound moved in my direction, whoever was driving put on the headlights, full beam, and blinded me. The only thing I've remembered since last night is that he must have been parked up round the side of the garage, where he wouldn't be seen from the road, in the gloom and shadows.'

'Do you remember talking to me before the ambulance left the scene?' asked Falconer, curious.

'Did I?' Roberts asked. 'I don't remember a thing from when I tried to throw myself out of the way until they were cleaning me up here, and very painful it was too, especially the stitches. Did you go to Mrs Bingham's house?'

'It was Mrs Bingham who called the station again, got Bob Bryant to summon an ambulance and phone me, then she went back out and put a blanket over you.'

'Well, even in these pyjamas, and with my head in an NHS turban, I look better than old Davey over there,' he stated, with no apparent relevance to Mrs Bingham's good deed.

'I'll tell you something about Carmichael, shall I, Roberts?'

Falconer said in a quiet, dangerous tone. 'He may dress like a crazy,' here the sergeant gave him a 'whose side are you on' look, 'but it's all part of his cunning behaviour.

'You may think he's soft in the head.' Again, that look from Carmichael. 'He is, in fact, very clever. If he dresses like a fool, people take him for a fool. They say things in front of him that they might not say in front of me, and, if he looks a bit simple, people will confide in him more readily.

'His simple disguises make him a genius at getting information out of people, just because of the way he dresses, so we'll have no more remarks like that, if you don't mind. I don't like them, and I'm not willing to put up with them. If you work very hard, you might, one day, be as good a detective as DS Carmichael here. In about twenty years' time, if you work hard at it.'

There was a silence, as the two others took in the meaning of Falconer's little speech, then Roberts thanked them for coming in to see him, but he was sure they had work to do. It sounded like the shot had hit home.

Outside the ward, on their way back to the car, Carmichael asked, 'Did you mean all that stuff in there, sir?'

'Most of it.'

'Which bit didn't you mean?'

'The bit about your clothes. It's your face that fools people. Now let's leave it at that, shall we? I don't want us to fall out, but I won't have him take a pop at you like that. You're a damned good detective, and sometimes you have strokes of pure genius, apart from the fact that you saved my life when we were investigating that ghastly hotel last year. Now, let it go.'

Carmichael let it go, not sure whether he had just been insulted or complimented, but giving the inspector the benefit of the doubt.

Shepford St Bernard

'We're going to have to re-interview everyone after what happened last night, and catch up with the people who were

132

out,' said Falconer as he entered the village. Indicating late and swerving right to turn into Coopers Lane, he added, 'And we'll start with that woman who was out. She may not know much about what happened to Lettice, but she could be of some help with what happened last night. She might have heard a car leaving the village at speed, or seen someone loitering in a vehicle with intent.'

'You're very optimistic this morning, considering that you're getting by on next to no sleep,' opined Carmichael, remembering the parlous state he'd been in after his unintentional binge.

'I think I'm running on pure adrenalin. I know I shall sleep like the dead tonight. In fact, I think I'll pick up a take-away on the way home, shove it down my throat, and go straight upstairs. Here we are,' he finished, drawing up outside Carpe Diem.

Gwendolyn was dressed when she opened the door to them, and invited them inside, after checking their warrant cards. 'What's this all about, then? Devious deeds in Shepford St Bernard? Criminal complications that require police investigation?'

'You obviously haven't heard what happened yesterday morning, or last night,' Falconer stated, looking her straight in the eye, to make sure she wasn't having him on.

'What did happen? You're really tickling my curiosity, now,' she asked.

'I'm sorry to have to inform you that Miss Keighley-Armstrong was found dead, outside her house yesterday morning, and Mr Twelvetrees was discovered dead, in his house, in the early hours of this morning. Miss Keighley-Armstrong's safe was also raided but, thankfully, the missing items have turned up now.'

Gwendolyn sat down with a whump, looking dazed. 'No!' she said, drawing the word out to an inordinate length. 'But I've had Toby round here this morning, and he didn't say a word about any of this: Toby Lattimer from next door but one, that is.'

133

'One of my officers put a card through your door yesterday, when he discovered you weren't at home, with a message to contact the station. That officer is now in hospital, having been deliberately run down by a car, in this very village, also in the early hours of this morning. Would it be acceptable for us to interview you now?'

'Perfectly,' she replied, her attention evidently still on what Falconer had just told her. 'I can't believe this, though. Shepford St Bernard's such a quiet little backwater. Nothing ever happens here.'

'Maybe that's why you've got a double dose, now, not to mention the damage to one of my officers. Let's start off with where you were yesterday.' Carmichael found himself a seat and got out his notebook, making sure he was out of her range of vision for the sake of discretion and not making her feel uncomfortable in her own home.

'I was at an antiques fair all day. I left very early, and didn't get back until nine, but I'd had a good day, so that didn't matter. Then I unpacked my remaining stock and went up to bed, absolutely knackered. I'm afraid I slept like a log, and heard nothing until I woke up this morning.

'I'd hardly got out of bed this morning when Toby came knocking at the door – just after nine; I ask you – then I grabbed a bite of breakfast, showered and got dressed, and here I am, the last twenty-eight hours completely covered. Not guilty. Sorry. But, tell me, what did happen to them both, and how's your injured soldier?'

Ignoring her flippant manner towards what had happened to Roberts, the inspector decided that there was no point in concealing the truth. It would be flying all round the village as they sat there. 'Miss Keighley-Armstrong had her safe broken into and all her jewellery stolen, then she was knocked on the head, and found dead outside her house several hours later. Mr Twelvetrees was found inside his own home, his throat cut, the missing jewellery spread out in front of him, and the whole scene set to indicate suicide.'

'But you don't think it was?'

'I'm certain it wasn't. We were supposed to think that Mr Twelvetrees had stolen the jewellery and killed Miss Keighley-Armstrong, then cut his own throat in remorse, leaving the sparklers out in plain view as an admission of guilt.'

'And you don't believe that's what happened?'

'Not for a moment. It was staged, and I'm going to find out who the author of this double-tragedy is, and make sure he or she doesn't try to orchestrate any more productions for a very long time.'

'I'm sorry I can't be more helpful, but I'll keep my ears and eyes open, and get in touch with you if I discover anything that may help you. Can I have one of your business cards?' she said, beginning to rise to her feet, to indicate that, as far as she was concerned, the interview was over.

Falconer evidently agreed, as he too rose, pulled a card from his inside jacket pocket, and handed it to her. 'You say you've already talked to your neighbour this morning?'

'Yes.'

'Then I'll go straight round there, in the hope that he hasn't gone out yet. Thank you for your time, Ms Galton, and don't hesitate to call us if you think it necessary.'

They found Toby Lattimer on his knees, on an old blanket, weeding the flower border at the front of his house. 'Good morning. Mr Lattimer, I believe,' Falconer greeted him, and introduced himself and Carmichael, as the man rose to his feet.

Shaking hands with them both, Toby kept his eyes on the inspector, then commented, 'You look awful. Bad night? Me too. I just couldn't get off, so I took some sleeping tablets that the doctor prescribed for me just after I retired from work. They get you off all right, but you feel like the walking dead the next morning. Dreadful chemical hangover.'

'Bad luck, sir. I look this way because I was awakened in the early hours to come out to a hit-and-run in this village. One of my officers, as a matter of fact; the one that came to speak to you yesterday.'

'Bad luck again. Was he badly hurt?' asked Toby, a mean

135

glint in his eye that indicated that he was a lover of bad news.

'Only a glancing blow, fortunately. He'll be back on duty again in no time,' the inspector informed him, watching closely for his reaction.

'Jolly good, jolly good!' was what he said, but his eyes wandered away from Falconer's face, and he suddenly gave a start, as if pulling himself together, and invited them inside.

Once settled, Falconer asked Lattimer if he would be so good as to confirm where he was, between eleven o'clock the previous evening and two o'clock that morning,' while Carmichael got his head in gear for taking notes.

'Well, that's an easy one. I went up to bed about ten thirty, but couldn't get off. Around midnight I gave in, and took something to help me get off, then woke up this morning feeling lousy.'

'Yet you were still on your neighbour's doorstep just after nine o'clock this morning, even though you were feeling hungover and tired?'

'Are you a collector, Inspector? Do you have a passion for amassing things in a particular category?'

'I've got a few favourite categories in which I sometimes collect pieces, but I'm not consumed by the idea of acquiring new items,' he replied, thinking of his Art Deco porcelain and a few other choice objects in his house.

Carmichael opened his mouth, but Falconer halted him by stating, 'I don't think Smurfs count in this case, Sergeant.' The mouth closed again, and settled into an embarrassed inverted smile.

'Actually, I think you're wrong there, Inspector, if you don't mind me saying so. You collect, but with no passion. I got the feeling, from the way your sergeant's eyes lit up at the mentions of collecting, that he is passionate. *What* he collects is immaterial. It's the enthusiasm that matters.

'And there, he's like myself. I am a very dedicated collector, and Gwendolyn next door but one went off on Sunday with a tortoiseshell box that is to die for. She'd shown it to me when she bought it, but I was trying so hard to resist buying it.

'Then, when she took it off to the fair, I realised that I wanted it more than I've wanted a little bibelot for some time. That's me, I'm afraid. If I collect something, I *collect* something, and nothing can put me off the trail, except for my own stupidity, trying to resist when I know I'll give in in the end.'

Carmichael's face was beaming after this little speech, and he offered to show his collection of Smurfs to the inspector sometime, and after his offer was rebuffed, regaled Toby with how he had found a nest of the little blue men at a car boot sale only a couple of weeks ago, and had got the lot for the paltry sum of a pound.

'That's the spirit, Sergeant. Follow your passion, and it'll give you a tremendous amount of pleasure. I'd be happy to look at your collection, any time. All collections fascinate me, and some of those little blue things are worth quite a lot of money nowadays.'

'Just to recap,' Falconer interrupted, 'and getting back to what we were talking about, you went to bed at ten-thirty last night?'

'That is correct, Inspector.'

'And did you hear any noise from the street, while you were tossing and turning? A car starting up, perhaps? Or maybe passing your house?'

'I sleep at the back of the house, Inspector, and can't hear a thing from the street. Sorry, but I can't be of any help whatsoever.'

'Never mind, sir. Thank you for your cooperation.'

Outside again, Falconer suggested, 'Why don't we park up outside the pub, then we can do the rest of our calls on foot, as it's such a beautiful spring-like day today?'

'As long as you don't mind being seen in public with me,' replied Carmichael, still stinging from Roberts' comments, when they visited him earlier that morning.

'I'll just tell anyone who asks that you're my slightly simple nephew whom I'm minding for the day to give my poor, beleaguered sister a day off.'

'But you haven't got a sister, sir,' retorted Carmichael in perplexity.

'That is correct. Ergo, neither do I have a nephew, but I don't think I'll have any problem being believed.'

Carmichael's lower lip stuck out in a pout while he considered the inspector's bald statement in silence, eventually relaxing his facial muscles. It might have appeared as an insult to some, but from a different point of view, he realised it could be seen as a compliment, in a back-handed sort of way. Maybe. Considering what Falconer had said to Roberts earlier. Definitely a compliment. Perhaps.

Sauntering along the street to Robin's Perch, it was a pleasure to look at how the front borders were coming to life in the recent sunshine, the storm having left the shoots undamaged, blossom now beginning to open the faces of its flowers towards the sun in rapture. Windows had been flung open to air the houses, so long shut up over the long winter, and lace curtains fluttered in the breeze like the sails of imaginary yachts on journeys to far flung shores that were no further away than the window-frames.

This blissful mood was shattered when they found no one at home, again, at Robin's Perch, but that was their furthest point of call at the southern end of the village. They turned, and began to walk back the way they had come, headed first to Sweet Dreams, on the south side of The Druid's Head, to see what Krystal Yaxley had to say about the events of the night before, or to be more accurate, the early hours of today.

Had they but known it, they were at the beginning of a fruitless exercise, very few of the residents being at home; probably out shopping, given that most of them were retired. They ended up at The Rectory, with little to add to their store of knowledge, except for the fact that Lettice's cat now lived with Violet Bingham, so its owner's tragedy hadn't resulted in it going to the RSPCA, such an old animal unlikely to find a new home this side of eternity.

On arrival at the vicar's residence, they were both frustrated

138

and fed up, and Rev. Florrie's smiling welcome and offer of tea and cake went some way to raising their spirits.

'I know it's a pain, knowing you've had a fruitless journey, but take a piece of cake, and try to see the positive side. You've had a lovely walk on a glorious day, and your interviews will keep until tomorrow,' she reassured them, handing round a plate laden with slices of Victoria sponge.

'We've simply got no leads, though. So many people had a possible motive, but there's no concrete evidence,' moaned Falconer, raising the jammy confection to his mouth.

'Don't forget you need to include me on your list of suspects,' the vicar declared, unexpectedly.

'Why ever should we do that?' Falconer spluttered through his mouthful of cake, and Carmichael stared at her, his mouth too full even to attempt speech.

'Oh, I thought I'd told you. Maybe not. Lettice told me, when she'd decided I was good enough for her parish, that she'd left a quarter of her estate, after death duties, to the church. She'd considered changing her will when I turned up, but didn't rush to do it, and then I turned out all right in the end.

'That'll mean I can get the roof into a good state of repair, and install a more efficient heating system into the bargain. I could even have the hall refurbished. It looked so shabby after I'd taken down the decorations after the party that I thought it needed a bit of a spruce up.

'Obviously, I've no idea how much it will come to, but I reckon it'll be a substantial amount of money, when the insurance pays out. So, you never know; perhaps I winkled the combination of the safe from her when I dropped her home, then cracked her on the head, emptied the safe, and took to my heels to hide the stash.'

'You are having me on, aren't you?' asked Falconer dubiously.

'Of course I am, but I've spent a lot of time thinking about it. It would have been easy enough for someone she was familiar with to turn up on the doorstep, saying she'd left something at the party, and they'd come round to return it in case it was missed in the meantime and she was worried about it. It could've been anyone who knew what she kept in her safe.'

'One thing you probably don't know, which hasn't been widely broadcast, is that the jewellery that was stolen was found on a coffee table, in front of the chair that Julius Twelvetrees was found dead in.'

'Oh, my good Lord!' she ejaculated with horror. 'What a very grim picture that paints. So it was he who killed Lettice?'

'I'm afraid it's not that easy,' said Falconer, bursting that hopeful little bubble of an easy solution, 'That's how it was meant to look: that he took the lot, then, when looking it over, was filled with remorse, and took his own life.

'Fortunately, Market Darley CID isn't that easy to fool,' he stated, feeling a slight stirring of guilt, remembering that it was Doc Christmas who had spotted the set-up. 'So now we're looking for someone who has killed twice, and why the jewellery was left there, out in the open, we don't have the faintest idea. Yet! But we'll get there, don't you worry.'

Chapter Eleven

Monday afternoon – Market Darley

Once more back at the ranch, Falconer suggested that, as he was a much quicker typist than Carmichael, he should type up the notes so far, while the sergeant ran all the village's residents that they'd spoken to through the CRB. It was a cunning suggestion of the inspector's, for he found CRB checks deathly boring, as they usually turned up nothing on this sort of case, and he found typing rather relaxing.

'Can you read my shorthand, sir?' asked Carmichael, knowing that, in the past, Falconer had pronounced his amalgamation of Pitman's (he had purchased a book at a jumble sale when he first joined the force), abbreviations and 'Carmichael hieroglyphics' impossible to unravel.

'You forget how long we've been working together now. I've finally broken the code, and feel as proud as if I'd solved the mysteries of the Rosetta Stone. Let me at them notes. I could do with doing something mindless, and typing's great for that: through the eyes and straight out through the fingers, without having to pass through the brain. Sometimes I've no idea what I've typed, until I read it through at the end.'

'I wish it was that easy for me, sir. I'm happy, though. I love going on 'villain hunt'.

'So, we're both perfectly content with our early afternoon tasks, then? That's good, and afterwards, we'll have a little pow-wow about what we've learnt so far, and see who we can make out a case against.'

Carmichael bent his head to his computer, and Falconer reached out to grab Carmichael's notebook from the edge of the sergeant's desk. For the next half hour there was silence, except for a mutter or two from one or other of them at whatever they had found. Falconer did query one of Carmichael's little drawings, which was a smiley face at the bottom of his notes about their visit to Tresore that morning, but Carmichael explained that he only drew that to indicate that he had found Toby Lattimer a very nice man.

'Smurf-lover!' Falconer muttered under his breath, in contempt, only to be interrupted about ten minutes later by a yell from Carmichael.

'Bingo!' he shouted, then fell to his computer again, to carry on his searches.

'What was all that about?' the inspector asked.

'I'll tell you when I've finished,' his sergeant replied, his eyes not moving from the computer screen.

Ten minutes later, Carmichael's voice was raised, once again, with the exclamation, 'Bingo, again!' This time Falconer ignored it, but when, only a quarter of an hour later, Carmichael shouted, 'Full house!' he could contain himself no longer.

'What on earth have you found to make you so excited?' he asked, giving up any attempt to carry on with transcribing his sergeant's notes. 'It must be good for you to have yelled three times.'

'Oh, it is, sir. Three of them have got records, and another one a warning. I didn't yell for that one, but the other three were irresistible. I just couldn't contain myself.'

'So, spill the beans, Carmichael. Which ones have got a record, and for what?' asked Falconer, slightly crestfallen that the glory of finding the records hadn't been his. When he checked he always came up with zilch.

'The first one I found was that antiques dealer, Galton. She's been in trouble for receiving stolen goods, but only the once. She got off with it, because they believed her story about buying in good faith, and her clean record before that.

'Then there was our latest victim, convicted for handling stolen goods. He bought some dodgy gear and sold some in his shop. One of our guys recognised something in his window when he went there to buy a gift for his wife, and old Julius coughed for the stuff he'd already sold as well. That seemed to be a one-off case, too, as he'd rung the station on at least one occasion previously to alert us to the fact that he'd been offered some hooky watches.

'And thirdly, our mysterious cove, Colin Twentymen.'

'A right cagey character he was, when we visited him. We'd have got more out of an oyster,' commented Falconer, wondering where on earth Carmichael had exhumed the word 'cove' from.

'Correct, sir. Well, it seems he's done time for theft and burglary. He was released on parole last year, which would probably coincide with when he moved to Shepford St Bernard.'

'We'll definitely have to have a rather firm word with Mr Twentymen – and the other two, of course. Who was it who received a caution?'

'The local witch – Wanda Warwick – of all people. Apparently, some zealous soul in our midst had a word with her about fortune-telling, invoking an ancient law against it, because he didn't believe she was genuine. I don't recognise the name reporting, but then I don't know every officer who works here, since the amalgamation, with all those extras bodies joining us from the little rural stations that they more or less closed down.'

'Very interesting, Carmichael. Good work! That'll give us food for thought, but now, I think we ought to have a brain-storming session, taking the suspects one-by-one and seeing how they might be responsible. Then, tomorrow, we'll go pay them all another visit.'

After a visit to the canteen to bulk up their blood sugar – very necessary in Carmichael's case – they got down to reviewing and speculation.

'Let's get rid of the obvious no-noes first. I can't see our nice lady vicar carrying out such violent attacks, can you? Two murders and a hit and run?' asked the inspector.

'I don't think we can exempt her from the list. Look at what she said to us earlier. That could have been a very clever double bluff, pretending not to know that the jewellery had been found. She could have religious mania, and have done it all for the money for her church. It's her first parish, she said, and she might have got a bit psychopathically involved with it.' This was from Carmichael, and surprised Falconer.

'Do you really mean that?' he asked, 'Or did you just not find her sponge cake to your liking?'

'No, sir, I'm only pulling your leg. I don't think she'd hurt a fly. I was just playing devil's advocate.'

Falconer was surprised that Carmichael had even known what the expression meant, let alone be capable of playing the part and coming up with a bizarre, but possible, candidate for the crimes. He'd have to watch him, or he'd be turning out a real smart-arse. And that wouldn't do at all; that was *his* job.

'What about Violet Bingham?' Falconer threw out at his sergeant. 'Can you make a case out against her?'

Carmichael thought for a minute, then drew breath, and said, 'If she knew she was being left the cat, what else might she think she has been left? And Miss Keighley-Armstrong would have let her in without a qualm, as would Mr Twelvetrees. Who would suspect an elderly lady of such dastardly acts?'

'Nice one, Carmichael, although I can't see an ice-cream's chance in hell of it being true. You're right about the will, though. We really must find out who thinks they might have been mentioned in it. It might make us look at things in an entirely different light, if we examine expectations rather than the reality.

'I must get on to that solicitor to find out if what we have got is the most recent will. And the insurance company. And we'll need to find a contact number for a gemologist to take a look at the jewellery, and give us an up-to-date estimate of its value. But that's not what we're doing at the moment. Who's next?'

'Let me see,' mused Carmichael, 'We've done the vicar and Mrs Violet. What about that Maude Asquith, who took such exception to DC Roberts?' he suggested, smiling at the thought of the DC's misfortune. Cheeky young upstart, insulting him like that, and taking the P.

'I hope you and Roberts aren't going to start squabbling every time you meet.'

'As long as he minds his manners and doesn't try to put me down again, everything will be just fine and dandy,' replied Carmichael, his face a mask of stubbornness. 'And Asquith's another old lady. I know we haven't met her yet, but she sounds more the sort to smarm round people with money than to knock them on the head. As for cutting a man's throat ... And why would she leave the jewellery there? In fact, why would anyone leave the jewellery there, sir?'

'Good point, Sergeant.

'Maybe it got too hot for them to handle, and they just wanted rid of it, sir.'

'Then why not just dump it somewhere in the graveyard? Why commit murder again? Somehow we're missing the connection between these two deaths, and there must be one. It can't just be coincidence, that two people get themselves murdered within a very short period of time, in the same tiny village, and with the jewels connecting each to the other.'

'And where's the knife that killed Twelvetrees?'

'Quite right, Carmichael: where the hell is it? It doesn't matter how I look at it, I just can't seem to find a common factor for murders, except for those ruddy jewels. What on earth was the point in seeing off the old lady, only to kill again and leave the jewellery at the scene of the second murder? Any ideas, Carmichael, because I'm stumped?'

'Nix,' replied his partner.

'I think we'll just have to consider all the suspects for the first murder, then sift through everything we have to try to identify why Twelvetrees was killed, and left in an Aladdin's cave of jewellery.'

'Weirdest murder scene I've ever come cross, but how about this, sir? Twelvetrees was the first murderer, but someone knew he'd done it, went round, maybe in a fury, because of how they felt about Miss Keighley-Armstrong. They catch him with his

145

illegal hoard right out in the open, not even any signs of concealment. Then they lose their temper and go for him, in vengeance.'

'And the knife, Carmichael? They just happened to have it on them?' asked Falconer, interested, but not convinced, 'We've still absolutely no idea where it came from, what it looks like, or where it is now.'

'Why couldn't it have belonged to Twelvetrees, and they just picked it up surreptitiously, then came at him from behind?'

'Stranger things have happened. But where did it go after the murder, even if it did belong to Twelvetrees? I give up, for the time being. In the meantime, I'm going to make those appointments with the solicitor and insurance company, and sort out a gemologist.

'Then we'll go through everyone again, with regard to the first murder, and see if we can find a link between the two. You go to the canteen and pick us up something nice and sweet, and we'll have a good old chew of the fat while we're having our coffee break.'

Carmichael returned, about ten minutes later, with a tray loaded with two mugs of coffee and a large plate, which held six jam doughnuts and two stout squares of lardy cake, and a hungry look on his face. 'Crikey!' said Falconer in surprise, 'are we expecting visitors?'

'No, sir? Why?' The sergeant really didn't understand the question.

'Oh, nothing. Now, make sure you don't get those mugs mixed up. I don't think coffee with six sugars in it is going to agree with me.'

'It's a big mug, sir. There're eight in it, so it's not too bitter. I can't stand bitter drinks. They make me shudder.'

'OK, let's get started,' suggested Falconer, wondering how Carmichael could even taste the coffee. When they were both seated, and each had in front of him a plate, Carmichael's piled rather higher than the inspector's, Falconer began with, 'We've just had a look at Twelvetrees himself being responsible for Miss Keighley-Armstrong's murder. We know he used to be a

146

jeweller. We also know he's got a record.

'I got Bob Bryant to take a brief look in the electoral register, and his home address is actually in Market Darley – one of those big, old Victorian places near the park, but it seems he's been spending a lot more time in Shepford St Bernard of late. We know he no longer has his shop, so it's a reasonable supposition that he's in the smaller house because it's cheaper to run, and times simply ain't so good now he's no longer working.

'He'd certainly have the contacts to break up the pieces, sell the stones – unidentifiable out of their settings – and melt the gold and platinum. Of course, he'd realise nowhere near their true value in their original state, but he'd certainly make a good little pile to see him through a bit longer.'

'That's fine,' replied Carmichael, spraying the inspector with sugar from his jam doughnut, 'but we know he didn't commit suicide. The only idea that's left is someone killing him in revenge for doing away with Miss Keighley-Armstrong.'

'OK, we can look into who that could have been later. Let's take the others, one by one, and see if we can find a better motive for them committing both murders. I've got a nasty feeling that I'm not going to like the solution to this case. It's got that feeling about it – dangerous, and liable to blow up in our faces.'

'That's not like you, sir,' commented Carmichael, sinking his teeth into a square of lardy cake.

'I know. I've just got that feeling. "By the pricking of my thumbs, something wicked this way comes". I'm not usually prone to that sort of superstitious stuff, but this one worries me.'

'We've discounted the vicar, haven't we, sir?'

'But can we really afford to? After all, she did take our first victim home from the party, and no one would turn away a vicar if they called late. She could have turned up at Twelvetrees' place and said – I don't know – that she'd heard a prowler, and she didn't want to disturb any of the older residents. She knew she could rely on a strong, silent man like him … Oh, this is just rubbish. Why leave the jewellery there?

147

In fact, if it was her, why take it in the first place?'

'Because she had expectations for her church from the will, of course. Doing away with Miss Keighley-Armstrong would just hurry along the inheritance.'

'Then why kill Twelvetrees at all?'

'Because, sir, he saw something that he shouldn't have done. Maybe he mentioned it to her, and was going to blackmail her for a share, or even all, of the money that was left to the church. Killing him would not only get rid of the only witness to the first murder, but would ensure that the insurance paid up promptly, because the missing items had been recovered.'

'Then wouldn't turning up at the witching hour alert him, and make him wary?'

'Not if she said she'd come round at that time because she didn't want to be seen, and that she'd come to agree terms with him – something like that, that he'd fall for, because he was greedy, sir.'

'Carmichael, did you join Mensa or something when I wasn't looking?'

'No, sir. It just seemed obvious to me.'

'Well, you can carry on being as obvious as you like. I'm all ears. Go on, do another one for me. What about – oh, let me see – that Yaxley crowd. Fancy anyone from that trio?'

Carmichael chewed for a minute or two, working his way through another doughnut, took a huge swallow of coffee to wash it down, then said, 'We do know that Mr Yaxley has walked out, and that his wife is very short of money.'

'That's right,' agreed Falconer. 'And life can be very hard when you've got twins to get through university. The fees must be astronomical, having the two of them studying at the same time. Something can probably be sorted out, due to her reduced circumstances – what is it these days, a loan or a grant – anyway, she's up Poo Creek without a paddle, and sees this opportunity.'

'Same thing applies, then, sir, for Twelvetrees. Or maybe he offered to shift them for her; find a fence – he'd no doubt have connections, with his past – then tried to fiddle the percentage his way. Maybe it was a secret meeting, and he got the stuff out, to point out that they wouldn't get much for them as they were, because they were too easily identifiable and traceable.

'Then he told her how much less they'd get if they were broken up. She thinks he's trying to take advantage, and does him. Then she just makes a run for it, leaving all the stuff on the table, because she'd terrified at what she's just done, and just wants to get out of there and save her own skin.'

'My turn, now,' said Falconer, really getting into the spirit of the exercise. 'I'll try Maude Asquith. So, what do we know about her? She's been sucking up to Miss Keighley-Armstrong in the hope that she'll be left something in the will, because life is difficult at the moment, as it is for most people her age, who used to rely on income from investments to help them get by.

'Roberts seemed to think she was some sort of hard-faced old besom. Was she hard-faced enough to kill the goose, because it wouldn't lay the golden egg at her convenience? We know that there's a military background in her family. Can we assume that a ruthless streak runs in her? It's not beyond the bounds of possibility, and she'd want the stuff found, so that the cash it represented could be freed up. Is old Mother Goose our ruthless killer?'

'This is just like playing Cluedo with the boys, sir. Now, my turn. I'm going to propose Violet Bingham.'

Falconer blew out a deep breath in admiration, and said, 'I wish you joy of that one. It's a very brave choice, and I'm glad she wasn't left for me.'

'Actually, it's very easy. Same as for the vicar. Miss Keighley-Armstrong would trust her simply because they're best friends. She could've come to the same deal with Twelvetrees and, when you're a little old lady, you can always call on a neighbour late at night, perhaps because you've had a fuse go, or the electric bulb in your bedroom needs changing, and you're too old to stand on chairs.'

'I'll grant you that, but why call the police, then?'

'So that the body didn't just lie around the house. Twelvetrees didn't really have any friends. He could've laid

149

there for days; weeks even, and she wants everything all tidied up, so that she can get to probate, and pick up whatever was left to her, sir'

'Well done. You're developing a very devious imagination, Carmichael. I applaud you for it.'

'Thank you, sir.' Carmichael was by this time just hoovering up the granules of sugar from the large plate and his own smaller one with a wet finger. He'd eaten all but one doughnut, which Falconer had taken charge of when the sergeant had first entered the office with his sugar-laden load and both pieces of lardy cake.

'If we consider the Haygarths, we could use the same theory as for Mrs Yaxley. Her boys couldn't have been involved, because they were doing the music for the party.'

'They could've done it afterwards, sir.'

'I find that unlikely, as they'd have to clear all their equipment away and get it back home: but the Haygarths have a failing business to prop up. We know they're at each other's throats over the smallest expenditure, and they could've done it, either together or separately. Who does that leave us, Carmichael?'

'The antiques fair lady and her neighbour – that refined gentleman collector who said he'd take a look at my Smurfs, sir.'

'Yes, Carmichael. There's no need to rub it in, that he said some of them – the rarer ones – could fetch quite a lot of money. Go on. It must be your turn, now,' he encouraged Carmichael, feeling a little guilty that they were almost turning the exercise into a game.

'Well, I believe the woman, when she says she was at an antiques fair the whole day. She can probably provide us with dozens of witnesses, just from the other dealers, and I don't think the old gentleman looked very well at all.'

'They've both had some sort of brush with the law,' Falconer reminded him.

'I know, but they're not like Twentymen, who'd done time. It sounded like they were one-off affairs, where they didn't

150

really know what they'd got hold of.'

'I tend to agree. Although with that sort of thing, it can't be used as a defence, although I really don't think there was any *mens rea* in their cases. It's just a hazard of what they do, that some people try to impose on them by using them as unwitting fences.'

'Precisely, sir. That just leaves us with Wanda the witch.'

'Don't even bother to go there, Carmichael. She's an absolute nutcase, and could have done either murder for some esoteric reason we'd never think of in a hundred years. We'll leave her on the back burner, and see if anyone else says anything about her.

'We'll have to go back over there, anyway, but I think we'll leave that till tomorrow. I still haven't made any appointments, I want a word with Doc Christmas, and we haven't even examined the insurance photographs that we brought back here.'

As he finished speaking, the telephone rang, and Doc Christmas registered for class as if he were telepathic. 'Hello, Harry boy. I've got the two of them done, if you'd like to hear the results.'

'I was just talking about you,' Falconer told him, marvelling at how some things just fell together.

'I thought someone must've been. My ears are burning like the very fires of hell. That aside, everything's exactly as we thought it would be. The old lady's heart gave out, and the other chap died from blood loss – exsanguination, as we posh fellows with a medical education call it. Oh, and the first weapon matched the wound, so we've got no mystery object to find there, but obviously we are still missing the knife, which I estimate as being only about three inches long but wickedly sharp. One thing, though, that keeps coming back to me about the old lady: why did she seem to be making her way out to the gravestones? It was almost as if she intended to hold on to one, as if leaving a message.'

'Who knows what goes through a person's mind when they're dying,' replied Falconer. 'Maybe she was just trying to alert us to the fact that there were stones in the house, but of a precious sort.'

'She wouldn't have made all that effort – her dying effort, mind you – to crawl all the way out there, if there wasn't something on her mind that she wanted to alert us to.'

'Who knows?' said Falconer, his mind already on the phone calls he had to make. 'We'll probably never find out.'

Noting down the list of numbers he'd have to dial, he asked Carmichael to search for any gemologists the police might have used in the past, and asked, in passing, how baby Harriet was getting along.

'She can hold her head up now, and she's a real smiler. We're all completely besotted with her. You must come and see her soon, because, after all, I've got a sort of date with the vicar to do the triple christening – oh, God, I hope it's not her, or I'll have to persuade another vicar to come to Castle Farthing,' he concluded, looking worried, as he turned to his computer.

'Don't worry, Carmichael. I'm sure Rev. Florrie is as innocent as the day is long – good grief! I'm starting to sound like my mother! Before she got all hoity-toity, that is.'

The insurance company could have a representative at their service first thing the next morning. The gemologist, whom Carmichael turned up, and who was attached to the local auction house, also agreed that he would be available in the morning.

The solicitor, however, proved more elusive, and couldn't see them until Wednesday afternoon, which was a real nuisance. Not knowing whether the will that they had picked up from the study floor at Manor Gate had been superseded by another one would definitely hold them back. Damn and blast! Who did these solicitors think they were, obstructing the police in their legitimate enquiries?

Feeling hard done by, Falconer sent Carmichael to sign out the necessary papers gathered from the first crime scene and had a bit of a sulk. His first sight of what was brought to him, though, revived his spirits no end.

'Look at this!' he exclaimed, running his eyes over the will, to which he had not previously paid much attention. 'This is only dated four months ago. It leaves the cat to Mrs Bingham, twenty-five per cent of the capital after all expenses and taxes to St Bernard-in-the Downs-Church, and five thousand each to Rev. Florrie and Violet Bingham, that they might treat themselves to something they would not otherwise be able to afford.

'The rest goes to the Cats' Protection League – as we discovered when we first had a brief sight of this – in gratitude for the company, and I quote here, "'that she has received from her many pet cats over the years, which has been vastly superior to that which she has received from most of her human companions during that time."'

Carmichael whistled. 'That's a turn up for the books for anyone with high hopes of being left something. Now we know a bit more about the inhabitants, I bet old Ma Asquith, for one, will be furious! It's lucky *she* doesn't have a cat, otherwise she'd kick it from here to kingdom come when she hears about this, sir.'

'I wouldn't fancy being the next person she runs into afterwards, either,' replied Falconer, looking at his watch and frowning. 'Time you weren't here, me laddo. You need to get home to that lovely family of yours. I'll finish up here. Tomorrow, we can drop in on Roberts early, then see the insurance company, but we'll have to pop back here first before we see the gemologist, so that we can sign the stuff out of evidence.

'We'll go back over to Shepford St Bernard after lunch. Maybe that Fletcher woman will be back by then. Who knows? Anyway, off you go, and have a good evening. I'll just look through the rest of the paperwork, and I'll be off, too. I've got a houseful of lonely cats who think I'm simply never there, and they aren't far off right.'

Chapter Twelve

Monday evening – Market Darley

With a look of absolute shock on his face, Falconer spread out the photographs of the pieces of jewellery, which were numbered, on his desk, and read the written description of each piece as he moved from photograph to photograph. Each description gave a weight in troy ounces for the gold or platinum, and a weight in carats for the stones.

Under his breath, he read out loud, 'Diamond choker set in eighteen-carat gold. That's a good weight of gold, but, look at this – how many carats of diamonds? Phew! That's a corker, and no mistake. What's next?

'Sapphire and diamond V-shaped necklace, with ruby and seed pearl flower decoration. Eighteen carat gold again, and about half a stone of gems. Daddy was a very generous husband to Mummy. Lucky old Mummy!

'Emerald and diamond bracelet with matching necklace, ring, earrings, and pair of clips. What are they? Let's have a look at the photograph. Oh, yes, those things you could clip on to either side of the neck of a garment. Very old-fashioned, but no less valuable for that. My God! This little lot's set in platinum, and I didn't know there were that many diamonds in the world!

'Graduated opal necklace with diamonds – oh, that's very pretty. Next, garnet and opal bracelet with matching necklace, ring, earrings, and another pair of clips. I think we're getting into the cheaper stuff now, but that's all relative.

'Mixed coloured sapphire necklace with detachable pendant, for wear as brooch, with matching bracelet, earrings, and ring.

Daddy didn't mess about when he gave his wife a present.'

He read on until he had examined each photograph against its description, let fall the last photograph, and whistled again. This was serious jewellery. He'd not seen anything of this quality since he'd gone on a school trip to the Tower of London to see the crown jewels.

There was also an additional description sheet of various rings and other baubles not photographed, and a note about loose stones. Good grief! Now it looked like there was a little leather pouch gone walkabout, with unset stones in it. They'd be a doddle to sell, if the seller didn't look like an out-and-out criminal.

The pieces themselves, though, would have been impossible to fence. Interpol would have been involved in searching for them, and the only way to deal with such distinctive items was to break them up. Who on earth, in Shepford St Bernard, would have had the contacts to dispose of this quality, and quantity, of treasure? There was more here than in some small countries' crown jewels, and they'd been kept in a safe in a tiny village in rural England for God knows how long.

Miss Keighley-Armstrong's solicitor must have been out of his mind for not insisting they were kept in a strongbox at her bank. And the insurance company was just as much to blame. She was lucky she hadn't been turned over years before. Silly old woman! What did she think she was playing at?

Well, she'd got her comeuppance good and proper now, and paid for her foolishness with her life, as had another resident of the place. He'd better get a patrol car to shadow them when they went to the auction house, or maybe he'd better give the chap a ring and get him to come to the station.

The thought of being out and about with such enormous riches made him break out in a cold sweat. No way was he getting coshed for this little lot, even with Carmichael by his side. Yes, the gemologist was definitely going to have to come to the station. There was nothing else for it.

A quick phone call and one of the photographs e-mailed to the auction house, easily obtained the gemologist's agreement and, with that settled, Falconer took a final look at the photographs, before putting them back in the evidence bag. What he hadn't noticed at first, being dazzled by the subjects of the pictures, was how old they were.

They must have been taken decades ago, but that was probably when the policy was first taken out. Why renew them, when there was no need? Jewellery didn't age or decay. And at least the gemologist was going to come to the station. With this arrangement made, his fears about having to walk around with a fortune in his briefcase had been allayed, and he went home in a less panicky state of mind.

When he got home he received an enthusiastic welcome from his cats, Tar Baby, the huge black, long-haired monster; Ruby, the red-point Siamese; Meep, the silver-spotted Bengal, and Mycroft, his original cat, who was a seal-point Siamese, and who had grudgingly ceded his personal space to include the other three as they joined the household.

After a scratch meal of baked beans on toast with lashings of brown sauce (divine), he sat at his desk writing cards for each of the suspects, then pinned them onto a cork board, and sat looking at them for some time, but nothing leapt out at him, and the cats were vying for his attention, starting little arguments and scraps to draw him away from what looked, to them, like a very boring pastime.

He eventually gave in, screwed a couple of used envelopes into balls, threw them across the room, then joined in with the scrum of cats, all vying to possess one of these prizes. He spent the next half an hour rolling round the floor with them, retrieving balls from them and throwing them to another part of the room.

At last, relaxed and in a much better frame of mind, he collapsed on to the sofa, and suddenly grew himself a thick, furry blanket with eight eyes. This was more like it. He might not be married with children, but he did appreciate the company of his cats, and knew exactly why Miss Keighley-Armstrong had left the bulk of her estate to their welfare.

Although he'd like a wife and children one day, and even had a candidate in mind when he could get his head round the idea, for now he was content. Cats had very simple needs – shelter, water, food, and someone to love them – so they weren't very different to him, and they served each other in these areas admirably for the time being.

Castle Farthing

Carmichael also got involved in rather a lot of rough-and-tumble after arriving home unexpectedly early. The boys were overjoyed to have him home before their bedtime on a weekday, and immediately initiated a tickling-wrestling game, which he joined in with enthusiastically, until Kerry upbraided her sons for hijacking him before he'd even had a cup of tea. All three looked suitably chastened, then winked at each other when Kerry turned away to go into the kitchen.

'We'll carry on after I've had my cuppa,' he reassured them. 'In the meantime, I'll catch up with little 'un.' Harriet was asleep in her bouncing chair, oblivious to all the shouting and laughter that had just gone on around her, but she didn't stay that way for long, for Carmichael lifted her out, and held her up in the air, booming, 'How's my little princess today?'

She replied by chuckling, then belching, the wind probably moved by her sudden elevation, and dribbled a sour stream on to his shoulder. 'That's my girl. Get it up, then you won't have a sore tummy when you go to bed,' he crooned at her, not a whit bothered about his clothes. Kids boaked a bit, sometimes; it was par for the course.

His arrival having suddenly turned the household upside-down, the two tiny dogs, Mr Knuckles and Mistress Fang, headed in his direction, followed by their three puppies, who had just woken up. They leapt about his trousered legs with the sort of joy that intimated he'd been away for a year or more and, as Kerry entered with his huge mug of tea, telling him that supper wouldn't be long, she shooed them down, and sent them, hang-dog, back to their basket.

'Daddy needs a sit down. He's been at work all day, and doesn't need to be bothered by you lot as soon as he sets foot through the door,' she declared, to all the residents of the house, whether two-legged of four. Monkey the Abyssinian cat, ignoring her completely, slid on to his capacious lap as he sat down with his mug, and curled up there, in clear possession should someone else want to question it.

'This is unexpected. Is that good news or bad news?' she asked, sitting beside him on the sofa.

'Neither,' he answered her. 'It's just the result of a natural break in the investigation. There was nothing more we could do for today, so I left the inspector looking at some of the paperwork and headed back here.'

'Didn't be need any help?'

'He told me to get off to see you lot, although goodness knows why,' he declared, then ducked as she lobbed a cushion at him.

'Because we're the lights of your life, oh powerful breadwinner, and your existence would be empty without us,' she told him.

'Amen to that,' he agreed, and leaned over to kiss her.

Shepford St Bernard

Gwendolyn Galton knocked on Toby Lattimer's door at exactly eight o'clock. She was quite looking forward to the company, as she lived alone, her only contact with the outside world being at auctions, antique fairs, and the occasional foray into junk shops. Goods in, goods out; lots of cleaning and tiny repairs, in between these didn't leave a lot for time for making friends and developing a social life.

Toby jollied her into the sitting room, where a bottle of red sat, already open to breathe, on a fine but, given the size of the room, rather overpowering credenza. It was the only large piece in there, and dominated it, commanding attention as soon as one entered the room.

'Come on in, beautiful lady,' he welcomed her. 'Sit yourself down and take a glass of wine with me, and then I shall put a little plan before you for our amusement this fine evening.'

Gwendolyn shrank inwardly, hoping he was not going to propose that they started a physical relationship. He was OK as a friend, but the thought of being intimate with him disgusted her. Her fears were unfounded, however, for, after handing her wine to her in a – good God! It was a seventeenth-century glass with a gorgeously twisted core running up the middle of the stem. Surely these weren't for everyday use? He then said, 'Let me explain to you a rather fun pastime, which we'll both enjoy.'

'I'm not up for grabs, Toby, if that's what you think,' she offered, boldly.

'Heaven forfend, dear lady. No, I merely propose that you should have a look at some of my finer bibelots and give me a rough valuation, then, perhaps, we could go round to your place, and you could show me your current stock of itsy-bitsy beauty. I may be in the market for a bibelot or two: something new to refresh my jaded sensibilities.'

'The tortoiseshell box wasn't a sufficiently tasty morsel?' she asked.

'No, no, no. It's a beauty. I just haven't acquired anything for some time, and thought it was time I treated myself. If I buy from you, I'll get my purchases at "mates' rates", and neither of us has to go out of our way to execute the transactions.'

'Sounds good to me. If I can make sales without having to pack everything up into that horrible little van, I'm all for it. Now, what do you want to show me? I'm happy to have a stab at valuation on anything. It'll be much easier than having to convince punters, on a windy field, that what I'm asking is fair. They seem to think that I buy everything at a quarter of what I'm trying to sell it for, and feel rooked if they can't knock the price down substantially.

'They never think of all the time and petrol spent looking for the stuff – it doesn't just fall into my lap, you know – and they completely ignore the iniquitous amount I've had to shell out for the pitch, and the effort of packing up all the stock, and transporting it there, only to then have to make an attractive display of it.'

'Oh, we are a grumpy old bunny this evening. Here,' he distracted her. 'Take a look at these Stanhopes I've managed to get together. One of them is rather racy. Rare, I'd imagine. Here, I've got a loupe for you as well.' So saying, he handed her a group of ivory, silver, and wooden articles, and removed a jeweller's loupe from his waistcoat pocket.

'Oh, these are darling, Toby. How long has it taken you to collect them?' She was instantly enchanted.

'It's taken quite a while. They seem to be getting rarer, and they have to be within my budget restraints, too. Look at this one,' he exhorted her, picking one out of the little pile on her lap. 'Just take a look through that, and tell me what you think.'

Gwendolyn raised the small object to her eye and looked through it, using the ceiling light to aid her vision. 'Oh, "what the butler saw", or what?' she exclaimed, smiling. 'That is a rather naughty one, isn't it? I don't suppose you've got any of those bronze ladies who are outwardly respectable, but when you move a piece of bronze, they're buck naked underneath?'

'By that chap who spells his name backwards on the naughty ones? No, I'm afraid they're way beyond my means, but I can lust after them, can't I?'

You can lust after anything you like, she thought, as long as it's not me. There isn't a fee in the world big enough to persuade me to take a roll in the hay with you.

An hour later, the wine bottle empty, he suggested they go round to her house, so that he could take a little look over her stock. 'Not a covetous eye, I assure you, my dear lady; merely a collector's eye, with a view to purchase.' How could she refuse him?

Back at Carpe Diem, Gwendolyn opened another bottle of wine, and brought a few boxes of trinkets for him to inspect, fetching her own loupe from her handbag so that she could point out any particularly fine work to him.

The first one he opened elicited a crow of delight, as he espied a nest of small boxes. 'Are they what I think they are?' he asked, his eyes alight with anticipation.

'You told me what you were interested in, so I got a group together, so that you wouldn't have to rake through all my packed stock. There may be a few other bits and pieces in the rest of the stuff, but I thought I'd start you off with a bang.' She finished speaking abruptly and blushed behind his back, hoping he didn't misinterpret what she had just said.

Toby, however, was not even aware of her presence, as he began opening boxes and examining their contents, puffing with delight at some of the tie and lapel pins she had offered for his inspection. 'I can see already that you are going to relieve me of some more of my precious stash of cash,' he said, but he said it with a smile, and the glint in his eye of the true collector.

'I didn't know you had a stash,' she replied. 'You're always pleading poverty.'

'That's because I only have money for pretty things. As far as anything else is concerned, I'm flat broke. If I were to let it fritter away on things that weren't important to me, I wouldn't be able to view this little treasure box with the certainty that I can make some of these exquisite objects mine.'

'Fair enough,' commented Gwen, the glint of profit shining in her eyes. 'Any interest in seals or watch fobs?'

'Bring 'em on, my girl. Bring 'em on. I say, why don't you come round for afternoon tea tomorrow? My collection extends well beyond what you've seen. The sitting room's not even a quarter of what I've got. Yes, that's the ticket. Come for tea; daylight hours, you see, so that you know I don't have any lecherous tendencies towards you. Three o'clock for three-thirty all right?'

'Done, you charmer. I'd be really interested to know what else you've got tucked away. It'll give me a better chance of finding things that suit your tastes when I'm out buying,' replied Gwendolyn, realising that she had an enthusiastic customer in Toby.

Market Darley

In the hospital, now on a general ward, Roberts tried to find a comfortable position, from which to inspect what had just been delivered to him. Failing in this respect, he sought the least uncomfortable one, for his bruises were really beginning to give him some pain now, and his head still throbbed where it was stitched under its dressing.

On the bed in front of him was a small pile of papers, the sum total of the notes on the case so far. He'd asked to use the ward phone earlier, and had called Bob Bryant, to see if Bob would print out everything on the case so far and have it dropped round to him by a patrol car, so that he could go through the notes and statements to see if anything jumped out at him.

He was, naturally, frustrated at being injured again so soon after he had returned to duty, and thought this mental exercise would aid in making him feel a little more connected, and not excluded by this unexpected return to a hospital bed.

First, he reread the notes of his own interviews, refreshing his memory of the characters he had spoken to, then moved on to those spoken to by Falconer and Carmichael, and his interest was pricked by the circumstances of the two families spoken to, the Yaxleys and the Haygarths.

Both families were in dire straits, financially: Mrs Yaxley because of the sudden departure of her husband from the marital home, the Haygarths because their business was in the process of falling victim to the current economic climate. The acquisition of a large sum of money would be a godsend for either household, and the tensions within those households might be enough to create a mood of reckless abandon.

Neither family, however, seemed likely to have underworld connections that could produce a fence capable of shifting such identifiable objects. Actually, that applied to everyone who had been interviewed and, although he had read the notes of those with some sort of form, he still couldn't see a connection between the two deaths. The only really shady character in the village was Colin Twentymen, who conveniently lived next door to the second murder victim.

The only conclusion he could come to was that Twelvetrees

had committed murder number one for the contents of the safe. Maybe Twentymen had smelt a rat, gained access to his neighbour's house, and confronted him, and then seen him off, perhaps after a furious argument, before realising that he couldn't call the police about finding the jewels, because that would put him in the frame for what he had just done . Roberts would have to discuss that one with the inspector when he came in to visit next, he thought, as his eyes slid closed, and he slid off the cliff of consciousness down the slope to sleep. Being hit by a car left one uncommonly tired, it seemed.

Shepford St Bernard

Krystal Yaxley knocked on the door of Ace of Cups with rather less trepidation than she had on the day of her tarot reading. That day, she had returned home considerably spooked after what had happened with the turning over of the last three cards, but she had spoken with Wanda Warwick on the phone since then, and felt much more comfortable returning to the cottage than she would have expected.

Wanda, also feeling very disturbed by how things had turned out on Saturday afternoon, had explained it to herself with the theory that the cards were as they were because of someone on the other side, trying to warn her that something tragic was about to happen in the vicinity. This, she was quite comfortable with, and was able not to dwell on it anymore.

She was also used to calling on Bonnie Fletcher a couple of times a week. Bonnie was the only friend she had managed to make so far in the village, and Bonnie had simply not been around. With a vague idea that she ought to say something to somebody about that, she had decided to ring Krystal Yaxley, and extend the hand of friendship.

She had had one of her 'feelings' that they would get on, and, even if they didn't, it would while away an evening, while she waited for Bonnie to return from wherever she may have gone. As Krystal used the door-knocker, she was straight up on her feet to answer the summons. Company at last! She really must get out more.

Tonight she was wearing almost normal clothes, in various shades of purple, and received an approving glance from her visitor when she let her in. She wore none of her symbolic dangling, jingling jewellery, and had a bottle of white wine waiting in a cooler beside two glasses. On the table beside it sat a bowl of peanuts and another of pretzels.

When Krystal sat down she felt almost at home, as if they had had a baptism of fire together which had bonded them. She had not been long in the village, and she, too, thought she might have found a friend at last.

By the second bottle of wine they were chatting away as if they had known one another for years, and it was Wanda who brought up the topic of murder for discussion. 'Who do you think has been bumping off our neighbours?' she asked, apropos of nothing, startling Krystal slightly.

'I don't know. I don't really know anyone well round here, but that Asquith woman from Coopers Lane is a nasty piece of work. I had a run-in with her in the shop one day about who was next in the queue, and I wouldn't put anything past her, the way she spoke to me.'

'She's a spiteful old gossip,' agreed Wanda, 'and she did her best to get into Lettice's good books, in the hope that the old dear would leave her something when she passed over.'

'Was Miss Keighley-Armstrong naïve enough to fall for that?'

'Not at all,' Wanda reassured her new friend. 'She was a shrewd old biddy who had everybody's number. She knew exactly what our Maudie was up to, and she knew she had a spiteful, wicked tongue. I'd have thought Miss K-A would rather have stuck pins in her eyes than leave that old bitch anything.'

'Who were her friends?' asked Krystal, genuinely curious.

'She got on like a house on fire with the Bingham woman, but then she'd known her for donkey's years. She came round to Rev. Florrie very quickly as well, after hating her like poison when she first took over the parish.'

'What about that woman dealer, and her neighbour, the collector. I heard tell the old lady had some fine pieces of furniture. Did she have anything to do with those two?'

'Pass your glass. You're empty again, and so am I,' replied Wanda, reaching for the last of the second bottle. 'I do believe the old fella might have bought a couple of bits off her. Let me see ...' Wanda poured the wine as she thought, upending the bottle over her own glass as she surveyed its emptiness with a rueful eye.

'Don't worry,' replied Krystal, closing one eye to focus on her new best buddy. 'I've got some in the fridge over the road. If I can use your phone, I can get one of the twins to run it over. Now, you were telling me ...'

'That's right, I was. A card table for definite. Oh, and what was the other thing? Think, think! That's it! A wine cooler, also Georgian. Rather chop 'em up for firewood, myself. What use are they in the twenty-first century, when we've got fridges, and you can play cards on your computer?' she asked, slightly belligerently, due to the amount of wine she had consumed.

'Couldn't agree more. Just old stuff. No use at all today,' agreed Krystal, as there sounded a knock on the door. 'That'll be our wine delivery. You stay there. I'll get it,' she said magnanimously, rising slightly unsteadily to her feet and weaving her way to answer the summons.

On the doorstep stood a twin. Krystal wasn't sure which one, because she had to squint to see only one of him, but he carried a bottle of white wine, so it didn't really matter which one it was. As she took possession of his delivery, he gave her a disgusted look and said, 'Drunk again, Mother?'

'You shu' yer face,' she replied, with as much maternal feeling as she could muster. 'Cheeky li'l mon ... hic! ... key!'

Chapter Thirteen

Early hours of Tuesday morning – Market Darley

Falconer moaned and turned over. As far as he was concerned, he was sitting immobilised under a pile of giant gemstones, while Nanny Vogel – a character from the early part of his life, whom he would rather forget – threw what looked like round, unknapped flints at him, yelling, 'Open your eyes, Dummkopf! Open your eyes!'

Eventually, he obeyed her command, and found himself in his own bed, sweating from the evil that had radiated from his old carer (!) in his dream. What on earth had brought her to mind, he wondered, lying there, waiting for his heartbeat to slow down to normal. The giant gems he could understand, but the flints, like Nanny Vogel, were a mystery to him. Still, that was the subconscious for you, ever oblique.

Turning over, he tried to get to sleep again, but every time he closed his eyes, Nanny Vogel threw another stone and yelled, 'Dummkopf!' at him.

Later that morning

When Falconer arrived at the office, he found a bleary-eyed Carmichael already seated at his desk. 'Have you been on another bender with your family?' he asked, surveying his sergeant's grey skin and baggy eyes.

'Baby woke up so many times last night I stopped counting. Kerry said it was because I was home too early from work, and got her all excited before she went to bed. She's got a point, I suppose. I usually go up to talk to her before she goes off, but she was still up when I got in, and I wanted to play with her for a while.

'In the end, I gave up trying to get any sleep, and left the house about half-past seven. What happened to you, sir? *You* been out with my brothers?'

'Not a chance!' replied Falconer, with a rueful smile to indicate that he, too, looked like he'd been out on the tiles the night before. 'Nightmares,' he explained.

'Nanny Vogel again?' asked Carmichael.

'Got it in one,' answered Falconer, groaning as he eased himself into his chair. 'I don't suppose you feel up to fetching us some coffee, do you? I've got this gemologist coming in this morning, and I can't face him feeling like this. By the way, I've arranged for him to come here, rather than for us to troll around with a king's ransom on us, just asking to be robbed.

'Then we can go off to the insurance office, and I've a good mind to just barge in on that solicitor as well. Damned cheek! Can't see us until tomorrow. I ask you? This is a double murder investigation, and I won't have him put us off just for the hell of it, because he fancies a power trip.'

'Take it easy, tiger,' said Carmichael, rising to fetch a large dose of caffeine for his boss. 'It's hardly his fault that you dreamt about your old nanny last night.'

'You're right, of course. Bring me big-big kalabash of magic juice, for make me feel better-better, boy!'

'Yassir!' replied Carmichael, tugging his short forelock, and bowing his way out of the office.

The gemologist arrived at nine-fifteen, a short, portly man in his early sixties with a completely bald pate, a bow-tie, and, of all things, a monocle. He knocked sharply at the CID door, and bustled straight in without being invited. 'Good morning, good morning, good morning, gentlemen,' he uttered. 'How may I be of assistance on this bright and beautiful day? I'm Chester Field – no laughter, please – the gemologist.' Catching sight of Carmichael, he exclaimed, 'Good grief, what are you wearing, young man? Are you in fancy dress?'

168

This last was addressed to Carmichael, who had worn the same trousers as he had the day before, but with a red, orange, and pink Hawaiian shirt today. 'You'll have to forgive my colleague's attire,' Falconer answered him, 'but he's not right in the head, and there's nothing I can do about it, equal rights for the disabled being in force here.'

Carmichael stared at him, but while the newcomer huffed and puffed about not knowing what the police force was coming to today, Falconer winked at his sergeant, eliciting a complicit smile in return.

'Can he read?'

'No, but he's not deaf, and his temper's a bit dodgy.' Falconer kept a perfectly straight face as he said this, and Carmichael slouched, his arms dangling loosely at his sides, his face set in a moronic mask.

'Er, shall we get on with what you summoned me to do? You are Inspector Falconer who spoke to me on the telephone yesterday, I assume?' Field was now backing away towards the door, and safety from the monster within.

'Correct. If you'd like to accompany me, I shall retrieve the items for your examination from the evidence room, then we can take a look at them in one of the interview rooms. They have lockable doors, so the items will be quite safe out in open view there.'

Falconer returned to his office, minus Field, his face chalk-white, his eyes staring, almost straining to escape their sockets. Carmichael took one look at him, and asked in a concerned voice, 'Whatever's the matter, sir? You look like you've looked death itself in the face.'

Slumping into his chair and dropping his face into his hands, he replied, 'I feel like I have, too. Every single stone, Carmichael. The whole damned caboodle. They're all paste – fakes!'

'What? They can't be!'

'They are. I have no idea whatsoever whether Miss Keighley-Armstrong has been the victim of a systematic thief

169

over the years, or whether she knew about it; contrived at it, even. The gold is plate, and the platinum is silver plate. It's all paste, and there's no way of finding out who did it, or when it was done. This case just gets more and more complicated by the day.

'We start off with a little old lady getting whacked for the contents of her safe, and now we're looking at large-scale forgery, with no time scale to guide us, and another murder on top of that.'

Both men sat in silence for a moment, before Carmichael said, 'Well, at least Mr Twelvetrees must've discovered they were fakes. He did used to be a jeweller. If anyone had known, it'd be him.'

'Carmichael, you're at it again!'

'At what again, sir?'

'Being a genius. If someone brought the stones to him to get them valued, and possibly broken up and fenced, and he rumbled quite quickly that they were just pretty glass stones, maybe the person who brought them to him killed him in a fit of rage, that they'd taken all the risk of getting hold of them, and now they had nothing.'

'That would certainly work, sir, and we wouldn't be stumped for a link between both murders, if it was a spur of the moment thing – not premeditated. Twelvetrees only got his throat cut because he was the bringer of bad news.'

'Precisely! Glory! That makes things a bit less complicated.' Falconer was regaining a little of his colour, as it sank in that the fact that the jewellery had been carefully copied and substituted at some unknown time in the past, didn't really have any relevance to what he was currently investigating.

'We've been barking up completely the wrong tree, looking for a complicated connection between the two deaths that simply doesn't exist. I want search warrants for Gwendolyn Galton, Toby Lattimer, and Violet Bingham's properties, and one prepared that we probably won't use, for The Rectory and the church. You never know what might not have ended up on that coffee table in front of its latest victim, for there's no doubt

170

that that jewellery has been the cause of both of these deaths, or the greed to possess them.'

'Why those particular properties, sir? Why not Wanda Warwick's as well? She's been in trouble with the police.'

'Obviously, because of the particular brushes with the law of the first two. Either one of them might have gone to Twelvetrees for his opinion on the sparklies. Violet Bingham, because she was Miss Keighley-Armstrong's best friend, and their circumstances were, apparently so different under the surface. Maybe Violet got tired of waiting for whatever she'd been left. And the church properties, purely because the church is a beneficiary.

'Chop chop, Carmichael! Let's get weaving. We've got an insurance company to visit and a solicitor. In fact, in the light of what the gemologist has revealed, I might just leave the solicitor until tomorrow, by which time we might have the whole thing wrapped up. That'll show him! It'll be a case of 'eat your heart out, Mr C. Batty', too-busy-to-see-us solicitor.'

'Best not to count your chickens, sir,' Carmichael intoned in a warning voice. Things weren't always the way they seemed, and it was best not to take anything for granted, he believed.

The representative of the insurance company received them warmly, then said he had some news that might prove rather surprising. Mr Horton, who insisted they call him Freddie, agreed that he wasn't surprised that all the photographs seemed to be quite old. Had the policy been continued ... Falconer's ears pricked up, and he prepared himself for some more unexpected news.

'Had the policy been continued with, the photographs would have been renewed regularly, and it would have been the company's advice that the pieces be stored in a safe deposit box at the customer's bank.

'Looking through our records for this policy, which is now defunct – may I draw your attention to the date it was issued – I find that coverage by our firm was terminated more than twenty years ago, when the original insurer died. I don't know what happened in the meantime, but we have had no contact with Miss Keighley-Armstrong for some time on that matter.

'She has continued to insure her house and contents with us, but she has not contacted us to revalue, even though we've sent her several letters to inform her that it is of the utmost importance to keep valuations up to date, in the event that she needed to make a claim.'

'Out of interest,' asked Falconer, realising precisely why the policy had not been kept up, 'what was the date of the last valuation of the property and contents?'

'Our records show that to have been just before she cancelled the special policy on her inherited jewellery. She carried on with the undervalued policies, but this is all before my time. I was still at school when all this was going on, so I can give you no personal slant on it.'

'Thank you very much for your time, sir,' said Falconer, ever polite, as he rose to leave, giving an almost imperceptible nod to Carmichael that they were leaving.

'I hope you find whatever you need, to solve your case. This sort of almost casual violence makes me feel sick. No one's safe these days, not even in their own homes,' were Mr Horton's – Freddie's – parting words.

At the offices of Strickland, Vanny, Batty, and Strickland, Mr Chris Batty, the person with whom Falconer and Carmichael wished to converse, was tied up with nothing more pressing than a cup of coffee and a biscuit and, therefore, felt obliged to see them today, rather than tomorrow, as they had taken the time to turn up in person.

'I'll show you through,' said the receptionist, a slight smile catching at the corners of her mouth, for no reason that they could identify, but were soon made aware of the source of her amusement.

'Opening a door, she pushed it open and announced, 'Detective Inspector Falconer and Detective Sergeant Carmichael for you, *Ms* Batty,' allowed them to enter, then closed the door quietly behind them.

'Good morning,' she greeting them, rising and holding out her hand in greeting. 'I'm sorry if my gender disappoints you, but I've been female since birth, and have no plans to alter that situation in the future.'

Falconer's face was a study in scarlet with embarrassment, as he apologised for making a rather sexist assumption. Carmichael merely smiled, finding the situation amusing, and storing it up to tell Kerry when he got home from work.

'I've pulled out Miss Keighley-Armstrong's file, and find that this firm was also her parents' representative as well. The family has quite a long history with us, but all of it before my time, unfortunately. It does make very interesting reading, however. Let me order us some coffee, and I'll tell you what I've learnt.

'Oh, and by the way, I really did have a meeting planned for this afternoon, but unfortunately, my client was unavoidably delayed by a ruptured appendix and was admitted to hospital during the early hours of this morning. I wasn't just playing hard to get. I didn't actually expect to be here.'

'Pressing a button on a console on her desk, she ordered coffee for three, and pulled a file from her desk onto her knee. 'Do you want the full history?' she asked, her eyebrows lifted in interrogation.

'If you wouldn't mind, Ms Batty,' agreed Falconer, still looking a little hang-dog.

'Just call me Chris,' she replied, smiled, and opened the folder.

'It would appear,' she began, having settled herself comfortably like an old hand at *Jackanory*, although she'd never watched the programme herself, 'that the family moved here from South Africa when their only daughter – the elderly woman about whom you're enquiring – was in her early teens.

'My colleague was informed, it says here in confidence, that Mr Keighley-Armstrong had been a gem dealer before relocating, and took some of his salary in stones. He had invested the bulk of the money he made in fine jewellery, which he smuggled over here in the horsehair stuffing of an armchair.

173

'It represented just about all of his worldly wealth, and customs and excise were not as well-equipped in those days, unlikely to suspect a consignment of household goods to be worthy of close scrutiny. Thus he avoided income tax in both countries.

'He worked for a while in Hatton Garden, but when he decided to retire early, he started to sell off the pieces he'd had made for his wife, to keep him in the style to which they'd all become accustomed.

'Another note, made for information given in confidence, says that he dutifully had each piece copied in paste, so that his wife wouldn't miss what she had previously been able to wear, although she was fully aware of what her husband was doing. They were particularly fine copies, and would have fooled anyone but an expert. I presume you've had them looked at?'

'Just this morning,' Falconer concurred.

'Funny, I should have thought that was the first thing you'd have done. No doubt they fooled you as well.'

'We never got the chance to look at them before, as they were stolen when Miss Keighley-Armstrong was murdered, and have only just turned up again. It was decided that they were the reason for her death. She was hit over the head during the course of the robbery.'

'Nevertheless, it's all out in the open now. And to continue, the daughter – your victim, I understand – didn't find out until her father's death that this had happened. She kept it a lifelong secret from her mother, whom she thought would have been devastated to find out that the more than generous gifts from her husband had only been a means of transferring money into England without incurring any tax charges.

'That her mother knew exactly what her husband was doing, and never let on to her daughter for the very same reason, Miss Keighley-Armstrong had no idea. No one here could say anything to her, because of client confidentiality. I hope that makes sense. It is a bit of a muddled story to try to follow. Families, eh? Who'd have 'em?'

'So, at least the mother died, happy and informed, which is

more than I can say for her daughter. This additional information is really useful as a history of how and why the replicas were made. My main reason for wanting to see you, though, was to check the most up-to-date will of your late client.'

'I've got that right here for you,' she said, smiling again, and picking up a document tied with pinkish-red tape, that had sat under the file. Here you are; have a look. Dated only recently, by the looks of it.'

One glance told Falconer it was the original of the copy that had been stored in the safe. One thing he hadn't noticed in his haste, however, was who the executor – or in this case, the executrix – was. It was Violet Bingham: why had she not said something about being Lettice's executrix? It would have made life a lot easier for him. Probably. Possibly. He wasn't sure, but the situation made him a little cross at being denied information like that which might prove pertinent to the case – cases. Plural! Blast!

They took their leave of Chris Batty, Carmichael's notebook stuffed with more information to add to the background on the first victim, and with high hopes of doing a little searching around suspects' homes.

These hopes, however, were dashed when, on arriving back at the station, they found out that the search warrants wouldn't be available until the following morning. Hand-cuffed from this angle, Falconer suggested they take a look in on Roberts, to see how he was getting on, and find out how long they intended to keep him incarcerated and off active service.

It had been nice, just for that very short time that he had been with them to have someone else to do some of the running around, instead of there just being himself and Carmichael, and he wanted an informed opinion on when that situation would be available to him again.

They found Roberts propped up in bed, his curtains drawn for privacy, and sheets of printed paper peppering the bed cover's surface. Looking up, as Falconer parted the curtains and the two detectives dragged chairs to the side of his bed, he crowed, 'Great! Visitors! And just when I wanted someone to discuss the case thus far with.'

'You've got the case notes?' queried Falconer, looking at some familiar sheets of printing.

'Got 'em copied and dropped over to me. I might be in pain, but that doesn't mean my brain's addled, does it? I've been mulling things over, and I think it's definitely that Asquith woman. And I'm not going to say anything about your joyful shirt, Carmichael. Truce? Please?'

'Truce,' replied Carmichael, slightly truculently, but hopeful that they would get along a bit better in the future.

'Why her?' asked Falconer. 'Explain your reasoning to me.'

'Well, for a start, she was definitely a hostile witness ...'

'She did make a complaint about you. How do you explain that?'

'It was just her attitude when I called round. Maybe I was a bit brusque with her, but no brusquer than she was with me. Anyway, to continue; she'd spent years sucking up to the first victim, hoping for a legacy in her will. Maybe she suddenly realised that she wasn't going to get one for a long time yet, the way the victim was partying at the hall.

'Perhaps she just got fed up, thinking the old biddy was going to outlive her, given the chance, and decided to hurry things up a little. She'd have gained admittance to the house, no problem, as she called round there quite a lot, and our Miss K-A could hardly *not* answer the door, if her lights were on, not given the days in which she was brought up. It would just be sheer bad manners.

'Things got out of hand, and she dotted her one. Then she decided to have a little snoop around, and found the combination to the safe. Being a nosey-bag, she'd be unable to resist opening it, just to have 'a little peek', as she'd no doubt call it, saw all the baubles, and couldn't resist having it on her toes with them. Does that float your boat?'

'Not really,' replied Falconer, watching the young man's face fall like a jelly sliding down a wall. 'I'm afraid we've got some bad news for you. The jewels were just paste – copies. They have hardly any intrinsic value.'

'Old Maudie Asquith wouldn't have known that, though, would she?'

'Probably not, but how do you explain the stolen goods turning up on Julius Twelvetrees' coffee table, with him beside it with his throat cut?'

'Oh, that's an easy one, guv – sorry, sir. She thought he was a dodgy character, and went to him to see if he could offload them for her, and when he told her they were worthless, she cut his throat.'

'She just happened to have a knife with her, did she? Little old ladies go around with knives in their handbags these days, do they? And he'd be happy with her strolling round the back of the chair he was sitting in, would he? Sorry, Roberts, but it just doesn't stack up to my mind. What about you, Carmichael? That ring true to you?'

'Sorry, Roberts, but I just can't see it. I can see her dotting the old woman over the head, but the rest is just too far-fetched,' replied the sergeant, choosing his words carefully, so as not to upset the DC.

'Sometimes fact is stranger than fiction,' Roberts retorted, then added, 'I'm clutching at straws, aren't I? Well, back to the drawing board for me. Where are you two off to this afternoon?'

'I suppose we'll go back to Shepford St Bernard and just call on a few people. We were hoping to have warrants for Bingham, Galton, Lattimer, and The Rectory plus church for this afternoon, but apparently we won't be able to lay our hands on those until tomorrow morning. I thought it might be a good idea just to make another visit and see if we could ferret out anything new in the meantime. Shake the branches and see if anything else fell out of the tree, so to speak.'

'Lucky you! I'm bored to tears in here. Still, I've got four fresh suspects to work on, given what you've just told me about where you're concentrating your energies.'

'When do they think you'll be out of here, anyway? I could

177

do with the use of your shoe leather,' asked the inspector, thinking of what he could have delegated if Roberts wasn't stuck in this prison camp, under armed guard.

'They say a few more days before they think I'll be able to manage at home, but it won't be straight back to work, unless you can find me anything to do that's desk-bound.'

'Typical!' Falconer snorted, and rose to leave. 'We'll call in again tomorrow; see what your imagination has come up with, given the current state of play.'

Chapter Fourteen

Tuesday afternoon – Shepford St Bernard

Before calling on any of those that particularly interested them now, Falconer and Carmichael stopped outside Robin's Perch, to see if Bonnie Fletcher had yet returned home. As they pulled up, they noticed that Wanda Warwick was just turning away from the front door, so maybe she'd been visiting, and the wanderer had turned up.

On this assumption, they both got out of the car but, as she reached the pavement, she shook her head at them. 'No sign of her yet, and I'm really getting worried now,' she said, before noticing Carmichael, after which a bright smile of glee lit up her face.

She herself was dressed in a long, tie-dyed, hippie-style dress that was multi-coloured and distinctive. Looking down at her own attire, then glancing over to Carmichael's neon trousers and gaudy shirt, she gave a low whistle, and commented, 'Looks like we've been asked to the same party, Sergeant, but don't tell the boss. He looks like he lucked out when they were giving out the invites.'

'About your friend, Miss Fletcher,' Falconer stated, defusing the embarrassment of the situation for Carmichael, 'Have you no idea whatsoever where she's gone off to?'

Suddenly serious again, Wanda replied, 'I haven't seen her for days, now. We usually meet a couple of evenings a week. Sometimes we stay in, or we go to The Druid's Head if we're feeling flush. She just doesn't do this sort of thing.'

'And we don't need to ask you whether she's been missing for more than forty-eight hours, because we called there ourselves on Sunday. If she doesn't show up pretty soon, I suggest you report her as a missing person,' Falconer advised her. He'd already bitten back a sarcastic retort about Wanda getting information from her tarot cards, and felt a twinge of worry himself.

'Put a note through her door,' he continued, 'Leave a message on her answer phone and her mobile and, if you don't get a response fairly soon, make it official. That way we can search for her, put out a radio appeal, something like that, and ascertain whether she's just sloped off somewhere and forgotten to tell anyone, or has put herself in danger somehow.'

'Thanks, Inspector,' said Wanda, her face a mask of uncertainty and worry. 'I'll start the process off straight away and, if I've not heard anything by the end of tomorrow, then I'll report it.'

When Violet Bingham opened the door to them, Lettice's old black and white cat wove in and out between her ankles, purring loudly. 'He seems to have settled in well,' opined Falconer, stooping to stroke the cat, which immediately turned into a raging monster and raked its claws across the back of his hand, drawing four lines of blood in his skin.

'That's only because he's known me since he was a kitten,' she answered, putting a hand across her lips, which refused to stop smiling, they having no understanding of the English belief that Schadenfreude should be enjoyed in private. 'The Bishop can be really naughty at times.'

'The Bishop?' queried Falconer, wondering how ecclesiastical matters had suddenly entered the conversation.

'The cat's called The Bishop. I should have explained, and I'm sorry about that, but you didn't give me a chance to warn you. This old kitty just isn't very good at making friends. Come in and wash the blood away, and I'll get you some antiseptic cream and a plaster – or two,' she finished, examining the length and breadth of the wounds.

'You come on in and sit down, while I show the inspector to the bathroom and administer a bit of timely first-aid,' she said, looking up at Carmichael, to make sure that he could hear her at that altitude. She was only five-feet nothing in her stockinged feet. Carmichael was like a giant beside her, and they'd only conversed in a sitting position before.

Carmichael made himself not-quite-comfortable in one of her tiny armchairs, his legs sticking out right to the hearth, like a giant hurdle to anyone attempting to cross to the other side of the room.

When the other two returned, Falconer had a wad of gauze-covered cotton wool across the back of his hand, firmly affixed with several sticking plasters. 'That's the inspector sorted,' Violet said, twinkling at Carmichael and walking round the back of the chair and inserting herself between a sofa and the other armchair, at the far side of the fireplace. 'Sit down, Inspector, and tell me how I can help you.'

But, before he could open his mouth, she asked him, 'Did the murderer take all her jewellery – I mean the whole lot – even what she was wearing?'

'She wasn't wearing any jewellery, Mrs Bingham.'

'She must have been!'

'Nothing, I'm afraid.'

'But she never took them off. Said that wearing them was better than a safe, any day of the week. I told her she was mad; it was too risky, but she said I was just fussing unnecessarily.'

'To what, exactly, are you referring?' Falconer asked, feeling that they were at rather cross purposes.

'To the bracelets and necklace that she always wore, of course,' replied Violet, getting agitated at their lack of comprehension.

'Those stones?' Carmichael asked. 'Those dull old stones?' not realising what he was about to bring down around his head.

'Those dull old stones, as you describe them, were uncut gems – diamonds, emeralds, sapphires, and rubies. Those were her real treasure. She'd never had them cut, thinking that, if she were ever in any real financial difficulties, she could always sell them. Where are they? They're really valuable.'

'Oh, my God!' exclaimed Falconer, 'that was the message

she was trying to leave.'

'Whatever are you talking about?' asked Violet, totally perplexed.

'When she was found,' Falconer explained, she'd managed to crawl out of the house and over to the boundary of the old graveyard. She had her arms reached out as if she was trying to touch something, and now we know what it was.'

'What?' asked Carmichael, knowing that light would soon dawn for him; it was just a case of waiting for someone to say something he understood.

'It was the gravestones!' Falconer exclaimed, with total comprehension, now.

'The gravestones what?' One minute they'd been talking about those dull old pebbles the old lady wore strung round her wrists and neck, now they'd somehow got on to the gravestones in the church yard.

'She was giving us the message that the most important things were those dull old stones she wore. That's why she crawled out to the gravestones – to let us know.'

'Why didn't she just take off the bracelets and necklace?' Carmichael was slowly getting there.

'Because the only other person who knew about them was Mrs Bingham here. Miss Keighley-Armstrong did something dramatic with her last ounce of strength and her final breath, to alert someone that they were not just some cheap holiday souvenir from her childhood. If we'd only had the forethought to tell her friend the position in which she was found, the connection could have been made right at the beginning of the case.

'If she'd just taken them off and put them on a table, they might have been cleared away, with no notice taken of them at all. They could have been packed up with the rest of the house and never identified. She was leaving a message for her best friend that the real stones had not been stolen. She was still wearing them.'

'Crikey! I don't know how you do it, sir,' said Carmichael in admiration.

'It was staring me in the face. I just didn't know what I was looking at, nor who to ask for an explanation. Thank you so much for your insight, Mrs Bingham. I don't know what we'd have done without you.'

'And none of the beneficiaries of the will are going to lose out either,' concluded Violet, with a 'hmph' of satisfaction.

Falconer, however, had disappeared off in to a brown study, suddenly visualising all those priceless uncut stones in a plastic bag in the evidence room, like so much worthless dross. 'I'm going to have to make a phone call about those stones. Before we go, though,' he said, his plans now shattered, 'Why didn't you mention that you were her executrix?'

'Because you already had a copy of the will from the safe. I'd have thought you'd have read it fairly thoroughly. I didn't know that you actually didn't realise the position.'

She was perfectly correct in her assumption, and Falconer felt the fool that he undoubtedly was, for his lack of attention to detail and observation.

'By the way,' she said, breaking in on his thoughts. 'I didn't think about it at the time, but Lettice always kept a goodly sum of money in the safe, just in case of emergencies.'

'Have you any idea of the amount? We certainly didn't find any cash.'

'Anywhere between four and five thousand, I believe. I told her it was asking for trouble, but she brushed me off, telling me I was like an over-anxious nanny.'

'Great! Glad you mentioned it!' Wrong-footed again. Why hadn't she said something sooner? Not that it really got them any further forward with regard to who the murderer was.

Back in the privacy of the car, Falconer telephoned the station and explained the situation to Bob Bryant, telling him to get the unremarkable objects out of the plastic evidence bag into their own bag, and safely locked in the station safe. It would do the reputation of the force no good whatsoever if a bag of valuable uncut gems was 'lifted' from the evidence room under their very noses.

After that shocking revelation, Falconer suggested that they went round to The Rectory and begged a cup of tea, using the excuse that they were just warning Rev. Florrie about the search warrant that would be executed on the morrow. Neither of them had any qualms about her knowing about this proposed search, for neither of them had any suspicions of her behaviour, or any doubts about her character.

Having refreshed their bodies, if not their souls, with well-brewed Darjeeling and the unexpected treat of sliced, buttered ginger cake, they left her to get on with writing her sermon for the following Sunday, and got back into their vehicle.

'Are we going straight round to the Galton and Lattimer houses?' asked Carmichael, as Falconer fired up the ignition.

'No, I think we'll just have another quick round of the runners in the race, just to make sure that we've asked everything we can, and to check the atmosphere in the households. They've all had more time to take in the fact that there have been, not one, but two murders, and I'd like to see if that has changed anything in their attitudes.'

'If we're just having a bit of a sniff around, and not actually searching, do you think I could ask Mr Lattimer if he'd come over to my place and have a look at my collection?' asked Carmichael, suddenly spotting a bright spot in the afternoon.

'If you must,' replied Falconer, in a resigned voice. He'd have to make sure he was not in earshot at the time, as he would find the whole thing very embarrassing. Smurfs! Whatever next? Barbie dolls?

Gwendolyn had gone round to Toby's house as instructed, wondering what on earth he could have that she hadn't yet seen – in the bibelots field, of course! She'd been in his sitting room and dining room. She knew he had a study, but it was a small one, the same size as hers, as the two houses had been built at the same time and by the same builder. There could be nothing in the kitchen. She was intrigued.

Her curiosity was not to be satisfied immediately, however, as Toby had the afternoon tea things laid out on the dining room table, there being no need to take it from a small table in front of the drawing room fire, as the weather was so spring-like.

He'd produced a proper old-fashioned tea, with cucumber sandwiches with the thinnest bread and the crusts cut off. A cake-stand held fondant fancies on the bottom and scones on the top. In the middle of the table was a silver tea service, hot water jug included, and fine porcelain waited to be used, with white, starched damask napkins rolled into silver napkin rings beside the plates.

'Oh, you shouldn't have gone to all this trouble, Toby. It looks rather as though you were expecting royalty, not just scruffy old me from two doors down.' Gwendolyn was astonished at his attention to detail, and the formality with which he had imbued the situation. 'I usually only manage a mug of tea and a custard cream myself, if I bother at all.'

'It's the least one can do for a lady guest with whom one wishes to establish a business relationship and, hopefully, a friendship as well,' he replied, with a self-satisfied smirk on his face. 'Sit down, do, and I shall be mother. I've made Indian; I hope you don't mind.'

'Sounds great. A teabag's the greatest luxury I allow myself,' replied Gwen, reaching for a chair only to find that Toby had pulled it out for her, and was waiting for her to sit, so that he could place it under her. Next, he removed her napkin from its ring, shook it out and placed it on her lap.

'Good heavens! I feel like I'm at the Ritz. Do you always do afternoon tea like this?' she asked, appraising the food with a greedy eye.

'Only on very special occasions,' he replied, causing her to blush. Really, he could be full of old-world charm, when he wanted to be. Perhaps he wasn't such a bad old stick after all, thought Gwen, watching the amber stream pour from the teapot's spout and into cups that were so thin that she could see the tea through them.

When she had eaten as much as she could and drunk three cups of tea, Toby placed his used napkin on his plate, and gave her a wolfish smile. 'Time for treasure!' he announced, rising

185

from the table. 'There are some downstairs things I'd like you to look over but, before we do that, I'll show you my upstairs collection.'

The smile and the word 'upstairs' had made Gwen wary, and she stared a challenge at him. Seeing her look, he smiled and reassured her, 'My dear, I'm interested only in my collections, and showing them to someone who will really appreciate them. These awful events in the village seem to have brought us together and exposed our like minds, don't you think?'

'Lay on, Macduff,' she uttered, at a loss for anything else to say. All she'd expected was a look through a few display cabinets, with maybe a few drawers full of items, and the contents of the glass-topped display table in the living room.

Toby led the way upwards, entering what proved to be the third bedroom – merely a box-room, in this particular house design. Every wall was lined with shelved, glass-doored units, each bulging with pieces of porcelain.

'I have some lovely little *Sevres* bits-and-bobs,' he told her, 'and my oriental collection will take some rivalling. Come in and have a look.'

In the centre of the tiny room sat a swivel leather chair, placed so that it was possible to sit and slowly rotate, allowing each cabinet and its contents to be admired one by one. It was a perfect little viewing gallery, and she'd never seen anything like it before in an ordinary, not over-large house.

Letting her eyes move round the room, she was overwhelmed with the bright display of Moorcroft pieces, from the very earliest to those from the sixties. There were even some early Macintyre pieces of Florian ware in his collection. Light from the window shone on some of the tube-lining, making it stand out proudly. The impression made was that she had walked into a rainbow, and she caught her breath in admiration.

'How long have been collecting this?' she asked, drawing in a deep breath of appreciation.

'I inherited the first pieces from Mother – she was a collector, too – and then I caught the bug as well,' he replied, smiling smugly at the expression of wonder on her face. 'I'll just visit the bathroom, and give you a few minutes to look around, then we'll go on to the next room.'

With the meaning of Lettice's message from beyond the grave now discovered, Falconer was given furiously to think, and when Carmichael spoke in the car, he heard not a word, a nudge of his knee from the sergeant finally bringing him back to the here-and-now.

'Sorry, Carmichael,' he apologised. 'I think the new pieces of the jigsaw are starting to settle in my brain. I was miles away. What did you say?'

'I said that I might as well try to confirm a provisional date for the christenings when we go to the vicar's tomorrow,' he repeated.

'Yes. Good idea.' The inspector had pulled up outside Three-Ways House, causing Carmichael to ask, 'So, we're starting here, sir, are we?

'Quite right. It's as good a place as any, and the closest to where we've just come from. As I said, I just want to take another look at everyone, before I reach any earth-shattering conclusions. If that's all right with you, Sergeant?'

'No problem, sir. You go where you think we'll get the most useful information.'

188

Chapter Fifteen

Tuesday afternoon – Shepford St Bernard

When they were invited inside the awkwardly positioned house, the Haygarths were in the middle of unloading the spoils of a mammoth shopping trip, foodstuffs scattered all around the kitchen waiting to be put away. The working surface boasted two packs of steak and a leg of lamb, the kitchen table half-a-dozen bottles of a rather acceptable red wine.

'Business looking up?' asked Falconer, eyeing the wares quizzically.

'Actually, we've just landed a big contract, and we've cut down on every side of our lives so much that we thought we deserved a celebratory splurge,' answered Belinda, caressing a pack of steak as she gazed at it lovingly.

'Couldn't have come at a better time,' confirmed Jasper, gently sliding the bottles of wine into the built-in wine-rack.

'Rather fortuitous,' remarked Falconer sarcastically, thinking back to the domestic stinginess that had existed just a few days ago. Here, indeed, was evidence of the acquisition of unexpected liquid funds. He'd have to factor that into his thinking.

'Anyway, how can we help you?' asked Jasper, the last bottle put away.

That called for a bit of quick thinking, as Falconer had only brought them there so that he could have a little nose around, to see if anything had changed. That done, he was a bit stumped.

'We just wanted to ask you if you've remembered anything else, from the night of the party. Any tiny thing, no matter how unimportant it seems to you, could be the vital piece of

189

information that solves the case.' This was Carmichael, who, for once, had proved quicker thinking than the inspector, and Belinda looked at him with a new respect.

'Actually, there was just a tiny something that looked unusual,' she volunteered, causing Jasper to look at her in astonishment.

'And that was?' asked Falconer, recovering his aplomb.

'It was just that Colin Twentymen; he hardly spoke to a soul. Even at the party, he kept popping outside for a smoke of his pipe, but just before he left to go home, I saw him shaking hands in a rather – furtive, I'd have to describe it – way with Mr Lattimer from Coopers Lane. It probably meant nothing at all. It was just so odd to see him shake hands with anyone, let alone look secretive when he did it.'

'Over-active imagination!' exclaimed her husband scornfully, pouring cold water on her big moment.

'Don't be so swift to judge, Mr Haygarth,' Falconer reproved him. 'It could prove to be very important in solving these murders, including Mr Twelvetrees' own demise.'

Toby led an already amazed Gwen into the second bedroom, where not a space remained on the walls, these being completely covered with oil paintings and water-colours, eighteenth and nineteenth century in the main. 'Bloody hell!' she blurted out, an unexpected lapse into profane language for her, she had been so surprised. 'It's like a gallery in here.'

'And that's not all,' Toby encouraged her. 'In the middle – look!'

A sixteenth-century table dominated the middle of the room, its top covered in pieces of Lalique glass. 'All pre-war,' he crowed. 'Wouldn't have a piece post-René's death in the house.' It was a rather boastful and snobbish statement, but he didn't care: this was the first time he'd really shown off the result of all the years he had devoted to his obsession.

'I'm just blown away,' Gwen said in an awed voice. 'It's a wonder you haven't been battered to death by burglars, desperate to get their hands on such an eclectic mix of collections,' then blushed at the thoughtlessness of what she had just said, in the light of what had happened to Lettice.

But Toby didn't even notice her gaffe. 'You're the first ever to see it.' He spoke softly, with a little smirk. 'I've not bought much since I retired, but I have been putting a bit by, so I hope to be buying just a few more bits and pieces in the near future. Now, let's go to my room.'

Uh-*oh*! Was this the pay-off, where he made a grab for her? thought Gwen, suspicious, once again, of his motives. If he was showing her *his*, would he expect her to show him *hers*?

Although it was hardly worth driving to Sweet Dreams, Falconer did so, for he couldn't leave the car on the road outside Three-Ways House, it being all corners, and nowhere being safe but the drive, and that seemed a bit of an imposition considering he was visiting neighbours and had finished his business with the Haygarths.

Today, Krystal Yaxley had a smile on her face, which was adorned with skilfully applied make-up, her clothes were smart, her hair tidy and sprayed mercilessly into place. This was a different woman to the one they had interviewed so recently, whose world had appeared to be in tatters.

'Good morning, Inspector. Good morning, Sergeant. Isn't it a lovely day?' she greeted them.

'Good morning, Mrs Yaxley. You look like you've had some good news,' Falconer countered.

'Just the simple joys of approaching spring, Inspector, and the fact that I've picked up some work in the village – just part-time for now, but I'm hopeful of finding something better, once I've got used to going out to work again. Would you like to come through, and I'll make a brew – oh, that rhymes, doesn't it? How clever of me!'

Her estranged husband had also put some money into the bank account – no doubt guilt money, but she didn't care. Money was money! He'd paid in the exact amount to cover all the household expenses. The only monies not presently resting in the bank account were her personal petrol and spending money allowances, but she'd be able to cover those herself now, with the bit of work she'd picked up, and that would still leave her time to look for something better paid.

Once settled in the kitchen, Krystal put on the kettle – something she seemed to have been doing endlessly since she was deserted. That, and tipping the gin bottle, she supposed. Falconer let his cynical eye rest on three bottles of good champagne, which sat on top of the fridge, waiting to be put away. She'd evidently had some ecstatic news, if those labels were to be believed.

When the tea was brewed – stewed, in Falconer's opinion – she poured. Carmichael wasn't bothered about the state of the tea, just happy to have a mug in his hands, and not some tiddly china cup. Krystal took hers, and sat down at the table with them, giving the inspector an interrogative look, as if to say, 'So, what do you want, now, then?'

'Just a quick call, to see if you've remembered anything at all that might prove useful, no matter how trivial the incident may seem to you,' he explained, as Carmichael spooned sugar into his mug, adding a seventh spoonful for luck, as it was quite a large mug.

'Oh!' She exclaimed. 'There was something that the boys said. Now, what was it? No, it's gone. Sorry. I'll have to give you a ring if it comes back to me.'

'I'd be grateful, Mrs Yaxley. Try to think, and let us know as soon as possible. I'll give you my card and write my mobile number on the back, and the sergeant's, just so you can get through without any bother. Belt and braces, eh? Better safe than sorry.'

Carmichael wasn't listening, however, as Mrs Yaxley had just got out a cake tin and three plates, and was rummaging in the cutlery drawer for a knife.

It was in trepidation that Gwen entered Toby's master bedroom, uncomfortably aware that she had entered first, and that her host was in prime pouncing position behind her. Her fears, however, were unfounded, yet again. The man really did have nothing on

192

his mind but his collections.

The bedroom contained only the bare minimum of furniture necessary for everyday function. A single bed was set against one wall, a wardrobe and chest of drawers, side by side, against another. All three items were, of course, antique, and French by the look of it. The rest of the space was taken up with several tilt-top tables, and valuable in their own right, all in their upright positions, and holding substantial pieces of silver.

'Toby!' was all she could say, her breath having been taken away by the sheer size of the pieces, and their multiplicity. 'No wonder you call your house Tresore. It is a veritable treasure house.'

'Pretty good, huh?' he smirked, smug as it was possible for a man to be. 'And after this, we'll go back downstairs, and I'll show you my collection of ivory. I keep it in a cupboard, out of the sunlight, and away from prying eyes.'

'I hope you're well insured.'

'I am. The premium is my major household expense, but I daren't let the policy lapse. Sometimes I resent the fact that, if I didn't have to hand over such large sums every month, I'd be able to collect a lot more.'

'But you bought from me, and said you'd like to make future purchases. You can't be flat broke,' Gwen challenged him.

'I told you, I've been saving my pennies,' he replied with a wide grin.

In the car on the short journey to Coopers Lane, Falconer was given furiously to think. The absence of the knife in Julius Twelvetrees' cottage had been constantly playing on his mind, and he kept coming back to why it had not been left at the scene. As they pulled up outside their next port of call, he had a blinding flash of illumination that made him realise that he had been totally blind. He was about to make a leap of faith in the darkness, and only hoped it paid off.

A fruitless attempt to gain admission at Carpe Diem drove the two detectives, next, to Tresore, but before they went up the front path, Falconer told Carmichael to go on ahead. He'd left something in the car and would join him as soon as he could. The sergeant watched as the inspector got into the driver's seat, opened the glove compartment, and appeared to fumble inside, then bend down, as if he were searching for something.

He'd already joined Carmichael by the time he had reached the door, and announced their arrival with a lively tattoo on the knocker. 'All sorted, sir?' he asked.

'No worries,' replied Falconer, a grim smile on his face. He thought he could see the picture on the jigsaw now, and he was determined to see whether the last piece fitted or not.

Toby answered the summons swiftly, and soon they were being shown into the sitting room, where the reason they had attracted no attention at Carpe Diem was explained. Gwen Galton was seated in an armchair in front of the fireplace, examining with a jewellers' loupe, a number of small, carved ivory objects, enthralled in her task.

'We've just had afternoon tea,' Toby informed his visitors. 'Would you care for any refreshment?'

'No, thank you, sir,' Falconer refused. 'We've got a few questions we'd like to ask you, but it would be better if we interviewed you in private, if you don't mind.'

Carmichael was confused. They'd got no answer from the house next door but one, then found the occupant here. Why wasn't the inspector questioning her first? And why did he want to speak to Mr Lattimer in private? A dark thought rose in his mind, and he wondered whether Falconer would be embarrassed about him, Carmichael, asking the man to view his Smurf collection. He didn't see it as different from any other collection, but the inspector, perhaps, wasn't so open-minded.

'I have nothing to hide from Gwen,' Lattimer declared. 'Ask whatever you like.'

'As you wish, sir,' Falconer replied, then surprised everybody by suddenly diving below a piecrust table, where something under the legs had caught his eye, glinting in the light. He emerged with a diamond ring in his hand, the stone approximately three carats in weight. 'My first question,' he said, 'is where did you get this ring?'

Quick as a flash, Toby had made a lightning grasp for an ivory-handled fruit-knife which he always carried about his person, grabbed Gwen tightly so that she couldn't wriggle free, and placed the knife at her throat. 'Don't think this is a bluff,' he spat out, 'for I *will* go through with it. It won't be the first time this knife has taken a life. It may be small, but it is *exceedingly* sharp.'

Something went 'ping' in Falconer's mind as he saw the knife. So he had been right, then. No wonder the weapon had not been left behind. 'How very clever of you, sir, to use part of your collection to kill the one person who could give you away, when he discovered that every piece of jewellery you had murdered to obtain was only paste.'

'What?' cried Gwen, real panic in her voice, with the sudden change in atmosphere and circumstances. 'Are you saying that Toby raided that safe and killed both people? For God's sake help me. I don't want to die. Toby, what the hell are you playing at? Let me go!'

'I'm afraid he can't risk that, Ms Galton. You see, if he does, we shall place him immediately under arrest for exactly what you've just asked about. Mr Lattimer did indeed commit both the murders, and the robbery. Has he seemed suddenly rather better off? According to Violet Bingham, there was between four and five thousand pounds in that safe, in cash.'

'The lying cow! There was only three thousand eight hundred,' yelled Toby in disgust, then realised that he'd fallen right into the trap set for him.

'That's why you were so flush, buying that tortoiseshell and silver box from me, and then saying you were interested in further purchases. You even looked over my stock yesterday.' Gwen was now sounding very indignant, distracted from the danger of her situation by this sudden revelation of why her neighbour had had a sudden change in his fortunes.

'Peanuts!' Lattimer unexpectedly yelled. 'If those gems had been real, I'd have been made for life; been able to collect whatever I wanted, and bought somewhere a lot grander than this pathetic hole in which to display what I had obtained.'

195

'And you were going to use Colin Twentymen's contacts in the underworld to fence the stuff, even though you'd have to break it up to sell it, because the items were too well-documented ever to appear on the open market. Before doing that, though, you wanted to run them past Julius Twelvetrees' experienced loupe, just to get an estimate of their real market value. You had no intention of being cheated, even though it meant you'd have to share the spoils.' The volume of Falconer's voice had reduced now, alerting Carmichael that he was now at his most dangerous and determined.

'And you bullied that old woman to give you the combination of her safe, didn't you? Maybe you should have been more wary of its contents, given that you didn't have to beat it out of her,' the inspector taunted him.

'I threatened to torture the cat, right in front of her, then kill it and throw it on the fire, for her to watch it burn. That made her give up the combination damn quick.'

'What a filthy, disgusting man you are,' croaked Gwen, shocked to her roots.

'Did you really think it would be that easy?' asked Falconer, a hint of contempt in his voice. 'Oh, and just for your information, the real gems were those bracelets and that necklace she wore. You know the ones? Looked like they were made out of pebbles?'

Bob Bryant had just received a very unsatisfactory call, in that he could react to what he had been told, but had not the least idea how to explain the actions he now had to carry out. He wasn't used to being spoken to in that tone of voice and, although he knew there would be a good reason for it, it nonetheless unsettled him.

This was certainly not conventional procedure, but the situation that had prompted such a call was, at this very moment, unravelling before him. It had been the right thing to do, making the call. He couldn't argue with that, and now he'd carried out his side of the bargain, he'd check up on what he'd unleashed, to pass on what information he had gleaned.

Krystal Yaxley was royally ticked off. She'd spent the time since the policemen had left racking her brains to remember what it was that the boys had complained about on Saturday night and, finally, it had come to her.

They had both gone off to the gents together – nothing odd in that. They did everything (well, almost everything) together – and one of them had needed the cubicle, but it was locked, and the weird thing was that there were hushed voices coming from behind the locked door.

When he'd rattled the door and urged the occupant to hurry up, as he needed the use of it urgently, there was a short silence, then the sound of a man coughing. Eventually, the door opened, and Mr Lattimer had come out without, the twins noticed, flushing.

Whichever one had been in dire need – her memory was getting worse – had rushed in, expecting to find himself facing a 'floater' belonging to the previous occupant, but instead, what he saw was a pair of boots disappearing out through the window; boots which he recognised as belonging to Colin Twentymen, and some very unpleasant thoughts crossed his mind as to what exactly had been going on in that cubicle.

She didn't think the inspector would be interested in a case of cottaging, but she supposed he was bound to uphold *all* the laws, not just the ones pertaining to the particular case he was investigating, so she had kept her promise and called his mobile number, only to be informed that he would not be able to take the call.

Not willing to impart the fruits of searching her memory to his answering service, and be deprived of his reaction to what she had to tell him, she dialled the number she had been given for that tall sergeant's phone, and hoped that he, too, wasn't engaged in some sort of chat with someone.

Lattimer roared with anger when he realised how close he had been to a real fortune, and just turned his nose up at it, not recognising it for what it was. He'd taken all the risks, committed serious crimes, and then been too blind to see what was right before his eyes.

As he swore at the top of his voice in frustration, pandemonium broke out. Carmichael's mobile rang, drawing the incandescent man's attention, and giving Falconer the chance to lash out at the hand holding the knife, knocking it from his grasp, and pull Gwen away.

Toby Lattimer charged like a raging bull, not giving up that easily, thus angering Carmichael, who had ignored the ringing of the phone: the back door suddenly burst open, and through the sitting room door surged a sea of blue uniforms.

'Game's up!' yelled Falconer, over the hubbub that had broken out, and Carmichael grabbed Lattimer and held him, while Falconer applied the handcuffs, having sent Gwen off to the door, where the newly arrived uniforms waited for instructions. There was enough going on inside the room, without them adding to the chaos.

With Toby immobilised, they were able to take him out to the car, after Falconer had read him his rights and effected the arrest, enumerating the charges, one by one, including one that covered his conspiracy with Colin Twentymen. 'There will be a similar reception at your co-conspirator's house simultaneous to this one, inviting him to a guided tour of the cells at the station,' the inspector told Lattimer with a glint of satisfaction in his eyes.

Gwen was led away to a second police car, to go to the station to make a statement, muttering as she walked out of the house, 'I just can't believe it. I just can't believe he did all that.'

As silence descended on the house, Falconer produced his mobile phone from his pocket, ended a call Carmichael didn't know the inspector had been making, and winked at Carmichael.

'Before we came in here, I had just about got things sorted out in my mind, and I thought we could be in for a rough time, so when I went back to the car for something, that something was a call to Bob Bryant, to alert him that I might be making an arrest imminently, and that there might be trouble, so I asked him to send a bunch of the lads over, to give us a hand, and that there may be two addresses that needed a call.

'Of course, I couldn't assure him that there would actually be a rumble. I just had what my mother's old cleaner would have called 'a feeling in my water' that there was trouble in the air.'

Before he could put his phone away, it rang, proving to be Krystal Yaxley, with her tale about what her boys had observed in the gents' on Saturday night. When he hung up, he retold it to Carmichael, adding that he felt that was the final nail in the coffin. They'd already been observed surreptitiously shaking hands on something. Now, there were two witnesses to the fact that they'd had a conversation in the cubicle of a gents' lavatory.

No doubt the knife that Falconer had knocked out of Lattimer's hand would produce traces of Twelvetrees' blood, as he had almost boasted that that was the weapon he had used, then cunningly concealed it back in one of his collections.

'Sir?' said Carmichael.

'Yes?'

'Shall we just have a look round while we're here, see what he's collected?'

'Why not?' replied Falconer. 'Shall we start with upstairs? He's not likely to have much up there, but we might as well take a look.'

Boy, were they in for one hell of a surprise!

Halfway up the stairs, Carmichael halted. 'Sir?' he said, again with an interrogative inflection in his voice.

'Yes, Carmichael?'

Falconer sighed, wondering what was coming next.

'I suppose this means he won't be coming over to look at my Smurfs now.'

THE END

199

An Excerpt From

Death in High Circles

The Falconer Files: Book 10

by

Andrea Frazer

PROLOGUE

The village of Fallow Fold is situated high on the Downs. In early spring, late autumn, and winter it is scoured by winds, but for the time in between these seasonal scourings its position is ideal, with panoramic views of the surrounding countryside, and clean, fresh air, which is a joy to breathe. It is situated about twelve miles south-west of Market Darley.

It is an old village which has retained its ancient buildings, having been discovered early, by both retirees and commuters, who bought the 'olde worlde' picturesque but unliveable wrecks and invested in them heavily. The result is a community so spick and span and well cared for, that it could almost have been designed by Walt Disney himself, to recreate ye olde England ('y' being a letter that, back in the mists of time, use to be pronounced 'th').

Many of its original retirees had now passed on to that great accountant's office in the sky, but their homes have passed on to younger family members, and the original commuters have found ways of living permanently in the village: usually by selling their London properties when a family came along, and it is now a well-inhabited community, with a much better balance of population than before incomers' money first arrived, and rescued it from demolition.

It is, on the face of it, a calm village, where the most disturbing events are squabbles caused by sibling rivalry, which produce the odd outburst on walks through its pretty lanes, and, superficially, seems to be an absolute paradise in which to live and raise a family.

It has also attracted a fair number of international residents, both from those who worked in England and those who had visited it on holiday. They had chosen it for a good place to settle into their dotages, so it has just a whiff of the cosmopolitan about it.

There is now plenty to get involved with in this village, as it boasts a number of hobby circles. The residents have a choice of joining like-minded others in a plethora of activities. There is a knitting and needlecraft circle, a book circle, a gardening circle, groups for growing both flowers (including arranging them) and vegetables, a bridge club, a classical music circle, and the church choir.

Their weekly, fortnightly, or monthly meetings take place in the village hall, one of the two public houses, or the larger properties of individual members. Each of these groups inevitably boasts cross-over members, as one's interests are rarely confined to one subject area. There is also an amateur dramatic group, like all the circles well-attended and enthusiastically enjoyed, but this latter definitely keeping itself to itself – its participants being much too absorbed in learning their lines and actions in the current production to have time to participate in anything else.

Chapter One

Saturday

The two men stood helplessly in A&E, disbelievingly watching the hospital trolley that was being rushed into the emergency admissions bay of Market Darley Hospital.

The shorter man, with mid-brown hair, bowed his head in despair, thinking how easily this dreadful thing could have happened to any of the team, and feeling guilty that he hadn't been able to do more at the scene.

The slightly taller man with the olive complexion was feeling as if he had been hit over the head with an iron bar. He was completely stunned, and simply couldn't believe what had happened, and with such swift, unstoppable inevitability. The man on the trolley was in a bad way, and the faces of those admitting him and in the ambulance had tried to reassure them, but their eyes were grave behind their professionally optimistic expressions.

He stood straight as a ramrod, as if standing to attention, wondering whatever he would do if the man didn't make it. What would happen to his family? Who would replace him in his job? But even more importantly to him, who would replace him not just as a colleague, but as the reliable partner he had become? In his own way, his partner was irreplaceable, and had carved a special place in his heart for the way he conducted both his personal and professional life. Sometimes he had driven him almost to distraction with some of his eccentricities, but he'd never worked with anyone better.

The shorter man grabbed the arm of a doctor who was rushing towards the room into which the trolley had disappeared, and asked if the patient was going to be all right.

'It's not a clear picture yet, but we do need to get him to the operating theatre to stop the internal bleeding. After that, it's all down to how strong his constitution is, and whether there are any complications that we don't know about yet.'

The taller man stood, still staring at the closed doors of the emergency admissions room, tears pouring, unchecked and unnoticed, down his cheeks, his heart breaking for what might have been prevented if either he or his partner had been just that little bit quicker thinking, or had made a move a fraction of a second before that terrible, deadly strike.

For the first time since he had been a child, he prayed silently, not even having indulged sincerely in this occupation during his years in the army. This was one compatriot that he couldn't bear to lose: his life would be so much the poorer for him to continue in any useful pattern, and it was something he knew he would never get over.

Although they rarely showed their respect and affection for each other, it was tacit in their good working relationship, and he couldn't believe that such a pointless attack might deprive him of this unique personality forever.

Chapter Two

Friday – Eight Days Previously

Spring had long since arrived, and was wending its lazy way towards summer. The treetops were a lush palette of mixed green salad, and the normally well-trimmed shrubs in gardens were bustling to throw out errant shoots, eager to destroy their manmade symmetry.

The weather was kindly in a way that is never taken for granted in this country; warm days, blue skies with candyfloss clouds and warm gentle zephyrs of breeze followed mild nights, and the countryside, thus cossetted, put on its Sunday best, and dazzled the eyes with its displays of wild flowers and lush verdant pastures, the call of the wood pigeons adding a soporific air to the next best thing to paradise.

It was during the early evening of his day off on such a day as this, that Detective Inspector Harry Falconer was just considering what to prepare for his evening meal, when there was an unexpected ring on the doorbell, followed by a rather urgent knocking on the door itself.

Wondering who on earth this unexpected visitor could be, he went to open it, and answered his own question when he saw a shape through the opaque glass that was as tall as the doorframe. 'Good evening, Carmichael. What can I do for you on this beautiful late spring evening? And why have you got a cat on your shoulder?'

He'd only just noticed this last interesting phenomenon, as he had been contemplating the dread possibility that Carmichael might have all his brood out in his car, just waiting to pay a visit, and thus turn his domestic harmony and tidiness on its

207

head.

'Davey' Carmichael was his DS in the Market Darley CID and, during their first case together he had met a young woman with two children in the village of Castle Farthing, where he now lived. He had courted her, married her, adopted her two sons (as their father was no longer living), and they had since produced a baby daughter who was immediately named Harriet for the inspector – who had, much to his horror, had to deliver the baby.

The Carmichael household also included a pack of tiny dogs and it would appear, at first glance, that this lithe little cat's arrival in their crowded household might have proved the last straw. Falconer set his face in a determined expression and waited for his answer.

'It's Monkey, sir,' Carmichael said, baldly.

'I know which one it is. How could anyone mistake an Abyssinian for any other breed? But what's she doing here with you?' Falconer could not conceive of a situation that would induce Carmichael to take his cat visiting.

'We can't keep her, sir, and I just wondered if ...'

'What's she been up to? I don't want any feline delinquents in my home.'

'Kerry can't cope. She's trying to wean Harriet, but if she leaves the bowl of baby rice for a moment, Monkey's in there like Flynn, and it's all gone by the time Kerry gets back to it. But the main problem is the dogs.'

'The dogs? How can there be a problem with the dogs? She's only a small cat. You coped very well with me there, and that great lump of a dog called Mulligan, all the time we were snowed in at Christmas. What's the problem with such a tiny feline?'

Carmichael had several dogs, all of them in miniature, and at complete odds with the enormous height and build of their owner. His current count was a Chihuahua, a miniature Yorkshire terrier, and their three unexpected offspring, as Carmichael had been too naïve and dilatory to get the original two neutered in good time. There were now three 'Chihua-

208

shire' terriers to add to his menagerie of minute canines, the pups romantically but impractically named by his wife as Little Dream, Fantasy, and Cloud.

'She might be small, but she keeps herding all the dogs, like they were a flock of sheep, and she chases them endlessly. She thinks it's a grand game, but the poor little dogs are terrified – even Mistress Fang and Mr Knuckles.' These were the parent dogs, but still extremely small. 'And I just wondered if you could find it in your heart to give her a home. I don't want to hand her into some anonymous charity organisation, for she's a beautiful cat, and I wouldn't like to lose touch with her completely.'

'Have you had her checked by the vet to see if she's got a chip?'

'Yes, and she hasn't, for some reason, so we've no way of knowing where she ran away from – and returning her to her original owners – which I'd do gladly if only I knew who they were – seems to be impossible. I even put adverts in the local rags, but no one got in touch.'

This was quite a heart-felt plea from Carmichael, who never asked for help unless it was the last resort, and Falconer took pity on the poor young man, replying, 'I'll give her a week's trial, but if it doesn't work out, you'll have to find another solution. That's the best I can offer.'

'Oh, God, thank you so much, sir. I don't know what I'd have done if you hadn't been a cat lover. Kerry will be thrilled that she'll still get news of the little tinker, but Monkey's just too difficult to manage, what with the dogs, the boys, and the new baby. Here she is,' he said, handing her over to his boss, where the cat immediately climbed on to his shoulder and purred loudly in his ear, a strange double purr that he'd never heard before from his other cats, of which he had already accumulated three to add to his original one.

Falconer's current register of feline house-mates was: Mycroft, who had been an only cat for a long time, and was a seal-point Siamese; Tar Baby, who was a huge black ball of fluff; Ruby, a red-point Siamese, the latter both inherited from

209

an escaped murderer on whom Falconer had developed a tremendous crush, and Meep (pedigree name 'Perfect Cadence'), a silver-spot Bengal he was caring for while its owner, another murderer, was in prison.

'Well, you've got five dogs, two stepsons, although they're adopted now, aren't they, and a new baby to care for. This will leave me with only five cats, so it's got to be easier for me to give her a trial than for you to send her away and never know how she's getting on. Come on, you little tinker, and we'll see what the rest of the gang think of you.'

'Thank you again, sir. I'll be getting back, and tell Kerry and the boys that everything's all right, now that she's living here with Uncle Harry.'

Falconer winced at this mode of address with which the boys had tagged him, 'I did say it was only temporary, Carmichael; remember that.'

'Oh, I know *you*, sir. You're so soft-hearted, you'd never give her up, once you get used to her winning little ways.'

'You mean like herding other animals, and stealing food?'

'Things aren't the same in your house, sir. In ours, they're much more chaotic. I know you'll manage beautifully and, before you know it, she'll just be part of the family.'

As Falconer turned to close the door, very aware of the furry little bundle now nestling on his shoulder, he left Carmichael tripping down the path, mission accomplished, and whistling for sheer joy at this unexpected success.

Entering his living room, one shoulder, of necessity, lower than the other, four furry lumps roused themselves from sleep, their nostrils informing them that there was an interloper in their midst, and they immediately informed their keeper that there was dissent in the ranks.

'Meep, meep-meep-meep!' piped Perfect Cadence.

'Meow-eow!' mewed Tar Baby, in protest.

Both Ruby and Mycroft joined their Siamese voices in their particular and unmistakeable call of, 'Neow-ow-ow! In reply, Monkey gave a little chirrup, and dropped gracefully to the ground, immediately identifying Mycroft as their leader.

210

She approached him, her belly slung low – what there was of it, for she was a very sleek brown brindled animal. She stopped a little distance from him and chirruped again, then lifted her head and gave a delicate sniff. The other three sat like statues, awaiting developments, Meep making a low growling noise in her throat.

Mycroft sniffed back and tossed his head as he smelt the superficial and unmistakeable fragrance of d-o-g-s, in the plural, then took one long, deep sniff, to investigate further. Then he sat for a moment, as if lost in considering thought, and gave a small yip of acknowledgement, that encouraged the new resident to approach.

Falconer sighed with relief. This was the moment he had been dreading. What if it had turned into a huge cat rumble, with them skidding and thundering all around the house in disapproval at the proposed change in the status quo?

But they hadn't, and if Mycroft gave the paws up to this little feline scrap, then the others would bow to his judgement as head cat.

In Fallow Fold, it being the time of year for planning the activities for the new season, timed to coincide with the academic year, the nominal heads of all the activity circles had their heads bent over calendars, and referred to letters containing dates that certain members couldn't attend. They also had replies to letters requesting that various local or nationally acknowledged experts in their chosen field come to speak at one of their forthcoming meetings, and all these had to be co-ordinated to produce the schedule for the coming season.

There was, of course, much swearing and cursing, as all the information was collated, and certain unpleasant circumstances raised their ugly heads.

Mabel Wickers of Sideways in Ploughman's Lays sighed theatrically in disgust. She could cope with letters of intention to miss certain meetings; what she was finding most frustrating was the in-fighting amongst the readers of the Book Circle about what books should be chosen to read over the next few

211

months.

And, for that matter, who would do readings for those they had already read together, for their day to shine in the village hall, when it was taken over for the best part of two weeks for each circle to publicly demonstrate what they had achieved during the past twelve months. That was a good way ahead, though, and does not come into this story.

Mabel was a short and portly elderly woman with a wicked, dry sense of humour, but this particular problem was an area from which she could derive no fun at all, nor see any bright side. On one side she had a group of readers who insisted that they should all read prize-winning novels, as they obviously had more merit than anything else.

From the complete other end of the spectrum, she had a few members who were vociferous about the sheer joy of 'Aga sagas', and pushed their case in a most unpleasantly pushy manner. Sometimes she felt like giving the whole thing up and just reading what she wanted to, with no interference in her choice, or opinions, of what she had read, from a crowd of silly women who were just squabbling to see who could get the upper hand.

In the end, she simply scribbled down on a piece of paper, *1066 and All That*, *Five Run Away Together*, and *Babar the Elephant*. Let them see how they like them potatoes! She'd had enough for one day. She could send along the dates of meetings to their collator, Melvyn Maitland, who lived just down the road in a house called Black Beams, and let him do the final timetable.

In fact, she decided to walk down there. At least they offered a good-quality cup of tea in that establishment, which was more than could be said for some other houses she visited on a regular basis, and if there were a biscuit or a slice of cake offered, she could always justify its consumption later by having decided to walk there and back.

At Black Beams, both Melvyn and Marilyn Maitland were at home, and it was Marilyn who opened the door to her, invited her inside and offered coffee and biscuits. Coffee? It wasn't quite what Mabel had expected but, no doubt, the coffee here was as good as the tea, and she accepted gratefully.

'Melvyn's in the study,' Marilyn informed her guest.

'He's got a lot of the stuff through for what we call "optional term four". That runs over the summer and is usually badly attended, but it doesn't mean he can skimp on it. So many people want to change times, days, and venues that I reckon he'll end up not only pulling out his hair but chewing off his own beard as well; positively using it like an oral set of worry beads. I'm sure, now that you've arrived, he'll be relieved to take a break and forget all about the whole beastly muddle for half an hour.'

When called for his coffee break, Melvyn appeared out of his study door cursing and swearing in a most venomous way. 'Those bloody Americans!' he yelled, not bothering to moderate his volume because they had a guest: it was only Mabel.

'What about them?' Mabel asked, intrigued to know what they had done to infuriate him so.

'They just don't honour their responsibilities in this village. I mean, Madison runs the Knitting and Needlecraft Circle, and a very good job she usually makes of it, even if her only interest in that whole craft area is quilting. We all know we have a lot of decisions to be made about exhibiting, and the dates for the optional summer term are always difficult, but she's just written me a little note – posted, I might add, not delivered by hand – telling me that their ghastly offspring will be staying with them for three weeks of July, then the whole bang-shoot of them are going back to the US of blasted A for the whole of August.

'That leaves Muggins, not only to work out the dates of the meetings, but also the exhibition. Well, I won't have it. She'll just have to appoint a deputy, and let *her* get on with it. I haven't got time for this! And all I get paid is a tiny percentage from subscriptions and weekly refreshments and membership money.'

Mabel had to admit that it was not much reward for everything that was expected of him. What she didn't know was that both the Maitlands were 'tax ghosts', who never stayed anywhere long enough to register in the cognisance of local bureaucracy, and were beginning to feel that their time in Fallow Fold was nearly at an end.

They had wandered their way around the world during the time they had been a couple, always working on the black, and in small ways. Thus, had they accumulated enough money to keep them on their travels, and made a little bit to put away in the meantime. Their expenses were low, and they were notoriously slow bill-payers.

Mabel made mental notes as Melvyn ranted and raved, took a sip of her coffee, shuddered, took a bite from a biscuit, and shuddered again. The coffee was very cheap instant powder, and the biscuits were soft. That was very unusual. Perhaps they were suffering financially because of the amount of time he had to give up to be archivist and record keeper for all the circles, and didn't have enough time left to do something better paid.

'Put yourself in my position,' she spat, feeling thoroughly out of sorts at the quality of refreshments she had been offered. 'That blasted Book Circle nearly drives me out of my mind with its two warring factions about what sort of books we should list for reading, and I don't get paid a penny. Sometimes I feel like chucking the whole thing up and just reading what I like.'

'Well, why don't you just do it?' replied Melvyn, still out of sorts with his own problems.

'I think I might just do that. And now, if you'll excuse me, I'll leave you to get on with enjoying your sulk.'

She rose, grabbed her handbag, and marched back to the front door. 'Don't leave us in a black mood, Mabel,' pleaded Marilyn.

'I shall leave in any mood I see fit to. No doubt I shall catch up with the both of you when Melvyn's not so peeved.'

When the door had finally closed on their grumpy visitor, Marilyn asked her husband how his schedule was coming along, and he sighed mightily, and said, 'I'll read it to you. I've already had to re-do it once because one of the damned groups planned to change the day of its meeting, but there was such uproar at clashes with other members about other groups they belonged to, that I've had to rearrange it all out again.

'If it's not right this time, they can all go to hell and blue blazes.' Wandering back into his study with Marilyn on his heels, he sat at his desk, lifted a large sheet of cardboard, and intoned, 'Knitting and Needlecraft, Monday afternoons in the village hall – weekly: Monday evening, Bridge at The Retreat – weekly. Tuesday evening, Books at Sideways – fortnightly: that's the only one for that day, thank God,

'Wednesday is Gardening Circle at The Dark House – fortnightly, and Thursday evening, Classical Music in the village hall – fortnightly. Friday's got Flowers in the village hall in the afternoon – monthly and Choir in the evening, weekly in the church. Saturday's the Am Dram meeting, but no one from that group belongs to any of the others because of the amount of time they have to find to learn lines, so thank the Lord for that. At least there won't be any clashes with the members of that circle.

'And that just leaves us with Vegetables in Tally Ho! for Sunday lunchtimes. What a tangled web. I've had enough for today, and I'm now going to have several large drinks to freshen my temper and my patience. I'll get this done on a poster for pinning up in the village hall, then I'm done with it for as long as I can get away with it. I feel like throwing the whole thing back in their faces and telling them to try to sort it out for themselves.'

'But we need the money, Melvyn,' said Marilyn in an anxious voice.

'And don't I know it,' replied Melvyn, and left the room actually growling.

In Rookery Nook, on the Stoney Cross Road, there were also cross words being exchanged about the regular meetings of the circles, and how it affected domestic life for them both. Martin Fidgette was not seeing his wife Aggie's point of view at all.

'I know you want to pursue your interest too, in retirement, but with all these meetings being weekly, fortnightly, or monthly, sometimes they all fall in the same week, and it's just not good enough,' carped Martin, his monotonous voice petulant with self-pity.

'Well, it's hardly my fault if that happens, is it?' snapped back Aggie, glaring at her husband. This week the monthly flower meeting had taken place in the afternoon, which meant that when she got home again on her sturdy bicycle, there was very little time in which to prepare the evening meal before choir practice, which was that same evening. The choir was run by Martin, and he magnanimously permitted them to take their small, elderly car to that particular event, which was a weekly one.

'And,' she continued, 'what about Sundays? You've got to be in the church well before time, to play for the earliest arrivals, then you go straight off to the Tally Ho! for your so-called Vegetable Circle meeting, which is every bloomin' week. I have to cycle myself down there, then heave all the way back home on my own while you're supping beer in the pub, and I just get to come back here and get the dratted roast dinner on for when you deign to return.'

'I really don't see that you couldn't give up one or two or your activities,' Martin replied ungraciously and extremely selfishly. 'A man does need feeding properly, after all.'

'Me? Why should I give up anything?' Counting carefully on her fingers, she declared, with a small sense of victory, 'I go to four clubs, you attend five different activities, and that doesn't include all the time you have to spend in the church just practising the organ. It's you who should give something up, not me.'

'You're my wife, dammit!' He shouted. 'You're supposed to look after me – remember, you promised to obey.'

'So when do I get to retire?' Aggie was getting really angry now.

'When I'm dead and gone, and then you'll still have to look after yourself. I won't have these rushed, shoddy meals! And I won't give up any of my interests. In fact, I'm going to phone old Lionel Dixon now, and join the bloody Bridge Circle as

216

well, and if that means I'm going to be offered a rushed and sub-standard meal on that night as well, because of your damned Knitting Circle, I shall eat at the damned pub instead of here. At least I'll get a good meal there.'

'You go over to The Dark House, but don't expect me to have any supper ready for you when you get home. I shall be in bed!' Aggie was really steaming now. 'And you can give my excuses at choir tonight. This unpleasantness has brought on a dreadful case of indigestion, and I think I shall take an early night. Don't forget to lock up before you go to bed.'

And with that, she declined to clear away the plates, and stalked straight upstairs, carrying her latest book up with her. Of course, she'd come down for a cup of tea when Martin had gone, but she wasn't going to tell him that, or about the fruit cake she had bought on her way home from the needlecraft meeting. That would be her little secret until she'd had a goodly wedge or two in private.

Chapter Three

In The Retreat in Ploughman's Lays, Lionel Dixon was already making plans for the next meeting of the Bridge Circle which wasn't until Monday evening. He had purchased new packs of cards for all the tables, with two spare packs, just in case of accidents. People were always misplacing cards, usually high value ones, which he was sure that they carried off in their handbags or pockets had they not had the chance to cheat with them.

His main problem was how to get the members to pay their fair share of what the packs had cost him. There was no point whatsoever in buying cheap playing cards for an enthusiastic group that met weekly; they lasted for practically no time. On this occasion he had bought top quality cards, but knew that they would balk at having to put their hands in their pockets, especially as there was a charge for refreshments, as these came out of Lionel's own pocket, and not courtesy of the WI, which it probably would have done had they used the village hall for their gathering. And much inferior that would have been, too.

He prided himself on his fondant fancies, sausage rolls, jam tarts, and sponge cakes, but the ingredients cost money which he wasn't willing to donate to what, on some occasions, could be a bunch of whingeing ingrates. And he so hated asking for money. A very shy man, he was bold and direct only at the card table. In all other areas of his life he was quiet and retiring, and not very sociable. It seemed to be one of only two aspects of his life where he came alive, these days.

He belonged to no other circles, finding that he had enough company and gossip in one evening to last him for the rest of the week, and had no further desire to seek out others for social intercourse in between these gatherings.

On hearing the telephone's urgent ringing, he cursed quietly and politely under his breath, put down the pack of cards he was checking, and went to answer the shrill voice of interruption.

When he ended the call, however, he was smiling. A new member would be joining them, and that would liven things up considerably, giving him an excuse to mix people up a bit in their fours, and make up another four. He had three odd members at the moment, meaning that three people always had to volunteer to sit out on some of the rubbers. Suddenly he was looking forward to Monday. Something told him it would be a thoroughly enjoyable day.

Two doors away, in Rose Tree Cottage, Ferdie and Heidi Schmidt were also in the midst of a disagreement. They jointly ran the gardening club, with fortnightly meetings on Wednesday afternoons in a back room at the public house, The Dark House, and Ferdie was not happy about the situation.

'It was you who wanted to do this crazy thing. I don't even like gardening. I want to go to the golf club north of Market Darley and play golf. Gardening is a waste of my time in an afternoon.'

'Is golf not the same?' asked Heidi, heatedly. 'You said you wanted us things together to do after we finished working. Here I have arranged for us something, together to do, and you do not want it to do any more. Why are you so selfish being?'

'Me? Selfish? It was you who were signing us up to run that club. You never asked me if I wanted it to do, first. I do not care for gardening. It leaves me hurting after so much work. I do not like talking about it, because it is you who all the garden work here do. I know nothing about the silly little plants. I want to play golf, and that is what I am feeling to do on that day.'

'But I thought you loved the flowers,' said Heidi, sadly.

'I love the flowers you grow and pick and put in the house in a glass vase. Growing them, I do not care for. I don't even know their names. You grow, you tend, you pick. Me, I shall care to play golf on the Friday afternoons now. It is my

220

decision. I have here and now made it. Jawohl!' Neither of them had managed to get the hang of English syntax as yet.

Heidi trailed dejectedly out into her beloved garden and flopped down on a bench, tears in her eyes, so that all the blooms that had arrived with the spring were blurred to her. Why did Ferdie have to be so inflexible? She had spent decades looking after him and now, in early retirement, he could not even spare a couple of hours to spend with her on what, she had sincerely believed, was a shared passion – but this was the first time they had ever had a garden together, as they had lived in an apartment in Germany.

No, Ferdie just spent all his time moving his investments around on the Stock Market, with the Bloomberg channel booming out in the background, and if he wasn't doing that, he was either having a nap, or planning to play golf. Life after work was not the golden experience that she had expected, and she rather wished she had stayed in Germany, where she had left so many girlfriends behind.

Here, she knew hardly anyone, and had hoped that running the Gardening Circle would expose them to new friendships, together. 'Scheisse!' she cursed, and continued to weep.

Inside Rose Tree Cottage, Ferdie got his golf clubs out from the under-stairs cupboard, and changed into his golfing clothes. He would do as he wished, whenever he wished. Women were inferior, and must learn to respect their betters.

In Lark Cottage in Fold Lane, however, there was nothing but joy and happiness in the air. Antoinette Chateau had spent twenty years working in England and, on taking early retirement, she had returned to France to settle again in her native country. She had found, though, that in her absence, her home country had changed so much, that she was now more English than French, and decided to make her home in a little village she had discovered during her time in her adopted country.

She loved her little cottage and garden, and was an avid member of the Classical Music Circle, the Knitting and

Needlecraft Circle, and the Flower Circle. All in all, she couldn't have been more content. She had within the last winter taken in a stray kitten, something she had vowed never to do, and now loved it like the child she had never had. Life was good.

As a non-English incomer, she could have experienced all sorts of resentment and negative behaviour from the other villagers, but she had a vivacious personality, was trim and elegant, and managed not to look at all her age, which was, in fact, seventy-eight. Her appearance, however, suggested she was a good ten to fifteen years younger, and she wafted expensive perfume, which she loved, wherever she walked.

When she wasn't adoring her kitten, Kiki, she listened to opera and sewed, being an expert needlewoman who loved her practical hobby, and had made all the curtains and chair covers for her cottage, and produced something wonderful and unique, rather than mass-produced. Today she sat outside in her back garden observing Kiki watching the birds, and trying her luck at stalking them.

So inept was the little creature that Antoinette had to laugh out loud at Kiki's face when she missed her target. She was such an entertaining little animal that she couldn't imagine why she had not got herself a cat before. Her delighted tinkling laughter filled the garden, as she took a break from the kitten's activities to survey the booming borders, and felt a small thrill of pride that she had created this little Eden all by herself, for she was not married.

Still in Fallow Fold, other residents were getting on with their Friday evenings in a rather more enjoyable state of mind. Dale and Sharron Ramsbottom, who resided at The White House in Fold Lane, had strolled down the road to their closest pub, The Dark House, and were sitting outside in the balmy evening air, taking an evening drink and discussing their plans for the coming week.

'It's going to be a busy one, and no mistake, Dale,' stated Sharron, pulling at her vodka and tonic with enthusiasm.

'You're not kidding, kidder,' replied her husband in his husky Cockney accent, draining his pint glass. 'You get a handle on how it's going to run, and I'll just get us a refill – fuel for the brain, you know,' and he headed into the bar to carry out this important task. A quick glance over his shoulder produced the query, 'Do you want any crisps or peanuts, while I'm in there?'

'Make it pork scratchings, Dale. I've got a sudden yen for a nice fatty mouthful,' she called after him, and thankfully he didn't reply in his usual ribald way. The Tally Ho! public house served only posh snacks, for which she had no relish. At least here, at The Dark House, you could get good old-fashioned packets of nibbles, with no pretensions to 'foodi-ness'.

She really enjoyed their involvement with growing and gardening. Instead of just selling produce now, they were actually growing it themselves and, even if it did take up a lot of their time, they always had so much to talk about when they had free time together. Early retirement had been a good idea, in her opinion, and the only fly in her ointment was the succession of weekly meetings of the Vegetable Circle in the Tally Ho!

She knew that it was really a lads' social, and that not much talk of vegetable production went on, and yet she was still expected to produce a glorious roast dinner on her husband's return, even though he normally just collapsed into a comfortable armchair and dozed off, after the number of pints he'd consumed. Still, he drank a lot less than when they'd lived and worked in London, and for this she was grateful, and knowing she wasn't the only wife in the village who had this cross to bear.

Also in the pub garden were Joanna and Wieto Jansen, the village's Dutch residents, but they were only concerned with getting a good few glasses of wine down their necks before going home to sample the organic 'weed' they had brought back from Amsterdam on their recent trip back to the Netherlands. They found its use very relaxing, and missed being able to go into a Grasshopper café, or similar establishment, to indulge themselves in this regular treat that they had enjoyed, before moving to po-faced England.

That evening, the telephone rang in Chestnuts in Ploughman's Lays, and Madison Zuckerman trilled, 'It's OK, Duke, honey. I'll get it.' On the other end of the line was Antoinette Chateau, all fired up with an idea she had formulated a little earlier during her time of contemplation in the garden with Kiki, and afterwards waging war against the ever-persistent weeds in her flower beds.

'I 'ad the most marvellous idea,' she informed Madison, 'to form an 'istorical society in the village. It 'as so much 'istory, but the English in'abitants don't seem at all interested in it. I wondered if you and Duke, as fellow non-English residents, would be interested to join me in this little idea, to see if we can raise any enthusiasm for it.' Antoinette was incapable of handling aspirates, even though her English had a better vocabulary than many native speakers.

'Hey, that's sounds like a great plan. Duke and I won't be available during July and August, but we could do some preliminary investigations as to levels of interest, and, perhaps, give it a go in the autumn. You can count me in. I'll speak to Duke after we've finished on the phone.'

At the other end of the phone, Antoinette smiled in innocent happiness. If things went well, she could have her own little circle to run; something she had wanted to try since she had first got involved in other hobby groups. 'We could search for 'istories of the buildings in local newspaper archives, and maybe find information on 'ow long some of the families 'ave lived here. You like the idea?'

'I love it!' replied Madison. 'Leave it with me, and I'll get back to you right after I've spoken to Duke.' Both women ended the call with a twinkle in their eyes and smiles on their faces. It was just possible that this could turn into a battle of wills over who actually ran and organised this proposed new group.

224

Back in Market Darley, Falconer had introduced his new charge to the litter tray, the food bowls, and water bowl, and now added another dish to the collection of feeding bowls on his kitchen floor. He at once decided that he would have to purchase two double bowls to take the place of the four individual ones he currently had. They took so much of his kitchen floor space that he was in danger of running out of places to walk, and he had no intention of moving out his kitchen table just to accommodate one more cat.

Someone had said once that a house without a cat was a home without a heartbeat, and he now had five extras heartbeats to keep him company. Approaching middle-age as he was, their lively and comforting company was some consolation for the fact that he still had neither a partner nor a family. They filled the hole in his heart he had always reserved for the eventuality of a life partner (wife, preferably, for he was unashamedly old-fashioned) and children, but he was definitely of a mind to think that he had, at last, met the person with whom he wished to spent the rest of his days and sire children.

If only he wasn't so reticent about matters of the heart, and could just churn out romantic sentiments, rather than being the pragmatic and, in the presence of beautiful woman, tongue-tied man that he was.

He decided that it was definitely time to sit down and get to know this Abyssinian furball a little. She didn't seem a mite phased at suddenly moving home and coming into contact with four strange felines, so he flopped into his comfiest armchair and sat her on his chest.

Immediately, she commenced her unusual double purr, and leaned up to lick his face. The regular gang of four slept on, with one eye open, to see what this interloper intended to do. Was she just visiting, or here for good? They'd have to see what they thought of her before making up their minds about whether she would be one of the gang – or, perhaps, the enemy.

After about fifteen minutes of cleaning his five o'clock shadow, Monkey dismounted from his lap and wandered off into the kitchen. She was probably in need of one or more of the cat facilities out there, and he let her go without worry. After all, what trouble could she get into in a kitchen?

He soon found out, as there was a thump followed by a very gentle but unidentifiable hissing sound, which were followed by the exit of the other four cats, in search of what was afoot. No sounds of confrontation or challenge met his ears, and it was another ten minutes before he went out there himself, to put on the kettle for a cup of coffee.

What met his eyes was simply unbelievable. There seemed to have been a blizzard, but at ground level only. Everywhere he looked was white, with the tiniest of blue and pink dots sprinkled in with the dazzling 'snow'. Then, he noticed that the giant-sized packet of washing powder that he always bought, to save having to make unnecessary trips to the shops, was lying on its side, its contents scattered everywhere, with all five of his pets enthusiastically joining in the game, and starting to sneeze from the effects of the soap powder.

It seemed that Monkey had been accepted as a welcome trouble-maker, by the others. It didn't look like he was going to have any say in the matter and, just for a moment, his sympathies went out to Kerry Carmichael, with her five dogs and three children. This extra trouble she just didn't need. With a sigh, he fetched the Dyson, and shooed the cats back into the living room.

After watching a documentary on the television, he switched off the set and noticed that he was completely alone in the room, but he could now hear a bit of cat hooraying upstairs. That needed investigation, although all the doors up there were kept closed. What mischief they could possibly have discovered to get involved with on the landing, he could not imagine.

When he got to the top of the stairs, he stood there, still as stone, horrified to notice that the bathroom door was now standing wide open, and he had another indoor meteorological phenomenon to cope with. He realised that Monkey was a cat clever enough to cope with the concept of door handles, and she had broken into his bathroom for the express purpose of egging the other four to help her shred the jumbo pack of eighteen

226

toilet rolls he had purchased recently.

This had happened before when Meep had first arrived, and he couldn't believe he could have been so naïve as now not to foresee a repeat performance, especially knowing how she had upset the usual running of the Carmichael household, which could cope with a little chaos if anyone's household could.

The white shreds of paper were everywhere. This would require a black sack before he could even consider using the Dyson. Determining to put hooks and eyes on the outside of his upstairs doors, he trudged resignedly downstairs to fetch the big sucky thing, as his pets probably thought of it, and shooed them down ahead of him, where he locked them in the kitchen, until he had things properly cleared up again.

Again, he had already done this once, to deter Meep's exploration, but as she had settled in, they had not been in use, and he had removed them all quite recently when he had had his woodwork repainted. Unusually for him, though, he hadn't put them away tidily, but had completely forgotten what he'd done with them – and didn't have space in his head to spare, thinking about their possible location.

The way he saw it, he could either spend the best part of two or three days looking for the things, or just go to the DIY store and get some more, for who knew what fresh mayhem Monkey could wreak in that elapsed time

In the Carmichael household in Castle Farthing, where things should have been really peaceful after the removal of Monkey's mischievous behaviour, things had taken a turn for the worse. Their neighbour's dog, whom they had doggie-sat during the big snow-in over Christmas, had been booked to stay with them again in the spring.

His owners were celebrating their pearl wedding anniversary this year, and their daughter had booked a week away somewhere warm, not just for celebration, but to compensate, both for the dreadful winter they had just endured and the fact that time had sneaked up on them stealthily.

A knock at the door, just after the children had gone to bed, revealed both the huge dog that was Mulligan, and his owner, on the doorstep, the latter with a big grin on his face. 'Thanks for offering to do this, Davey. You know how much it means to us and to our daughter's family. Here's his leash, his bowls, and his blanket. I'll whizz you down some chow for him in a minute, but then we'll have to get to bed. We have to be up at five thirty for the trip to the airport. You know how inconvenient travel is, now it's so easy to do.'

The Falconer Files

by

Andrea Frazer

For more information about **Andrea Frazer**
and other **Accent Press** titles
please visit

www.accentpress.co.uk